Elizabeth's
Landing

Katy Pye

Pyewacky Press

Mendocino, California

This is a work of fiction. Names, characters, businesses, places, events and incidents are either the products of the author's imagination or used in a fictitious manner. Any resemblance to actual persons, living or dead, is purely coincidental.

Pyewacky Press
P.O. Box 265
Mendocino, CA 95460

First Printing, 2013

Cover photographs:
 Oil slick, copyright © Matthew S. Rambo/ iStockphoto
 Turtle and shell copyright © Adrienne McCracken
 Camera copyright © Katy Pye
 Footprint copyright © Tomas Hajek/ Depositphotos
 Author photograph: Laurie MacMillan
Title page photograph, tire tracks: copyright © SV Luma

Cover design copyright © 2013 Katy Pye
Cover design: Laurie MacMillan, Sunfield Design
http://www.sunfielddesign.com/ and Katy Pye
Book design & Production: Pyewacky Press
Sealife dingbats: Denise Clendenin/ Sassygraphics

Publisher's Cataloging-In-Publication Data
Pye, Katy.
  Elizabeth's landing / Katy Pye.

   p. ; cm.

   Summary: Adrift, 14 year-old Elizabeth sparks Texas-sized trouble, fighting power and history to save sea turtles, family, and find her way home.
  Interest age level: 10 to adult.
  Issued also in eBook and Mobi formats.
  ISBN-13: 978-0-9890973-1-4 (pbk.)
  ISBN-10: 0-9890973-1-5 (pbk.)

  1. Teenage girls--Texas--Juvenile fiction. 2. Sea turtles--Conservation--Texas--Juvenile fiction. 3. Real estate development--Texas--Juvenile fiction. 4. Families--Texas--Juvenile fiction. 5. BP Deepwater Horizon Explosion and Oil Spill, 2010--Juvenile fiction. 6. Beaches--Texas--Juvenile fiction. 7. Teenage girls--Texas--Fiction. 8. Sea turtles--Conservation--Texas--Fiction. 9. Real estate development--Texas--Fiction. 10. Family life--Fiction. 11. BP Deepwater Horizon Explosion and Oil Spill, 2010--Fiction. 12. Beaches--Texas--Fiction. I. Title.

PZ7.P94 El 2013
[Fic]   2013904967

Printed in the United States of America

For Virginia

*"Tell me, what is it you plan to do
with your one wild and precious life?"*

—Mary Oliver, "The Summer Day"

The last word in ignorance is the man who says of an animal or plant – 'What good is it?'
—Aldo Leopold, *Round River*

CHAPTER ONE

Port Winston, Texas
Saturday, April 3, 2010

"STRAIGHTEN THAT GIRL OUT before it's too late, hear?" Grandpa's trapped Dad inside the swayback garage behind our dump of a rental house. Another one of his "I know best" lectures spews out the open window. Only this morning's gripe isn't about dragging for shrimp, Dad's landscaping job, or Mom being gone. It's about me.

I straddle my bike, bend low, and roll in close, listening for one more reason to hate this place.

Grandpa's smoker's hack rips through the air. "By God—" He coughs and huffs a second for breath. "At fourteen, I was workin', not lazin' around Highland Beach, or poutin' like I was owed better. My Daddy made clear I had to amount to somethin'."

My cheeks sting. I press my chin hard onto the bars so I don't blow up. The old crank deserves it, though. Four months and six days since Mom, Dad, and I moved here to help out him and Grandma Linnie. Waste of time. Nothing stops his carping about everything and everybody.

A match snaps. Smoke from Grandpa's cigarette snarls over the sill. I pinch my nose against the stink and wait for Dad to stick up for me, for us.

Go ahead, tell that walking chimney this relocation plan is over. Mom gets back, one U-Haul and three days we're home in Coulter City. Back to the way things were before he ruined our lives.

"Give it a rest, Pop." Dad's voice is frayed. "If you want to fish tomorrow, I've got an engine to fix." The toolbox lid clangs shut. Screwdrivers and wrenches clunk together as he drags the box off the workbench. I wait for him to say more but all I hear are his footsteps as he heads toward the door.

I slam my fist against the garage wall. "Thanks for nothing, Dad!"

Gravel spins under my back tire as I jam the pedal hard. I career past Dad, standing in the open doorway, hand raised, maybe to protect himself from flying rocks, maybe to slow me down. I flash a "see-ya" wave over my shoulder.

"Elizabeth," he hollers. "You've got chores."

The front wheel wobbles. I swerve, barely missing the front bumper of his truck on my way to the street.

I'm not listening. And I won't be at Highland, if you come looking.

Six blocks down, I glance past the beach and Ghost Crab Bay, to the far shoreline at the Gulf. Traffic is light on Preston Street. I ride hard, away from downtown glitzy offices, restaurants, and tourist shops, toward Wayward Landing Beach, five miles out. Dad would kill me if he knew where I'm going. With Mom gone and Grandpa breathing down his neck, he's turned into Super Worrier Dad. But by the time he's home from working on the *Linnie Jean*, I'll be safely back in my boring room, counting oak leaves on the tree outside my window. For now, I'm free. From chores and not measuring up.

I kick out my feet and sail onto the county road, head back, sucking in warm air. The salty tang of drying sea grass fills my nose. Through gaps in the high dunes along the road's edge, I glimpse flashes of grey-green Gulf under bright blue sky.

Three miles from the Landing I flatten over the bars to pick up speed past the development I call Mansionland. A thick sea mist floats toward the scattered line of fake brick driveways, stone pillars, and locked gates with scrolled names like Lost Resort, Pirate's Wake, and Eagle's Rest. Like overloaded freighters, dozens of white and pastel-colored mega-homes ride the sand. "For Sale" signs litter the beach alleyways between houses.

I hit my brakes in front of the six-by-eight-foot billboard. It wasn't here three weeks ago. The black-trimmed gold letters holler, like all-caps in an e-mail:

Opportunity of a Lifetime
1.5 miles of Beachfront Bliss
Multiple or single lots
Contact Pioneer Development, Inc.

A dragonfly, the deep red-orange of sunset, buzzes onto a morning glory stem winding between the sign's wooden legs. Before I reach my camera, the bug catches an offshore gust and is gone. Bliss for what? Next year bulldozers could be scraping out driveways for Mansionland II. Like almost happened to the forest around Picketts Pond six years ago. Almost, but didn't thanks to Dad. Lately, it feels like that Dad, the one with the guts, stayed behind in Coulter City. I push on through the layer of sand retaking the roadside. Port Winston's not my place. So, not my problem.

The road gives out under a dune, unstopped by the red and white-striped reflective barriers or the VEHICLES PROHIBITED sign. A joke, since all beaches here double as sandy streets. I chain up my bike, shoulder my daypack, and slog to the top. The breakers land as soft thuds against the shore. The fog bank two miles away has swallowed Mansionland. Eerily empty, the beach north toward Pelican Bay draws me, slide-hopping down the slope.

I jog the long beach and wade into the Gulf. Waves lap my knees and the outgoing current pulls sand from under my toes. Arms out for balance I worm my feet into the shifting sea floor and breathe the briny air. Balance. That's what's gone. Back home everything was solid. Back home tall and photo geek equaled me, and okay. Here, I'm "Tripod Legs," which equals bottom of the pile. Back home Teresa and I were tight. Now she's slipping away. Coulter City High's spring formal is next week. "Everybody's going," her text said. But not, "Wish you were." Everybody used to mean her and me. Now she's got a group. Our forever friend Brad is her date for the dance.

A tangle of yellow-green sargassum seaweed bumps against my legs. I lift and gently shake it over my hand. A tiny silver fish and a shrimp drop to my palm. Two baby crabs cling to the beaded grass and each other's pinchers.

You guys want to make it? Stick together, and don't leave home. I set them back on the clump and release it to a wave.

The sun hangs above me. Straight-up noon. Three hours taking photos and I'm hot, tired, and hungry. I scan the look-alike ridges for the one hiding my bike and the road. On the long ride home maybe I'll figure out how to keep from getting grounded for running off this morning. Not that restrictions from friends I don't have and places I don't go will change much.

A quick scuttle near my feet makes my heart jump sideways. It's only a Ghost crab, no bigger than two dimes laid side-by-side.

"Hey, watch who you're scarin'," I say. Stationary eyes on long stalks stare at me. I stare back, taking in the spotted detail of its shell. I blink and, like a shape shifter, the crab disappears against the sand. My gaze falls to the track under my feet that begins at the water and runs toward the dunes. It's too simple for a car tire, and the outside edges, like a string of commas, frame a single line up the middle. Maybe my bike's over the hill ahead. I take a picture and start walking the line.

A few yards from the end I lurch to a stop. In a shallow dugout is the biggest turtle I've ever seen. Two feet long and almost as wide, it's nothing like the freshwater sliders or snapping turtles in Picketts Pond. This one has flippers.

And that. A Twinkie-sized box is glued to the turtle's back. I ease onto my hands and knees and wait for the turtle to move. Nothing.

Escaped experiment?

Chin tucked, front flippers half-buried in sand, the turtle looks dead. I ease up my camera, focus, and shoot. Click. Not a blink.

Yep, it's a goner.

A deep grunt from the turtle's throat snaps me alert. I shuffle around behind it, out of sight. The broad back flippers lay spread-eagled inside a deeper hole. I wait for the turtle to slap the sand, get mad that I'm so close. It lies still, then grunts again. A soft plop poofs up from the hole. I stretch and peek in as two ping pong ball sized eggs, covered in clear goo, slide from under the tail and land on the growing pile.

A mom!

Goosebumps race up my skin.

I've never seen anything born. Wait, does this count? They're eggs, so maybe not. Who cares? Sea turtle, laying eggs are two firsts in my book.

I rest my chin on my arm and breathe in. She smells clean. A mix of saltwater and sea grass, warm sand, and essence of fresh fish. Another grunt. Three more eggs.

I ache to run my fingers over her shell, to touch the leathery tail.

Grunt. Plop. Inches from her tail, I angle the camera over the half-hidden hole and take a five-shot burst of the glistening eggs. If anyone from school saw my face stuck in the butt end of a turtle, my new nickname would go way past ugly.

A few more pictures and I'll leave her alone. I crawl to her left side, rising to my knees for another shot. The front flipper lifts out of the sand as her head twists toward me. A quick stab of light freezes my camera mid-air. The eye of a large stainless steel fishing hook juts from the corner of the turtle's mouth. The shank and barb are buried inside. Line trails from the metal eye, twisting, loop after loop, around the flipper, binding the muscle. The pale pink edges of deep cuts send a sickening jolt through my stomach. A thin pool of tears rims the turtle's sand-crusted lid. I sit back on my heels and turn away, blood pounding at my temples.

You can't creep out.

The turtle grunts. More eggs. I swallow and pivot toward her.

The box. Someone knows about her. I unzip my backpack, pawing through my stuff. *Call 911.* Water bottle, wallet, apple, banana, notebook—

Phone. On charger. In my room. *Crap!*

Another grunt. I throw my camera in my pack. Mansionland isn't far once I get to my bike.

Not freaking likely they'll buzz in a kid, blathering about a turtle.

More eggs plop. She'll be in the Gulf before I get back. I stare at the hole.

We're doomed.

The engine's tight distant whine moves closer, then roars as three ATVs burst from the mists of Mansionland.

I whirl up off the sand, waving, and sprint toward them. "Over here!" Leaping piles of drying seaweed, I cover ground fast.

The ATVs crisscross the sand, weaving back and forth, then run straight, side-by-side, swooping to the water's edge. Spray flies, like nets of stars, behind them. In what seems an instant, they close in on me. I stop and lower my arms. The drivers are high school guys, maybe older. Sweat lines slide down my cheeks.

"Hey, girl, what's up?" the blond leader calls. Shirtless, his skin glistens with salt-water drops. He switches his head sideways, tossing hair away from his eyes as he drops the ATV into neutral in front of me. "You must be new." His look roams slowly from my face to my feet and back. "I like 'em tall. And hot."

My skin tightens against his stare. I'm not what guys call hot—not how he means. And he sounds drunk. Leaning back he pops the clutch, bouncing the front wheels a few inches off the ground.

I turn and walk quickly away from him.

He guns the engine and guides the machine next to me. His friends circle around, one going one way, one the other, trapping us in the middle.

"How 'bout lettin' Pete take you for a ride?" he says, revving the engine.

I walk faster, not sure where I'm going. A gap opens in the circle. I dart through, eyes focused straight ahead, squinting against the lightly blowing sand. I pull air hard through my nose, fighting the burn in my calves.

"Where ya goin'?" Pete pulls beside me again. "Climb on up here. I'll take ya." The other boys move beside him, making a line three across.

I step up my pace. They match it. Pete reaches for me, but I dodge out of range. If I bolt, they're on me like desert dogs on a jackrabbit. Ignore them. Maybe they'll find another toy.

Like the turtle.

I lengthen my stride, stay mid-beach, scanning the base of the dunes for signs of my pack or the turtle.

None. Good.

"Come on, Ernie." The guy with the buzz cut calls above the engine noise to the one driving beside him. Buzzcut's not wearing a shirt, either. Tattooed across his chest, a leering, orange-haired clown squeezes drops of blood from a dark purple heart. I swallow but my mouth's so dry nothing slides down.

Ernie follows Buzzcut in a last circle around us before they speed together toward the surf. Pete doesn't follow.

"Go away," I say, pitching my voice low and narrowing my eyes to show I'm serious, as opposed to what I am, which is scared spitless. I stare ahead to get my bearings, or find the track the turtle made dragging herself from the water.

"That's not very nice." Pete tips his head back toward Mansionland. "You and me could have some real fun. My girlfriend's parents ain't home . . . she ain't either. Nice place. Big pool."

"Not interested."

"New girl playin' hard to get?" The engine purrs. I glance over my shoulder. Pete slows, watching his friends idling along the surf.

"They're waiting for you," I say.

He hesitates, then grins. "I think you're right." He stands up on the running boards, punches the throttle, and swings away.

I shoot for the dunes and spot my pack and the turtle. She's still in her nest. The guys are far away at the water. I grab my pack, lie down beside her, and listen for plopping eggs over my heavy breathing. Nothing. Then, slow and deliberate, a back flipper swipes sand into the hole. The other flipper moves. More sand in. The first, then the second. She's covering the eggs.

She's done. She's leaving!

The engines roar at the water. I flatten onto the sand, wanting to crawl in the nest with the eggs. In battle-line formation, Pete, Buzzcut, and Ernie ride up the beach toward me, yipping and shouting like warriors.

"No!" I stand up, planting my feet wide in front of the turtle, reaching for my only weapon—the camera. I hit ON, hold the shutter release, and take ten shots of their race toward me. I jog out from the nest, and catch the curtain of sand Pete's ATV throws onto the turtle. He jerks to a stop six feet from her. I get that, too.

Head lowered, the turtle rests her back flippers on the sand and is still. Sun flashes off the hook.

Pete throws his leg over the seat and grabs up a stick of driftwood.

"What the hell you doin'?" he says, stutter-stepping toward me. "Gimme that thing."

"Get her, Pete," Ernie says.

I hold the shutter open again as Pete lunges toward me, teeth bared. One hand grabs at the camera, the other flails the stick in the air between us. I move away in tight, snaking patterns that throw him off balance in the deep sand.

Ernie laughs, slapping his hands against the handle-bars. "Move your fat butt, man."

Pete stumbles halfway to a fall, then gives up trying to run. I slip the camera in my pack and clutch it to my chest.

Buzzcut swings off his ATV.

"How cute. Miss Nature Girl's got herself a pet." His kick rains sand down on the turtle's head. "Not for long. Ernie, help me flip this sorry thing."

"Leave her alone!" My dead-center charge knocks him flat, landing me pack down against his chest. My fists pummel his face. A fingernail catches his cheek and draws blood.

"Hey! Get her off!"

Hands grab me from behind. I hold the pack tight as Pete and Ernie yank me backwards onto the sand. Pain screams through my right shoulder.

"Give it." Pete snatches the pack strap, raising his fist above my face. I grit my teeth and thrash sideways, twist-ing my head and shoulders trying to get loose. His punch grazes the back of my head.

A truck horn blasts in the distance. Pete stops pulling.

"Let's go." Ernie revs his engine once and takes off.

Pete jerks the pack straps again. "I gotta get them pic-tures." I twist against the pull.

"Pete," Buzzcut yells. "Another DUI, you're hosed." He disappears in a cloud of sandy dust. I squeeze my eyes shut.

The tension on the strap releases. "Don't think I'm done with you, brat."

I wait for a final blow, but get only the whine of his engine in my ears as he follows the others. I lie still, chest heaving, listening to the sound of tires flying across the sand in both directions. A minute later an engine dies near me. Two doors slam shut.

CHAPTER TWO

I OPEN MY EYES. The woman kneeling at my side slips off her sunglasses and scans my face. Wisps of dark chocolate-colored hair stick out from under her sand-colored ball cap. *Port Winston Marine Science Center* is printed over the brim. Embroidered in dark blue thread above her shirt pocket is MARIA, *Staff Biologist.* She's Mom's age or close.

Lines deepen above her eyebrows. "Are you hurt?" she says.

I look past her at the thin layer of clouds, the dull ache in my shoulder spreading through my neck. I slowly shake my head, my brain and mouth disconnected.

"Let me help you." Her arm sliding under me moves the pack. The memory of Pete's jerk on the strap zings through my skin. I squeeze my eyes shut against the image of Buzzcut's tattoo as my legs stiffen then start to shake.

Maria's fingers lightly grip my shoulder. "Shhh. You're safe." Her voice is calm, but firm. "I won't hurt you."

I hesitate, then sink into her.

"There you go. Deep breath. Slowly."

I breathe in and out until my head clears.

"You ready to sit up?" I nod and let her steady me.

"Where did you come from?" I say, hardly above a whisper.

"Tom and I were on nest patrol when he saw something going on up here."

Now I remember. That poster with the turtle track on the grocery store bulletin board. Report All Nesting Turtles, it read with a phone number underneath.

"The turtle's hurt." I say. "At first I thought the boys would help."

Maria glances down the beach and scowls. "I know." Her gaze lifts past my face and settles on the turtle. "Not to worry. The Center's got the best turtle vet in six states."

The knot in my neck slowly loosens. The muscles in my thighs tingle. I push the pack free of my arms.

Maria stands. "There's work to do. Trust your legs yet?"

"I think so." She offers me a hand. I wobble so she stays close as we walk toward a man in serious conversation with the turtle, which isn't moving. He turns and I see he's on a cell phone.

"The sheriff doesn't have anyone close to go after them," he says, punching off the phone and reaching toward me. "Tom Mikels," he says, pumping my hand when I take it. "You okay?"

Ow. My eyes water. "Yeah. I'm fine."

"Maria and I were too far away to see exactly what was going on," he says. "Riding ATVs on the beach is illegal, and it looked like you could add an assault charge. Am I right? Can we get them for wildlife harassment, too?"

My shoulder throbs. I scan the beach toward Mansionland, my thumb tracing the pack's zipper. My photos are evidence for sure of the ATV thing, maybe the turtle, too. "I've got—"

Don't. If I tell them about the pictures, the sheriff will end up with them. If I tell them about my arm, I'll have more trouble, since I'm not supposed to be here in the first place. Even if the guys were harassing the turtle, she's safe now and so am I. All I need is to find my bike, get home, and forget the whole thing ever happened.

"I'm okay, really." My voice jumps. I try again. "They mostly just scared me."

Maria raises an eyebrow, like she doesn't believe me. Why would she? A few minutes ago I was falling apart in her arms. Tom shrugs with an easy look, as if rescuing teenage girls and turtles is something he does everyday.

"Just checking," he says.

I swipe sand off my rear. "Yeah, no. Thanks for showing up. I'm Elizabeth."

"You, too," Tom says, "otherwise this turtle might have been in real trouble."

"No problem." My voice squeaks partly in excitement, partly relieved they're not pushing for details about what happened. "What kind is she?"

"A Kemp's ridley," Maria says. "The most endangered of the seven sea turtle species and our first nester on Wayward Landing this year."

The turtle plops a front flipper onto Tom's shoe. She hasn't moved since they got here. "Yes, ma'am," he says. "Time to go." He pulls his foot loose before she bears down and inches forward. The fishing line cinches tight in the cuts. Her head dips, easing the tension of the hook on her mouth. I turn away, preferring to watch Tom walk to the truck.

"I'll let the Center know we're bringing in a patient," he says over his shoulder. "You can help us load her up."

Maria pulls a small camera from her pants pocket and points it at the turtle. "Hold on, momma, I need your picture." She presses the shutter release and frowns at Tom when nothing happens. "Sure would be nice if someone recharged the battery when he runs it down."

Tom's on his cell again, but obviously hears her. He points at his chest and mouths, "Who, me?"

"I'll do it." My camera is out before Maria can object. As soon as I get the turtle in focus on the LCD screen, the tension in my body dissolves. I take shots from above, then drop eye-level in front of her for a good angle on the hook, line, and injured flipper. No more feeling sick looking at the cuts. Now they're photo subjects. On a moving target. Nose straight out, the turtle crawls toward my face.

Okay, so I'm just another lump to crawl over on your way home.

I scoot backwards on my elbows and knees, trying to ignore the pain in my shoulder. Behind the nest, I take shots of the flipper swipe patterns next to the egg hole and the white shells peeking out of the thin layer of sand.

Tom laughs, dropping a round plastic tub onto the sand. "Hey, enough. We're not shooting a documentary."

I shut off the camera. "Sorry. I get carried away."

Tom winks. "No, thank you for saving my hide from the wrath of the camera warden." Maria stands by the nest, latex gloves in her hand. The turtle pushes the tub aside.

"Your girlfriend is escaping," she says, tossing one set of gloves to Tom, another set to me. We put them on and he grabs the rim of the turtle's shell on one side. Maria takes the other. I reach for a place to hold on near the tail as the turtle's flippers wave wildly.

"We've got her." Maria's quick comment backs me off. Tom ducks a flipper whap to the face. In one quick move they lower her into the tub.

"Whew," Tom says, removing his gloves.

Maria retrieves her sunglasses from the beach.

"You didn't let me help," I say.

Tom points to the back of the tub. "Grab on there." They take the side handles and lift. I stumble forward and

"I know, but ecosystems need both prey and predators to stay balanced. Even when things are going well, only one in a thousand hatchlings make it to adulthood."

"Still, people should have done more."

"People did," she says, her arm half-buried, reaching for the bottom of the hole. "Have you heard of the Head Start program?"

"Like for little kids?" She nods and lays three more eggs on the heap. "I don't get it."

"Over thirty years ago, Mexico allowed U.S. scientists to bring thousands of Kemp's ridley eggs to Texas to incubate and spend the first year at what's now Padre Island National Seashore. The hope was the hatchlings would imprint to the island and the year's head start would improve survival rates. If all went well, years later the adults would come back to lay eggs. Over time, this would build another major nesting site, in case something ever happens to Rancho Nuevo."

"Has it worked?"

"The number of Kemp's nests on the island increases almost every year. On other beaches in Texas, too."

"Do a lot of Kemp's nest on the Landing?"

"Only a few so far, and none from our program yet. It's too early. We've only released hatchlings from the Landing for five years and they won't reach maturity for another five or more.

"Why do turtles come here instead of going back to the island?"

"We don't know. Maybe this turtle's mother saw this was a safe place, too. Now her daughter has returned."

"So, even though you take the eggs, you're messing with nature in a good way."

"Exactly. Until the species recovers."

I reach toward the hole. Maria catches my wrist.

"You need proper training to handle the eggs," she says.

"I promise not to hurt them."

"You wouldn't mean to, but the spot where the embryo attaches is very fragile. If it isn't done right the growing turtle can break loose and die."

"I didn't . . . I wouldn't . . . sorry."

Maria lifts the last egg and holds it in her palm. "You want it to hatch, right?"

I nod, my chin quivering before I can stop it.

"It's okay." She raises the egg toward me. "A gentle touch, but don't squeeze."

The egg's already dimpled, like a beach ball with a tiny leak. I stroke the soft leathery shell with my finger and imagine 40,000 turtles crawling onto a beach like the Landing, each one looking for a spot to nest. Eggs plopping, sand flying, then all of them crawling back into the Gulf. It's too much. Today one sea turtle was like total chaos for me.

She tops the eggs with a layer of sand. "The hatchling release is open to the public," Maria says. "You should come."

"Hello." He nods, walking past me without a glance. Tom drops the tailgate and the two of them hoist Sunny's tub off the end.

"He's all business when he's working," Maria says, as if reading my thoughts. "Come on."

We follow Sunny and the men into an examining room where they rest Sunny on a stainless steel table. The pale green walls wash almost white under the strong overhead lights.

Sunny twists and bangs her flippers on the table, scratching for traction on the slippery surface. Tom and Maria each catch a side of her shell to hold her still. I wince and look away as Dr. Nguyen pulls and rotates the injured flipper and presses the skin around the cuts.

"What are you going to do?" I say.

"I won't have to amputate." A smile tweaks the corner of his mouth—a little vet humor. So much for Dr. All Business. "We need vitals: shell measurements, heart rate and rhythm, and blood tests. I'll cut the line out and scrub the wound clean."

I steady myself against the supplies counter.

He and Tom pry open Sunny's mouth and lay a short stick across the back corners. Dr. Nguyen shines a light down her throat. She doesn't move when he touches the hook. "She's dehydrated and will need surgery to get the hook out without doing more damage."

"Will you do radiographs and the gastroscopy today?" Maria says.

I can't stop a giggle. "You test her for gas?"

Tom laughs. "You'd be surprised all we test for."

"Hold Sunny, please" Maria says. He zips his hand across his mouth, sending me into more giggles. I sober up when Maria flips open a binder of photographs.

"This is the inside of a turtle's throat," she says, pointing to a picture of weird, fleshy tube things. "And this one with the soft, pinkish ridges is a stomach. See that strand-like line?"

"Yeah."

"It's fishing filament. The radiography—the x-ray—only sees solid objects like hooks. The gastroscopy feeds a little movie camera down the throat into the esophagus, stomach, and upper intestine to find what x-rays can't see."

I stifle the creeping yucky feeling I get when my doctor uses the tongue depressor to look deep in my throat. "Sounds nasty."

"More like magic when you see the images on the screen," Maria says. "Better for her since we don't have to open her up to find out if she's swallowed garbage."

"Garbage? Like what?"

"Pieces of hard plastic and plastic bags are what we find most often."

"Turtles aren't very smart if they eat that stuff."

"They didn't last a hundred million years being stupid," she says. "We've tricked them with ocean trash that looks like their favorite foods. Think how much a plastic bag in water looks like a jellyfish."

"Miss Braveheart, I hear," he says, shaking my hand. "An honor."

I blush, but am so loving Braveheart over Tripod Legs. "Thanks."

Maria picks a spot in the back right corner of the twenty-foot square pen. Bud starts the hole. At a foot down he kneels and swipes his hand around the top to widen the opening, then scoops out sand until he's elbow deep.

"Okay, scribe." Maria hands me a long wooden marker. "Transfer the egg retrieval data from the chart onto this stick: the number of eggs, the date, time, and location."

Maria and Bud fill the hole with eggs. I'm still amazed they all fit inside one turtle. Tom said Sunny could lay another clutch before the season's over.

Bud covers the eggs with sand and I plant the stick where he says it won't punch into the nest.

"How long will you keep Sunny?" I say, handing Maria the clipboard as she pulls the corral gate closed and snaps the padlock shut.

"If she doesn't develop other problems, ten days to two weeks."

I wish she could stay here, safe forever.

On the front patio, Maria and I find shade and an empty table under a lean-to for lunch before she goes back to work. I watch three kids near the water turning bucket loads of sand into castle turrets. A barking dog splashes after a ball in the shallow breakers while a man's kite dips with the wind. The morning's stress slides off my body like an outgrown snakeskin.

Maria holds out half her sandwich. "I'll share. If you like hummus, lettuce, and cheese."

I'm starving and the banana and apple in my pack are trashed from my landing on Buzzcut. "Sounds great." I've never heard of hummus and the first hit of garlic and lemon on my tongue is a killer. "Not bad," I say, covering my mouth to hide the bread sticking to my front teeth.

Maria tears off the edge of cheese poking from her sandwich. "You're not from here, are you?"

"How could you tell?"

"Gulf kids know about sea turtles."

"We moved from Coulter City, Missouri in January."

"Are you liking the high school?"

I gaze at the ridgeline of a wave rolling across the bay. "It's okay. I'm still trying to fit in." A lie, but better than telling her I gave up the second week.

"And your family?"

"My Dad grew up here. He runs crews for a landscaping company. Right now it's just him and me 'cause my Mom's in Mexico researching an article on how immigration affects families left behind. My grandparents still live here and, well, Grandma's fantastic but Grandpa had a heart attack last year, which is why we moved. But he's really . . . he and Dad . . ." No sense blabbing to a stranger how Grandpa's an opinionated, ornery, pain in every inch of my nerves. "That's about it."

Maria sips from her metal water bottle. "You obviously love photography," she says.

"It's sort of a habit."

She smiles and hands me half her cookie. "Do you like photographing nature or people best?"

"Nature. More of a challenge. I can't make a bird hold a pose or a flower stop moving in the breeze. I guess part of it's 'cause my Dad and I spent a lot of time around Picketts Pond when I was little. Besides, nature doesn't get all full of itself in front of the camera."

Maria laughs. "I hear you. What's Picketts Pond?"

"A one hundred acre pine and oak forest around this really cool lake near our house back home."

"Sounds nice, spending time with your dad."

"Yep. Sundays were our days. We'd pack a lunch and spend all afternoon together, him trying to teach me everything about the woods. He owned a landscaping business, too. Mostly designed native plant wildlife gardens. I helped sometimes, but had a hard time remembering the plant names. My Mom bought me a camera so I could put pictures with the words. Did I say she's a photojournalist?"

"Not exactly." Maria rests her chin on her hand. "But she sounds interesting."

"She is. Anyway, everyone says I'm really good at photography. Mom says it's because my Grandma's an artist—was one before marrying Grandpa—and I have her eye for detail and composition; she's no slouch, either.

Whatever, I've won lots of prizes, but honestly, I mostly like roaming around looking for things to shoot."

Maria stares at me.

"Boring. Sorry. I mentioned I get carried away."

"Never apologize for being excited about what you love. Do you go to the Landing a lot?"

I'm not sure why she's asking, but explaining about being angry with Dad and Grandpa feels like ancient history.

"I went once before, but it's pretty far from our house."

She folds up her wax paper sandwich bag. "I understand needing a place like your pond to hang out, but it was very dangerous trying to protect Sunny—if that's what you were doing. Some people might say foolish." Her gaze locks on me and I know she's searching for more than I copped to at the Landing.

"I thought about leaving," I say, "but she was all alone. What if those guys were out to hurt her? Or her eggs. I figured whatever happened we were better off facing them together, you know?"

"Yes, I do. Still—"

"Don't worry, once was enough. I'd like to put the whole thing behind me."

"I understand, but—"

"Except for Sunny, of course. Can I visit her sometime?"

"Certainly. We need teen volunteers. The training is free and the bus and trolley system to get here is cheap.

The school bus even stops up the street. What do you think? Have you got time?"

"I'll make time."

"Good. Now, back to work for me." She tosses her lunch papers in the trash. "Meet you back here at five."

I watch her push through the doors into the atrium. Protecting turtles. Busy. Teen volunteer. That ought to shut Grandpa up.

CHAPTER FOUR

"WE'RE JUST RENTING THIS place 'til Dad can look for something better," I say. Maria pulls up behind Grandpa's pickup in front of our house. I open the door and step out, hoping she won't stay long enough to notice the paint peeling off the porch rails. Long enough for Grandpa to come out and make a scene 'cause I'm late.

"It's nice you're near the beach," she says, leaning across the seat.

"Yeah, but Highland's not the Landing." I lift out my bike, trying to ignore the sharp ping in my shoulder. "Thanks for the ride and the Kemp's book."

"See you soon," she says.

"Definitely." Maybe. I was supposed to be home a half hour ago to set the table and help put supper together. I stash my bike in the corner of the porch as she drives away. Hunger and jitters about facing Dad chew at my stomach.

The house is quiet inside. Barbeque smells and voices drift into the kitchen from the backyard. I pick up the place settings Dad's stacked on the kitchen table. Snatching the salt and pepper shakers off the stove, I step onto the back porch and stop inside the screen door. Grandpa's settled in the Adirondack chair under the gnarly oak tree next to the picnic table. He draws on a cigarette, then swallows the last of his iced tea. Smoke fills the empty glass as he breathes out through his nose.

Could you be more disgusting?

I stand still, hoping any minute he'll stand up, head out the gate, and go home. Last thing I need is him shoveling more opinions on top of whatever Dad's got waiting for me.

Dad squirts water at a flare-up under a chicken leg, then brushes sauce on all the pieces. The corners of my mouth turn wet. He glances up from the grill as Grandpa fiddles at his shirt pocket for the cigarette pack.

"The doctor told you to quit smoking," Dad says.

Grandpa lays the pack on the table and tops it with a book of matches. "Like I told you this mornin', first thing you should be worryin' about is your little girl. Her momma was here, you wouldn't have to."

Dad stabs a piece of chicken, moving it away from the dying flame. "My family's my business, Pop, not yours."

Go, Dad. About time you told him where to get off.

My stomach growls. Grandpa looks toward the door. No way he heard me, but he raises his chin and stares down his nose in my direction. I plaster my face with a protective smile and push open the door.

"Smells good out here." I hop down the worn wooden steps to the patio bricks.

Dad's head snaps up. "Elizabeth, where have you been? And don't say you didn't get my message."

I plunk the dishes onto the table. "Sorry. I was too busy to check." Even if I'd had my phone. Sliding onto the end of the bench farthest away from Grandpa, I grab a glass of iced tea and a handful of carrot sticks from the tray in front of me. "Wait 'til you hear what happened at the beach."

"Hold it," Dad says.

I shove a carrot in my mouth and try looking innocent.

"I know you heard me tell you not to leave," he says.

I chew fast and swallow. "Yeah, but I didn't think you meant do chores that minute." Grandpa coughs but doesn't say anything. Any other time, I'd let them think I went to Highland, but I can't tell about Sunny without mentioning the Landing.

Dad ignores the glob of red sauce that plops on the ground when he waves the barbeque fork at me.

"You're too old to chase after. I expect you to listen. And we're not paying for a phone you won't answer."

"I know, but stuff happened."

He frowns and Grandpa lights another cigarette with the one he's finished but not put out. I dive ahead.

"I was at Wayward Landing—"

"What in heaven's name possessed you to go way out there?"

"I just did, okay. Don't you even care your daughter's kinda, sort of a hero?" I bat away the cigarette smoke floating by my face.

"A hero?" Dad sits on the bench across from me, white knuckling the fork handle.

"Well, I did a really good thing, anyway. I was on my way home—you'll be happy to know—when I found weird tracks in the sand. They dead-ended at a sea turtle who'd hauled out to lay her eggs."

Dad shakes his head. "A sea turtle is why I didn't get a phone call?"

"Yeah, a sea turtle. You know, four flippers, stubby tail, hard, grayish shell?"

"Don't be cute."

"I was taking pictures when Sunny, that's the turtle's name, kind of came unglued. At least she swatted her flipper at me like she thought I was going to hurt her. The flipper was all torn up with fishing line. That was nasty enough, but when I saw the huge fishing hook sticking out of her mouth, I came unglued." I stop for a swallow of tea. Dad stares at me, lips tight.

"Nobody was around to help her except me. A couple of guys came by, but—"

"Elizabeth Susan Barker," Dad says. "Why didn't you have the sense to take someone with you?"

Where's he been since January? There isn't anybody. Mom knows I'm the new kid reject at school. She says be patient, but they ticked me off calling me names.

"Everyone was busy, okay?"

He shakes his head, "Not a smart move for a smart girl." He gets up to rearrange the chicken over the coals.

"What's that supposed to mean?"

"Port Winston is not Coulter City," he says, "and the Landing is too far to go on a joy-ride. You don't know your way around yet. Anything could happen."

"What *did* happen is everything turned out fine."

Grandpa's staring a hole in my head. The old Opinionator's been quiet too long.

I shorten the Sunny and egg rescue story and what I learned about the Center's turtle conservation program. No way I'm bringing up taking pictures of Pete and the guys, my hurt arm, and how, if Maria and Tom hadn't come along—well—being grounded for the rest of my life might look like a blessing.

Neither Dad nor Grandpa chimes in when I come up for air. I push on.

"Sunny's got a satellite transmitter on her back," I say, "and Tom tracks her along the coastline. Maria says scientists have turtles tagged all over the world to learn where they go and how they live. Some countries regulate fishing during the breeding and nesting season so the turtles don't drown in the nets."

"What happened with those guys you ran into?" Dad says.

The guys? Talk about me not listening.

"They took off." I don't dare look at Grandpa. "Like I said, everything turned out fine." I draw a line through the moisture beads on my glass and think about Sunny lying on the operating table. "More than fine. And since I signed up as a volunteer, when Sunny's eggs hatch, I can help release the baby turtles from the Landing. Isn't that great?"

"Hogwash is what it is," Grandpa says, shifting to the edge of his chair.

Here we go.

"Waste of time and taxpayer money." He grinds the cigarette between his shoe and the patio brick. "Them bleeding heart friends of yours care more about an animal that never amounted to a hill o' beans than they do people. Ain't nobody liftin' a finger to help the shrimpin' families goin' under every day."

"Pop, I think Elizabeth was trying—"

"She's the one said it about regulations. They've all but killed shrimpin'. But nobody's stoppin' farmers or plastics and chemical plants and the oil industry from pollutin' our bays and the Gulf. Damn cheap Asian shrimp run us out of the big markets years ago." He turns his head and spits. "You got any idea what it takes to run a shrimp boat, missy?" I shake my head. He looks at Dad. "When's the last time we saw the price of fuel or parts go down?"

Dad doesn't answer.

"Them turtle excluder devices are money down a rat hole," Grandpa says, his voice pitched to a sharp edge. He coughs hard, focusing a wide-eyed gaze on the bricks in front of him. Red-faced, his lips tighten above the edges of his teeth. I can tell he's not finished.

"Good men can't earn a livin' anymore," he says, "but you expect me to stand still for shrimp swimmin' out of my net 'cause of them turtle savers?"

My thoughts twist like a kite caught in a wind gust. I'm not sure how much of his rant is aimed at me and how much is about everything else wrong in the world. All I know is he has a choice about what he does to survive. The turtles don't.

"Take it easy," Dad says. "The TEDs are better de-signed now. If used right, there's no evidence many shrimp escape. Truth is, there aren't enough shrimp out there to go around anymore."

Grandpa's breathing staggers. He glares at Dad. "You sound like them government scientists. Well, your 'no ev-idence' don't match my evidence." He coughs, spits again, then is quiet, his grade-A hissy fit hanging between us. He hates turtles, I couldn't care less about his shrimping issues, and Dad's stuck in the middle.

I pour myself another glass of tea, but don't offer Grandpa any. No sense giving him a reason to stay longer.

Dad covers the plate of chicken with foil and walks into the house. I trace the weathered grooves on the picnic ta-ble.

"Sunny worked so hard laying her eggs," I say. "If you saw her hurt, Grandpa, you'd think differently."

"I've seen plenty of turtles, alive and dead. What I ain't seen is any work out of you." He palms his cigarette pack. "Running away from chores. Home too late to help make supper."

I watch for Dad, hoping for a rescue.

Grandpa aims the unlit cigarette in his fingers at me like a warning dart. "You go off worryin' people," he says. "then come back whimperin' over somethin' that never gave me nothin' but headaches. Your responsibility's to this family and your schoolwork, not gallivantin' off on some animal do-gooder hooey."

I peer up through the tree branches. *You won't make me cry.* Leaning forward, I lock him with the kind of stare he turns on Dad to drive home a point.

"I didn't ask to leave everything I love to come here," I say. "None of us did. Mom's lucky to get out!" My voice cracks the air.

"What's going on?" Dad says, coming down the back steps, holding the salad bowl.

I bolt from the bench, grabbing my glass. Grandpa pushes to his feet. Jaw muscles working, the rise and fall of his chest quickens. For a second he wavers, then locks his knees to steady his six-foot frame. I'm only two inches shorter, but no mistaking that look. I'm an irritating insect, deserving a swat.

"You speak for everyone, do you?"

"It's stupid how you argue Dad to death about everything. I'm . . . we're sick of it. You aren't the only one with an opinion. Or a life!"

"Elizabeth!" Dad says. "That's enough. Pop, time you went home."

Grandpa starts toward the backyard gate, then turns and glares at me. "You remember who puts food on your table and a roof over your head. Show more gratitude and drop the sass."

I open my mouth to ask where he'd be without us. Dad fixing stuff on the *Linnie Jean*, taking him fishing weekends 'cause Grandma's scared he'll forget something important if he's alone, do something stupid. Or worse.

"Forget it." Dad reaches for my arm.

"No." I block him, probably tagging on a week to whatever jail term I earned already. "I won't give up the one thing here I care about." I slam the glass onto the table, splashing tea over my hand. "You think I'm so worthless, Grandpa? Don't know how to work? You watch."

"Elizabeth, you're finished," Dad says.

Grandpa flips the latch. The gate slams behind him.

I run up the back steps, yanking open the porch door. Upstairs, I flop on the bed, jamming the pillow over my head like I can stop the voice screeching inside.

Dad's knock is leaden on the bedroom door. "I want to talk to you."

And I don't want to hear it, but no way he'll back off after what just happened. Since Mom's been gone, his parental overtime makes him cranky and me nuts. My stomach rumbles against the mattress. I sit and grab tissues from the box on the bedside table and blow my nose.

"What?" I drop back down, my back to the door.

The smell of barbecue smoke walks in first. I don't turn over, still mad he let Grandpa treat me like a nobody twice in one day. Used to be, Dad and I were close, closer than Mom and me. Here everything's changed. Feels like he isn't on my side anymore.

"I know you're upset," he says, sitting on the bed, "but I've got enough trouble without you riling up your Grandpa."

I flip over and stare at him. "What about me? I was trying to tell you guys about my fabulous day and he ruined it. He ruins everything." I swipe at my tears. "We were so happy back home."

He looks toward the window. I watch the corners of his mouth slacken, maybe remembering how much. He's got to know we don't belong. I'd give up anything, even Sunny and the Center, if we could get out of here.

"I know these months have been hard," he says, "but I promised your grandma I'd see her through the rough spots with Pop until we can convince him to retire."

"Sounded tonight like he's got good reasons to quit. Give him a shove in that direction and let's go."

"That's just complaining," Dad says. "He doesn't know any other life, and he's not the sort to spend every day at the coffee shop jawing with other old men with nothing left to do."

"Dad, you're miserable and I bet Mom wouldn't have taken the assignment if we were still at home." I know that's not true, not with her career finally taking off. Main thing is she and Dad have been super tense with each other since the day we got here.

I sit up and lean against the headboard. "Grandpa's never going to change no matter how long we stay. Please, can't we go home?"

"You think it's so simple. Just load up the truck." He sounds even more tired than this morning in the garage. "As much as I might want that, we have to stay. Your job is to show your Grandpa more respect."

"Why? He doesn't show me respect. Or you."

"I know and I'm sorry." I watch the pool of energy empty behind his gaze. "He's sick, and angry, and I can't will him different. Try to find a way to understand."

"His being sick excuses him from being mean?"

"No, but we need to avoid any more conflicts. Turtles, for example, are a liability in his mind, so he'll never understand your enthusiasm.

"I didn't ask him to like turtles, but he acts like only his precious shrimp should be allowed to exist. Anyway, he's not going to tell me what to do."

Dad sighs and rubs his hands over his knees. "Then don't give him reasons to think he needs to. Watch your mouth and stay out of his way. Okay?"

"I'll try."

"Good. About your running off this morning. I'll give you a pass this time, as long as you double-time getting your chores done tomorrow. And no pulling that kind of stunt again."

"I will and I won't." What bought me that get-out-of-jail card?

"And never, ever go to the Landing alone. Otherwise, you won't see another sea turtle until you graduate high school. Understood?"

"Yep." None of this is the same as telling me I'm right and Grandpa's wrong, but I want to see Sunny, so I keep my opinions to myself. "Can we eat now?"

He stands and I step into the crook of his arm as we walk to the top of the stairs.

"Grandma sent over a chocolate angel food cake," he says. "And vanilla whipped cream."

"You should have told me. I could have made Grandpa mad a lot quicker."

I hang up the dishtowel and head for my room to organize today's photos from the Landing. Dad's in the living room watching an old movie and looking lonely. I know he misses Mom.

Lost in my photo files I delete the not-so-great pictures, and sort others into different folders: *Birds, Flowers, Insects.* Sunny has her own file. The pictures of her turned out great. A huge surprise, considering I was buku nervous and nauseous one minute and ripping excited the next. The headshot with the hook catches my breath. I save copies of everything to a CD for Maria then run a set of prints, plus a few shots from Pelican Bay. I guess that's showing off, but she seemed interested.

A folder labeled *School* near Sunny's reminds me to look for pictures I took my first few days here. A plea went out Thursday during announcements for candid shots from the beginning of the year. The yearbook photographer's hard drive died and he hadn't backed up anything.

I open the file and scale up three early morning pictures of the quad. The sun's backlit a tree by the bench a clique monopolizes before school and during lunch. Not the money, brains, looks, college future, sweet clique. The other one—maybe money, maybe smart, but definitely the-edge-of-nasty clique. They aren't why I took the picture. I liked the contrast between the school's no-window, prison style walls and the dark, bare limbs. Like if I could climb the tree and walk off the branch tips, I'd be free.

I zoom in. The usual crowd. Perfect for the yearbook. Julia, the witch from P.E. stands in the center. She makes fun of my jeans and T-shirts, my camera, Missouri, and anything else that crosses her mind. Not like I ever did anything to her. She's looking over her shoulder at the dark-haired boy walking toward her. I up the zoom.

OMG. Pete. I didn't recognize him on the beach because he's bleached his hair. Julia's pose is rigid, like she's bracing for something. I study her face. No smile. I shift to the next photo. The kids in the group are more animated, some talking with their hands, some mouths open, laughing. Pete and Julia are clearly a couple. His arm, crossed over Julia's shoulder from behind, encloses her neck. His hand has her face pushed sideways. They're kissing. More like he's trapped her in a lip-lock. My heart double beats. He tried to get me to go with him today. First with charm, then cajoling, finally through fear. I try not to imagine what works on Julia.

I close the files then swipe the cursor over the last set of thumbnails. One click to capture them, a second one to send Pete, Buzzcut, and Ernie into the trash. I stare at the screen. Last month a kid at school ratted out a couple of bullies. Three days later they beat him to a pulp in the bathroom. No pictures, no trouble.

An e-mail from Mom says she's staying longer in Mexico to visit more villages. She's interviewing kids about how immigration affects them when a parent goes to the U.S. looking for work. I'd like to tell her how the kid she left behind feels. Instead I send an edited version of today at the Center and about being a teen volunteer. She'll like that. I attach a photo of Sunny, and send Mom a hug as the doorbell rings. No one ever visits except Grandma or Grandpa, and he usually walks in without so much as a knock. I hear Dad at the bottom of the stairs.

"I'll get her, officer."

CHAPTER FIVE

"ELIZABETH," DAD CALLS.

I walk to the top of the stairs. "Yeah?"

"Come down, please. This gentleman wants to talk to you."

A man in a pale grey uniform, looking like fog pierced by a silver star, stands next to Dad. His official hat's caught up under his arm. I step off the bottom tread.

"Good evening, Miss, I'm Deputy Kirkland," he says, flipping his notebook open and clicking his pen. "I understand you ran into trouble at Wayward Landing this afternoon."

Pete's final warning, about his not being done with me, zings through my head.

"Not trouble," I say, glancing at Dad. "Just guys goofing off, trying to scare me."

"The Marine Center folks said it looked like the boys may have been rough with you. Is that true?"

"What's this?" Dad's face flashes past serious to seriously upset.

My shoulder twinges again. I shift my hands to my pockets.

"It's okay, Dad. Maria and Tom misunderstood. Don't get me wrong, I'm glad help showed up when it did. Just in case. I was trying to distract the guys is all. I thought they might bother the turtle. I'm fine." My smile at the deputy goes over like yesterday's oatmeal.

He taps the page lightly with his pen. "Did the boys call each other by name, or have any identifying marks? Scars, tattoos?"

I tilt my head like I'm thinking, afraid describing Buzzcut's tattoo could lead the deputy straight to him then to Pete. "It happened so fast, I don't remember much. They were older than me, riding ATVs . . . but I'm sure Tom told you that." I pause a second, hoping the deputy will spill what he knows. His steady stare presses back at mine. The back of my neck tightens. I'm stuck.

"The blonde had on light blue shorts, I think. The biggest one had a buzz cut and was wearing jeans. The third guy . . . um, ordinary . . . brown hair, about my height. He was the only one wearing a shirt. Plain white tee." I try another smile. "Nothing identifying about that."

Officer Kirkland writes on his pad. Dad shifts his feet, latching his hands behind his back.

"Ms. Sanchez, Maria, told me you take pictures. I don't suppose you got any of these fellows or their vehicles?"

I scramble through what he just said. Tom and Maria didn't see me taking pictures or they would have told the deputy. Or asked to see them when we got back to the Center.

"Any details could help my investigation. You don't want them bothering other people, do you?"

"Of course not. I was too busy worrying about the turtle to think about anything else." I've never told so many half-truths and untruths, but no way I'm risking my life snitching on Pete.

"Be sure, Elizabeth," Dad says. "Sounds like these boys are trouble."

"I already told him everything."

The deputy looks at Dad, then at me. "All right, young lady." Kirkland hands me his card. "If you come up with anything else, give me a call."

"I will." I slip the card in my pocket and look away. "Sorry I wasn't more help."

"Thanks for your time," he says.

Dad shuts the front door. "Reassure me you told him the truth."

I turn on the stairs, knowing he needs an answer he can swallow. I can't give him one. Fear of those guys is bigger than whatever he'll lay on me if he finds out what really happened or what's in my computer.

"I did my best. Can we drop it now?"

He sighs. "If you say so." He settles onto the sofa and picks up the remote. "I'm just glad you weren't hurt."

I back up a stair. "I'll be smarter next time, promise."

He nods. "I'm glad to hear it."

Sunday, April 4

I roll over, away from sunlight pushing through the crack in the curtains. Nine o'clock. I'm stalling on starting my chores.

My cell phone buzzes on the glass-topped nightstand. I catch Sunny's eye in the photo across the room as I sit up to answer. The phone rattles again.

"Good morning, sweet girl." It's Grandma Linnie. I bet she's been working in the garden since sunrise.

"Hi Grandma, what's up besides you?"

"I wondered if you've got some free time to help me this morning?"

I glance at the pile of clothes and towels by the bathroom door. "I promised Dad I'd do laundry." My cash box is hatching moths, meaning empty, and Grandma usually slips me a little when I help out. "But that can wait."

An hour later, I park my bike inside Grandma's garden gate and lean against it to catch my breath from the two-mile ride. Her gathering basket sits by the strawberry bed. Spring peas, sugar snaps, red chard, onions, young garlic, and lettuce fill beds nearby. Next to the gate, raspberry canes run over trellis lines along the fence. I swear there's nothing she can't grow.

I pop a strawberry in my mouth on my way past a bed and open the screen door into the laundry porch. The sweet-smelling kitchen beyond is quiet.

"Grandma?" No answer. "Grandma, you here?" I peek through the door into the living room.

"She's upstairs." Grandpa's in his green, leather chair that faces the picture window overlooking the porch and front yard. Grandma's oil painting of the *Linnie Jean* hangs on the wall behind him. A man in his kingdom.

"Morning, Grandpa." Stay cheerful. Keep it short.

"Elizabeth," he says, snapping out the crease in the Wood Carver's Digest he's holding.

"You carve?" I say. "What stuff have you made?"

His lips narrow, like he's deciding whether to be irritated. "Your Grandma thinks I need a hobby durin' my so-called recovery."

"Do you like it? Carving, I mean, not your recovery. But you're getting better, right—you're reading the carving magazine, so I guess you do—like carving?"

Motor mouth.

"She paid good money for the subscription. There might be somethin' worth doin' in here, but I just picked it up when you come callin' through the kitchen."

"Sorry. I'll find Grandma."

He nods. I slink past him and up the polished, oak stairs.

Grandma's grandparents built this house a hundred years ago, and I love it. The family owned retail stores, mostly, and had money. Her father was a druggist with his own pharmacy. She inherited the house from her parents, even though Dad said her folks weren't happy about her quitting college to marry a shrimper. My guess is they objected to Grandpa in particular.

The walls upstairs are covered with family photos and Grandma's art. I run my finger over the simple wooden frame around a pencil drawing of Grandpa she drew the year they were married. He was handsome then. No smile, but his eyes look confident. There's mischief in them, too. Wonder where it went.

A watercolor of the house hangs next to one of the bedroom doors. I look closely at details in the flowers painted along the front fence. Initials—not Grandma's, but R.B.—lay in the lower right-hand corner under the edge of a bush.

"Did I hear you, Darlin'?" Paper rustles in the big bedroom down the hall. Grandma's standing among cardboard boxes, a stack of newspaper, and an assortment of stuff on the floor.

"What are you doin'?" I say, sitting on the end of the bed.

"Clearing out junk and collecting things for the hospice rummage sale."

"How can I help?"

"We need to get these boxes filled with giveaways, then take them to the truck. I was just about to start on the closet." She fingers a stack of folded cloth in a yellowed, paper box on the bed. "My Nana embroidered these napkins for my mother when she got married. Haven't used them, or the matching tablecloth, since I don't know when. Maybe you'll use them someday."

I pick up a napkin, tracing the flowers embroidered in white thread. *Probably not.*

She looks at me and walks to the closet.

"They're pretty" I say, not wanting to hurt her feelings. "You should keep them." I cover the napkins with tissue paper and close the box.

"What a mess," she says from deep in the closet. I look inside. "Haven't cleared this out in nearly thirty years. Not since the boys finished high school." She stares for a second at the ceiling. "Well, never mind. Today's the day."

The closet holds more than I thought possible—sort of like Sunny carrying all those eggs—things just keep appearing. Down come Christmas decorations, embroidered pillows, and four boxes of outdated hats that match ten boxes of outdated shoes.

"Can you believe I once wore these things to work everyday?" She holds up a pair of high heels.

I put on a wide-brimmed, lemon-yellow, felt hat and green stacked heels, then parade in front of the mirror. They're stunning with my shorts and T-shirt. I try on every hat and shoe combination. We laugh so hard my ribs ache.

Grandma hangs my armload of clothes back on the rod. I watch her hesitate before sliding a two-foot-long, four-inch-high box, tied with a black ribbon, to the far end of the closet shelf. "Roy" is written on the side of the box facing out. Uncle Roy died when he and Dad were teenagers. That's all I know. I want to ask Grandma about the box, but don't. No one ever talks about Roy, and she didn't bring him up with the box staring her in the face. There must be something I'm not supposed to know.

"Those cartons of shirts go downstairs," she says. "Time for lunch."

"You baked this morning, huh?"

"Strawberry-rhubarb tart."

Next to gardening and painting, what my Grandma does better than anybody I know is cook. I stack and lift the boxes. "Race you downstairs."

Grandpa's filled the iced tea glasses and is pulled up to his place at the table when we get to the kitchen. A pile of Grandma's bread and butter pickles overlap like a nest on the side of his plate. I scoot out quick to the truck with the boxes so I don't have to talk to him. When I get back, Grandma's added plates of bread, chicken salad, and lettuce to the table. Next month the tomatoes will be ripe and we can have BLTs. Only Grandpa can't have the B. Bacon fat's not good for his heart.

"What were y'all doin' up there so long and so loud?" he says. "And where am I haulin' them boxes?"

Grandma sits across from him. "We were cleaning out closets. I'll take everything to the hospice store tomorrow afternoon, so look around the garage for what you can add."

"I ain't got time for that," he says, spearing a lettuce leaf. "Got boat work 'cause Steven and I are goin' out next weekend. I swear that boy's forgotten more than he ever knew about fishing the bays."

"Your blood pressure's still up, James. The doctor said you're not strong enough to be going out so often. Besides, Steven works hard all week. Don't you forget he needs a life of his own, and time with Elizabeth."

Red streaks rise in Grandpa's cheeks. "There's nothin' wrong with my memory," he says. "That doctor's never been on a shrimp boat, so what's he know about what I can do? And it was your idea draggin' Steven down here to help me out. So let him."

"The doctor doesn't have to be a shrimper to know what's best for you. Speaking of which, take your pills."

She puts three in front of his plate. He swallows two and leaves the third.

"Come on," Grandma says, "the doctor says that one, too."

"Nothin' wrong with my attitude, so I ain't takin' no pill for it."

Grandma stares at him, though he's not looking. "Too bad you can't see your 'attitude' from this side of the table."

The sandwich and pickles that tasted so good a minute ago are vinegar on cardboard now. I finish and take my dishes to the sink.

Grandpa trundles back to his chair in the living room. I wash and dry the dishes while Grandma adds a scoop of vanilla ice cream and a dash of cinnamon to my dessert.

"Can I take mine out to the swing?"

"Of course, you go on."

I grab my tea and plate and head out the door.

The glider swing sits at the far end of the yard, over-looking the back of the house and the garden. The pillows are wide enough to seat three, but work best for two when you want room to stretch. The summer I was eight, Mom and Dad sent me here to visit for a week. Grandpa was off shrimping most of the time so I didn't see him much. I was Grandma's tag-along through the house chores and in the garden. Every day after lunch we'd swing, me curled up, her reading aloud until I'd fall asleep. I loved it here then.

I push and glide forward, wishing I could go back to being eight and Grandpa could go back to shrimping.

Grandma hands me a container of strawberries from the refrigerator. "Don't go hitting any big bumps on the way home." She gives me a hug. "It was fun having you with us today. I haven't laughed like that in years."

"Me neither." Not since moving here, anyway.

"I'll collect my purse."

"For what?" Grandpa says, coming in from the living room where he's probably been eavesdropping.

"To pay her," Grandma says, opening her wallet.

"We're family. She ought to do it for nothin'."

"It's all right, Grandma. I'm glad to help you."

"James said you're trying to help the sea turtles," she says, closing her purse in the cupboard.

Grandpa snorts. "Wasting her time is what I said."

I shoot him a warning glance. *As if Grandma was talking to you.*

"Let's take these last two boxes to the truck," Grandma says, following me to the back door.

Grandpa starts toward us. "I can take those."

"They're not heavy," she says, holding tight to the one in her hands.

At the truck, Grandma hands me a folded, ten-dollar bill.

"No, that's too much. Besides, you heard Grandpa."

"He doesn't make my decisions. You do what you want with it."

"Thanks." I hug her and swing onto my bike, thinking how many bus trips to the Center are in that green and white treasure in my hand.

"Love you," I call back at her as I ride out the driveway, sure Grandpa's watching me from behind the picture window.

CHAPTER SIX

Wednesday, April 7

I STEP OFF THE trolley into a warm breeze at the Center. A lab tech inside says Tom and Maria aren't back from nest patrol, so I stop in the atrium to look at the displays. Port Winston is packed. Spring Break has brought down the tourists. Most are outside, looking for an April tan to take home somewhere north where it's still winter. Several dozen visitors mill around the kiosks reading about the bays and the Gulf. I wedge my way through them, out into the sun.

I stop to watch a group of guys hammer a volleyball back and forth over a net. A young boy, standing a dozen yards away, waves a baseball in my direction and winds up to pitch.

Me? I rise on my toes and take off. Half sun-blind, arms stretched, hands cupped, I track the spinning ball as it sails high, then starts its drop.

"Mine." A girl's voice calls across my path. I see the wheelchair too late. Pain flares above my ankle. I crumple to the sand, curling like a car-conked armadillo.

"Hey, I thought you'd veer off," the voice says above me.

Through eyelid slits, I stare at her. "Hey, you need better timing." Grimacing, I slowly sit up, giving the footrest that nailed me an extra glare.

"Sorry, I was in the moment." She's my age, but looks older. Her thick, walnut-colored hair, swept up and fastened behind her head, frames her half-grin. Maybe she thinks this is funny. *New York City Athletic Club* is stenciled in dark green on her pale yellow, well-filled tank top. The baseball rests in her hand. "How's the leg?"

"I'll live." My toes tingle, not so sure. "You?"

She pats her thighs. "The damage is already done." I try not to stare at her thin, olive-skinned legs bent over the chair's seat. Legs that don't match her upper body, which isn't just a fact of nature. She's earned that shirt. Sandaled feet, with sunshine sparkle toenails, prop on the evil footrest.

Her side-arm snap hurls the ball back to the kid. "Awesome, thanks Becca." he says. "See you tomorrow." He sprints back to his beach towel. I wasn't his target, so I sprawled myself down here for nothing.

The girl reaches toward me. "Let's try this again. I'm Becca Calderman."

Instead of shaking hands when I grip hers, she pulls, forcing me to stand. My ankle throbs. I make a lame attempt to smile.

"And this is Midge," she says, patting her compact wheelchair. The oversized battery and double set of hard rubber wheels are wide enough to manage the sand. The fabric-covered armrests are printed with fire-engine red musical notes and the slogan: *Rock and Roll.*

"Elizabeth Barker." I wipe my sweaty, sandy hands on my shorts. "I didn't expect someone out here in a wheelchair." *Good one. Brilliant.* "I mean, I've never even known anyone—"

"Expect the unexpected is what I learned." A grin tweaks her mouth, again. "And I love surprising people, though usually there's no pain involved." She fans her face with both hands. "Do you live around here?"

"Yes. Well, no, not exactly. We're on the other side of downtown, near Highland Beach." Like she'll care.

"I don't know it, but we've only been here four days." She sweeps her hand back toward the housing development, one of several surrounding Forster Boulevard. "We rented a condo in the last tower on Primrose Circle."

Of course, Spring Break.

"Isn't this a great beach?" she says. "I've been down here every day to people-watch and play games with the kids."

"Games?"

She wiggles her fingers. "Catch. Footraces, Frisbee. Whatever."

I look again at her ten perfectly painted toenails. "Footraces?"

"Personal joke." The laugh at herself feels honest. "Frisbee's good. As long as the guy on the other end knows how to aim." She points to the slowly maturing bump on my lower leg. "First class ankle shiner."

"Hardly notice it." Really, it's beating a bass drum, but I'm not going to wimp out around someone who probably can't use her legs at all. "You always been in a wheelchair?"

"Nope." She rubs her hand over her knees. "Midge and I bonded three years ago after a car blew me out of a crosswalk." She touches a toggle switch on the end of the armrest and the chair's seat rises until she sits almost eye-level with me. "That's better."

"You get ten surprise points for that one," I say.

"Stops people from looking down on me, in more ways than one." Without a glance to see if I get it, she rolls toward the water. "Time to cool off." She points over her shoulder at the back of the chair. "I don't allow just anybody to touch the chair—it's the same as touching me—but grab on if you need to."

"Thanks, I can make it."

"Suit yourself."

I have to hobble fast to keep up. She slows on the hard, damp sand. We move side-by-side, the cooling breeze ruffling the front of my thrift store, navy blue T-shirt. Looks every bit the embarrassing buck-and-a-half it cost.

"I was flying kites yesterday with a couple of kids," Becca says. "The kite lift I got, full throttle . . . like a skate boarder leaving the end of a ramp."

"You've got such a good attitude. I'd be . . . well, awful, I think."

"You're toast in New York if you lose your sense of humor. My Dad says the city's motto is: 'Don't whine.'"

Why does my life suddenly feel like it's still bolted to training wheels? "We moved from Missouri a couple of months ago and I still hate going downtown. I'd be wacked out in a week finding my way around New York."

Becca laughs again. I love that it was something I said. I wipe away the trickle of sweat running past my ear.

Might as well find out now. "You're here for Spring Break, right?"

"No, until the beginning of June. My Dad's consulting for some business in town. Big-time marketing job. My folks are into new experiences so they dragged me along to check out the great state of Texas."

"Are you going to Port Winston High?" I say. "Tenth grade?"

"Ninth. My Mom's playing home school teacher. What about you? Missouri, huh? Now Texas. Any thrills you can talk about in either place?"

The joys of life in Coulter City get a quick skim. As much as I miss home, it sounds really boring compared to what I imagine as Becca's life. She asks a few questions and looks like she's listening. Then I tell her about Sunny's rescue. She lights up like a Fourth of July sparkler until I bring up the near miss with Pete, Buzzcut, and Ernie. She clamps a death grip on my wrist.

"Take it from a big city girl. Bow to the moon and pocket your lucky stars."

I don't bring up the pictures, even though she'd probably understand my dumping them.

"I *really* want to see Sunny," she says, her big city, no-whining voice replaced by a ten-year old's. "Can you get me a pass?"

"Follow me." Puffing out my nominal chest, I lead her to the Center.

Maria walks through the atrium doorway as Becca and I reach the patio. "Glad I caught you," she says. "We found two nests at the Landing this morning."

"All right." I give her a high-five.

"Becca Calderman." Becca extends her hand before Maria can ask.

"Can I take her to see Sunny?" I say.

"Sure, I'm headed that way."

We follow through the atrium into the main room. Becca peers into the empty operating room. "Elizabeth said Sunny had surgery."

"Yeah, how did it go?" I say.

"Good. The hook's out, along with another, smaller one he found further down. She has a small wad of fishing line in her lower intestine, so we'll see how that goes."

"What do you mean, 'we'll see?'" I imagine something stuck in my gut. If it feels anything like the cramps I get with my period every month, poor Sunny.

"The line should pass naturally through her system."

"How will you know if it does?" I say.

"You collect poop samples, right?" Becca says, parking next to me.

"Exactly," Maria winks at Becca. "I'm sure Elizabeth will volunteer as a lookout."

"I believe I volunteered for occasional feeding, emotional support, and portrait photography. Poop patrol was not on the sign-up sheet."

"Too bad," Maria says. "Here I thought you were a budding turtle biologist."

"It's my first week, give me a break."

Maria laughs. "Come on, then."

We follow her to the rehab area. Sunny paddles slowly around the edges of her pool, then crosses the center. I want her to know I'm here, but as usual, she doesn't seem to notice anything around her.

"She's adorable," Becca says, swinging in sideways to the tank. "You're so lucky to be the one who found her." She reaches toward Sunny when she swims near. I point out the DO NOT TOUCH sign. We lean on the edge and watch her rhythmic swimming, front flippers gliding up and down, back ones trailing behind. In the water she's as graceful as a great blue heron gliding across Pelican Bay.

"What happens if Sunny doesn't lose the fishing line?" Becca says.

"Dr. Nguyen will do surgery. For now, she's on antibiotics to get her white blood cell count down."

I snap out of daydreaming about birds and bays. "I thought you said it was just fishing line, no big deal. Is she really sick?"

"Just a little infection. Chances are she'll be fine, but we're in 'wait and watch' mode for a bit."

I'd like to believe her, but I'm the wait and worry kind.

"How did Sunny's photos turn out?" Maria says as Becca and I follow into her office.

"I almost forgot." I dig out the CD. "Here." I spread the photos from Pelican Bay and of Sunny onto the worktable. Becca maneuvers her chair in the tight space. She moves forward a foot, turns, backs six inches, turns the front wheels again. There's nothing to clear out of her way, nothing to do, but my chest tightens like I'm supposed to fix something. She stops next to the table, looking as relaxed as if she's walked in on two legs and sat down.

Maria picks up the picture of swipe marks Sunny's flippers made trying to cover the nest.

"I love this. The sun sparkling off the sand grains around the nest and the eggs peeking out of the hole. Magic. My shots always turn out dull—grey turtle on grey-brown sand."

Becca fingers the corner of the headshot of the hook and line. "This one is really sad. Sunny's crying."

"The tears aren't about sadness or pain," Maria says. "They flush excess salt from her body."

Becca pushes the picture away. "They still look like ouch tears to me."

"Barbara," Maria says, signaling to a woman walking by in the hall, "come look at Elizabeth's pictures."

A middle-aged woman, dressed in a light blue blouse and tan slacks, doubles back into the office. She stands next to me and looks through the photos twice.

"They are very good," she says. "May I keep them?"

"Sure. I can make more."

"Barbara is the Center's executive director. We call her 'Top Turtle,'" Maria says. "This is Elizabeth's friend, Becca."

"You're both signed up as volunteers, yes?" Barbara says. It's not really a question.

"Give me the paper," Becca says. "Elizabeth can't be the only turtle hero around here."

I push away a twinge of competition.

"Excellent," Barbara says. "There's a required volunteer training Saturday. See you then."

Becca and I park by one of the tanks in the atrium. She tucks the copy of her completed volunteer paperwork into the chair's side pouch and tickles the underside of a sea star through the glass wall.

I shift my backpack on my shoulder and check outside the window for the trolley.

Take a chance. "You want to maybe hang out sometime?"

"How about Saturday after the training?"

We exchange cell numbers and e-mail addresses. Becca glances at the clock above the gift shop door. "Yikes, I'm late to meet my Mom at the pool for our workout. I'll call you."

I watch her zoom down Forster Boulevard. Ms. Hot Wheels.

I close the front door and am across the living room when I first hear him.

"Amy, you're not listening." Dad's barely controlled anger behind the kitchen door stops me on the bottom stair. He's on the phone with Mom. Maybe she called because of the e-mail I sent the other night about Sunny. Maybe Dad wrote and filled her in on Deputy Kirkland's visit, the big detail I left out.

"What do you mean, you've about reached your limit?" Dad says. "You're not even here—No, that's not what I meant. I never said you had to be." A cup bangs against the kitchen table. Chair legs scrape the floor. I brace myself to fly up the stairs if the door moves. "What do you expect me to do? Pop's convinced it's only a matter of time before he's shrimping full-time again."

Good, not about me. Bad, Grandpa's still causing trouble.

"Be reasonable," Dad says. "You and Elizabeth seem to think I can pack up and leave. It's not like after Roy died."

I lean back against the banister, heart pounding. What's Uncle Roy got to do with it?

"Calling Pop delusional doesn't help. He's agreed to only go out fishing if I'm along."

Mom's right.

"Look, if nagging him worked, he'd have quit smoking already, so back off."

Dad's right.

"I don't need a reminder your job is keeping us afloat. You wanted this assignment. Your career, remember?"

Hey, you encouraged her, no problem, you said, we'd manage. Now you're one frayed wire.

"This conversation is going nowhere," he says. "We'd better hang up. Okay, I'll tell her."

Silence, then the back door slams. I stand frozen, as if handcuffed to the railing. What did she mean about reaching her limit? My phone buzzes against my hip. I pivot and run up the stairs. What if it's Mom?

"Hello," I drop into my desk chair and lay my head on the desk.

"What's with the whisper?" It's Becca.

"Sorry, I thought you were someone else. What's going on?"

"I've been crazy on the Internet since I saw you. There is tons of stuff about sea turtles. You probably already know that."

"Umm." My attention lingers downstairs.

"Hey, don't be too interested."

"Sorry, what did you find?" So far I've only looked at the pictures in the book Maria gave me.

"All seven species of sea turtles, worldwide, are in deep trouble. Even though tons of people are trying to protect them."

"Maria mentioned it." Mom and Dad hardly ever argued before we moved. She usually says how it is and Dad pretty much goes along with it. This place, his being around Grandpa—

"Listen to this," Becca says. "'Shrimp trawl nets often scrape the sea floor clean, destroying habitat for shrimp and numerous other species. For every pound of wild shrimp that ends up on your dinner plate, up to fifteen pounds of other sea life, called by-catch, is caught, much of it killed, in the trawling nets. Thousands of sea turtles drown in these nets every year, seriously compromising recovery and conservation efforts.'"

"Hold on, hold on," I say. "My Grandpa's a shrimper and he was making a huge deal the other night about how he has to use something called a TED in his net that lets turtles get out so they don't drown."

I hold my breath, waiting for the fallout on the other end.

"I read about those things, too. But lots of turtles are still dying. Maybe not every place has the same laws about using TEDs. Then, not everyone obeys the law, right? Even coming from Missouri, you're not that naive."

"Of course not." Not after last Saturday. Possible harassment, threats, assault, lies. Dad's right, I'm not in Coulter City anymore. I get up, walk to the window, and look down into the backyard. The oak tree's branches stretch toward me, filtering my view above and below. Through the leaves I catch a splotch of red plaid. I squirrel around for a better view. Dad sits at the picnic table, head in his hands.

"Hello?" Becca says. "Did I lose you again?"

"Yeah. No. Can I call you back? Dad's waiting on me for supper."

"Sure. I'll see what else I can find out. Later." She's gone.

I shut off the phone and start my computer. A new e-mail from Mom. I stare at the "Hello" in the subject line. My stomach flutters. What does she know? I don't want her yelling at me, too. The screen door below squeaks open and shut.

"Elizabeth?" Dad calls. "You up there?"

"I'm here."

"Supper." Tension from the argument has deepened his voice.

"Okay, be right there." I open the e-mail.

Hi Honey,
Your news about the turtle is wonderful. I knew you'd find something fun to latch on to. Sounds like you'll have plenty to keep you busy this summer. Calling your dad in a few minutes. Hope you'll be there so we can talk. I can't wait to hear more. Love you.

It doesn't sound like she knows anything more than what I wrote. Still, Dad could have told her other stuff when they talked.

"Elizabeth. Now." I scoot out of my chair and take the stairs two at a time down to the kitchen.

The colander in the sink holds a glob of dull grey shrimp bodies. Some of last year's catch from Grandpa's freezer. I think of what Becca just told me about by-catch and turn away from the sink, barely hungry anymore.

Dad's sautéing onion and garlic in the big frying pan. Two lemon halves lie on the cutting board. As soon as the onion is clear-looking, he'll put the shrimp in and cook them until they're all pink.

"I can't eat those," I say. He stops stirring and rests a balled-up fist on the counter ledge.

"I've had a long day, Elizabeth, don't be difficult. And since when do you turn up your nose at shrimp?"

"They just don't sound good tonight. I'll make myself scrambled eggs, okay?"

"Fine." He hands me the smallest pan from the over-head rack.

Nothing in here feels fine. I beat the eggs and two slurps of milk together in a bowl, melt the butter in the pan and slide them in. We stand side-by-side, stirring, yellow in one pan, grey and pink in the other. Dad scowls down at the shrimp changing color under the wooden spoon. A pot of veggies from Grandma's garden steams on the back burner.

On top of the silent treatment I got at the stove, we sit wordless at the table filling our faces for three whole minutes. I watch the clock as another minute clicks by. I can't stand it.

"So, you want to hear about my day?" I reach for the pepper and count to five. "Of course, Elizabeth. Maybe you can cheer me up."

"I'm sorry, Sweetheart," he says. "How was your day?"

"Terrific. I made a new friend at the Center. Her name's Becca, she's really great, and even though she about killed me, we're going to hang out."

He looks away from the deep green swirl of Swiss chard on his plate. "I left you a note about extra chores."

"I know, but I had to see Sunny. She's got fishing line knotted in her gut and elevated white blood cells. I'll do the chores tomorrow, I promise. Don't be mad at me."

"I've heard that before."

"I promise, promise. I'll even have supper made by the time you get here. How about that?"

"Sounds good. So, is this girl local, and what's this about almost killing you?"

"She's from New York City and I tripped over her wheelchair's footrest trying to catch a high fly ball. See?" I plop my foot on the chair between us and show him the deep purple and blue knob on my leg.

He whistles. "Gonna be a nice shade of yellow-green in a week."

"Thanks for that charming prediction."

"A New Yorker, huh? I'm surprised she talks to a small town, Middle America girl like you." He smiles and gently pulls on my big toe.

His tweak makes my leg hurt, but I keep quiet. He's finally lightened up, and I don't want to spoil it. "For your information, Becca thinks this Middle America girl is pretty amazing for helping save Sunny. Did I tell you she's in a wheelchair?"

"Sunny?"

"No, silly, Becca."

"I believe you mentioned it. What happened to her?"

"Pedestrian accident. She's so positive, cruising all over the beach, talking to anybody, playing with kids. Like nothing's wrong with her. I mean, just like anybody else."

"She sounds practically perfect. I'm very happy you've made a friend." His expression clouds. "I forgot to tell you, Mom called earlier."

"I know." It slipped out. "I didn't know she actually called, I got an e-mail from her saying she would."

"She was sorry to miss you and sends her love." He takes his dishes to the sink. "I need a walk. You want to come?"

Something tells me he'd rather be alone, and I don't want to work so hard talking if he's going into another funk. "You go. I need to get ahead on some homework."

He crumples his napkin and drops it into the trash can at the end of the counter.

"Dad, did Mom say anything else?"

"Such as?"

"Like when she's coming home."

"She doesn't know yet. Depends on a lot of things." He lifts his ball cap from its hook. The door closes gently behind him. The kitchen feels hollow and empty. Except for a very small me and the cold, soapy sponge in my hand.

I catch Becca's call on the fourth ring. "We're going to the volunteers' training Saturday, right?" she says.

"Rats, I forgot. I'll ask my Dad when he gets back from his walk. If he says no, I'll call you."

"You're the only friend I've got down here. Don't let me down."

"I won't." Only friend. Go figure.

It's dark when Dad gets home. I'm forcing myself to work on math when he stops in my room to say goodnight.

"Can I go to the training at the Center Saturday?" I say.

"What kind of training?"

"For volunteers. CPR training in the morning, then Maria's going to teach us about the Center's programs and stuff about turtles in the afternoon. That way we'll know what to tell visitors. They're feeding us lunch, then Becca and I are hanging out afterwards. I promise to be home by five."

"What does it cost?"

"Nothing except my bus ticket, but Grandma more than covered that. The trolley's free."

"Sounds like you made plans before asking me."

"I kind of had to. The training's mandatory for working with the turtles and Becca's depending on me."

"I don't know. It seems like you're getting awfully caught up in this all at once."

I bristle. "How can you say that? You were happy I found a new friend, and I want something better to do than hang around here all the time."

He runs his hands over his face, then through the short curly hair that's close to matching mine. "I know you need your own life. I just don't want you wandering too far from ours."

"Does that mean I can go?"

"I guess so."

I kiss his cheek. "I love you." He looks surprised, in a good way, but it lasts only a second before his expression turns distant.

"Sleep well." He holds my arm a second longer than I expect before letting go.

CHAPTER SEVEN

Saturday, April 10

BECCA'S SITTING NEXT TO Sunny's pool when I get to the training. She turns and waves when she sees me. Today her tank top is army green. The logo—a gold tiara and *Crown Boxing Academy* in black letters—stretches across her chest.

"Hey, E. Guess what? Tom let me help with Sunny's blood draw."

"Help? How exactly?" Sunny pokes her nose along the edge. I drum the air above the pool with my fingers, trying not to feel jealous.

"I didn't do much," she says not reacting to my snarky tone. "Tom and this other guy wrestled her for the sample and I wrote her stats on the vial label." She makes kissy noises in Sunny's direction. "Pretty soon you'll be in the Gulf catching blue crabs won't you, sweetie?"

Oh, please.

She wags a finger at the water. "But, no more hors d'oeuvres on hooks, young lady. We can't save you every time you get in trouble."

We?

She smiles at me and moves away from the tank. "You ready for class?"

I drop in beside her. "I guess."

"What's wrong?"

I look away. "Nothing, just tired." *And not sure what you're about.*

Everyone else in the class is forty years old, at least, with this middle-aged cliquey thing going on around the center chairs. Becca chooses an open spot in front to park. I sit, stifling a yawn. She turns to say something, but I pull a brochure from the packet so I don't have to talk to her.

WHAT IS CARDIOPULMONARY RESUSCITA-TION (CPR)? the cover says. The picture shows a man leaning over someone, his hands crossed on the person's chest. I stuff the brochure back in the packet. *This is going to be a riot.*

Maria walks to the front of the room. "Good morning, everyone. Welcome to one of our favorite events around here: launching a new group of volunteers." She motions forward a guy in shorts and polo shirt. He's got a swimmer's build and a summer's worth of tan already. "Greg is your CPR instructor from the American Red Cross."

Becca pokes me. "Woo-hoo," she whispers. "Things are looking up."

Greg may be a woo-hoo to her, but his five-minute introduction slides me dangerously close to zoning out. Until he plants himself next to Becca. She beams up at him.

He scans the group. "Does it seem odd to anyone that Becca's in a CPR class?"

Whoa, dead body on the doorstep. Nobody says a word. It never occurred to me Becca shouldn't be here.

"She's in great shape, but in a wheelchair," he says, "so how can she manage rescue techniques that require mobility and strength?" Not a peep. "The answer is she can't."

Oh, my God, he's going to kick her out.

Becca stiffens and sits straighter against the back of her chair, smile gone.

So much for being the center of attention.

"But," Greg says, "in an emergency, she—all of us— can do a lot. Obviously, the first and most important thing is to call 911. Almost anyone can do that." He looks down at Becca. "Right?"

"I believe so." Her smile is wary.

"In a crisis," he says, "Becca could instruct others in CPR techniques or direct people away from the scene." He puts his hand on her shoulder. "I imagine her as the calm voice a frightened child or anxious adult may need to hear."

She gives him gaga eyes.

Really?

"Let's get started," he says. "Becca, for now you're my partner. The rest of you pair up and clear enough space on the floor for half of you to lie down when we get to the resuscitation exercises."

Becca follows Greg to the front of the room, the same self-pleased look on her face I saw when she told me about helping Tom this morning. I turn and look over the crowd for a partner.

The only choice left is a man Grandpa's age. I glance back at Becca. Greg's hands are doing half the talking, his gaze locked on hers. She nods, looking serious. The Grandpa clone is heading my way.

No surprise, Becca is really good at giving directions. I hate to admit she makes the first half of the morning fly by. Greg can't stop us laughing when one drill gets out of control and we pile into each other. Between her "People!" and spouting orders like a traffic cop, Becca gets us back in line and through all the moves. Her style makes us feel easy. Even me.

By lunchtime the group's working like a real team. I like it—a lot, mainly because everyone treats Becca and me like we're adults. My partner, unlike Grandpa, thinks I'm a turtle hero.

Greg stands at the head of the food table as we load our plates with sandwiches and salad. "Great job everyone," he says. "You are now prepared for an emergency."

First rule in emergency prep—don't leave your cell phone at home.

Check.

"How about some bocce?" Becca says after we finish Maria's training.

"What's that? A drink or something?"

"No, it's an Italian ball game. I play it with a group once-a-week in Central Park." She points a thumb over her shoulder. "Get the balls out of my pack."

I check my phone. Three o'clock. "Maybe I shouldn't. My Dad expects me home by five." Since he didn't ground me Saturday, it's stupid to take a chance on being late. Now that I finally have a friend and someplace to hang out.

"Come on, this won't take long" she says.

"An hour and a half, max." If the trolley's on time, I'll squeak in the front door as planned. I lift out a string sack of four red balls, four blue, and a smaller white one.

"This spot is perfect," she says, rolling to a stretch of sand not covered with blankets, chairs, umbrellas, and people. "Drag out a rectangle. Fifteen giant steps straight up, eight feet across, then back toward me fifteen. I'll make the throw line here."

My lines drawn, I watch Becca shuffle the shiny white ball back and forth on her palm. "This is the 'jack,' or 'pallino' in Italian," she says. "Toss it out there anywhere, just keep it inside the boundaries. We can dump the rules for now."

My throw arcs the ball through the air, dropping it with a soft thud midway between the two sidelines.

"Now roll your first ball as close as you can to the pallino. I have to get mine even closer or knock you farther away."

"Sounds easy enough." I push my toe into the line, drop my hand back to start my swing, then stop. "Oh, great."

"What?"

"It's Julia and her accessory pack from school." The procession of five girls glides along the water's edge in our direction. "She's made me the butt of her stupid jokes since the first week of school."

"Why?"

"Just because I'm not Texan, I guess, and not rich like her."

Becca watches as Julia and her crowd close in. "They slithered past me the other day when I was playing wave tag with a couple of kids. She met up with a big blonde guy at the refreshment stand. He had his hands all over her." Becca turns back to the throw line. "Nothing new. Big boobs, bucks, and attitude. She's harmless."

"Oh, right, as a swamp full of cottonmouths." I shiver. "The blonde is her boyfriend, Pete. He's one of the guys who went after Sunny and me."

Becca scans the beach around us. "Doesn't look like he's here, so relax."

Not yet.

Julia's packed into "look at me" baby blue short-shorts and a white belly-shirt. The sun flashes off the gold chain around her neck and set of bangle bracelets. The girls laugh and bounce behind her, then, like a flight of sand-pipers, they veer in our direction. Julia stops a couple of yards away from us. She slides her dark glasses up onto her head with the tip of a dark red fingernail.

"Well, if it isn't Elizabeth, 'Mizery pants,' Barker. What are you doing on this side of town?" She switches her attention to Becca before I have time to throw back an answer. Not that I have one. I squeeze the bocce ball, so close to smacking her with it my knuckles hurt.

Julia points at Becca's chest. My breath catches. "What's that supposed to mean, you're a boxing queen? Who'd you beat, Elmo?" The girls giggle in unison. It's then I notice the fading yellow bruise, covered in extra make-up under Julia's eye. I remember the picture of Pete and her I took at school, what looked like his forced kiss.

Becca's mouth turns into an easy smile. She gazes at Julia like a cat locking onto a careless bird. "Wrong class," she says. "Elmo's a featherweight." She scans Julia up and down, stopping at her face. Her smile disappears. "It can be dangerous getting in the ring with the wrong opponent."

A frown flicks the inside edges of Julia's perfectly plucked brows. Becca sits still, waiting for her bird to fall off the perch.

Julia is the first to look away. "Go back to your stupid game before Barker-brains forgets how to play." She drops her glasses back on her nose, flares out her chest, and walks off, hips in overdrive.

Becca smiles. "That girl's got a lot to learn."

"Come over for a few minutes." Becca's punching numbers in her phone, not waiting for my answer. "Hi, Mom. I need a ride—because Elizabeth's coming over and she doesn't have much time."

I'm stuck, again. I call Dad and leave him a voicemail that hanging out with Becca includes going to her house and I'll be a little late.

Mrs. Calderman is already parked in the handicapped spot in front of the patio when we get there. The center van door is open and a lift for Becca's chair rests on the street. She rides onto it, swivels to face the door, and locks herself in place.

"This is my mom, Jenny," she says.

Becca's mom doesn't look like how I imagined a fancy New York lawyer. Big smile, pleated pink shorts, white button-up blouse, and dark hair clipped back at her collar.

"I feel like I already know you," she says, shaking my hand. "Becca's hardly stopped talking turtles since you two met."

"I'm an info freak," Becca says behind me.

Primrose Circle ends at a grassland buffer that runs the length of Elliot Bay and the half mile between all the houses and the beach. We park in the ground floor garage in a handicapped spot reserved for condo number 1201. Becca glides out of the van to the elevator.

"Going up," she says, pressing the button.

"I'll be back from the store soon," Mrs. Calderman says out the van window. "Fresh herb tea and juice are in the refrigerator."

"I know, Mom. Bye." Becca jabs a finger against the elevator button again.

We ride to the twelfth floor—the top of the building. Becca leads the way down the long corridor to the last apartment and opens the front door onto a large living and dining room. Sunlight bounces over cream-colored walls. Thick area rugs decorate the wooden floor around furniture covered in light fabrics with faded aqua, tan, and pink flowers. Faded on purpose, not because its old and worn out. Two cushy swivel chairs and an overstuffed couch cluster round a coffee table. A bar counter separates the dining area from the kitchen. I hate Julia, but she's right, I'm definitely on the "other side of town."

Becca wheels past the dining table. Everything is arranged in open paths to make room for her chair. "The furniture's tacky, but it rents with the place." She glances back at me in the doorway. "You coming?" She disappears behind the counter into the kitchen.

I close the door. If I were alone, I'd roll around on these soft rugs, then plop on the couch, eyes closed, and do nothing but breathe luxury for an hour.

Becca's head and shoulders rise above the counter. I slip around the end of the bar and watch her get two glasses from the upper cupboard.

"So, what's it going to be?" She opens the fridge. "Herb tea, okay?"

"Great. Can I help?" I walk toward the open refrigerator, but she moves the chair, blocking me.

"Nope," she says, filling the glasses.

I follow her onto the patio, feeling put off—until I look at the view. The brick-colored tile roof of the Marine Center stands out against the green water and blue sky. A small wetland in the buffer glimmers through reeds growing along the end of Elliot Bay near where it flows into the huge Ghost Crab Bay. A hawk calls above us. I hold my breath as it drops from sight into the green and brown grasses not far off the beach. I settle into a chair cushion. "Snagged a mouse, I'll bet."

"Really?" Becca wrinkles her nose.

"Bird's got to eat."

"Yeah, but some poor little creature is out there getting ripped to shreds."

"No mouse, no bird." I sip my tea and listen to the water break against the beach. "You are so lucky with this to look at every day." No way I'm inviting you to my house. Ever.

"Granted, it does have a few things over my usual view of the Hudson River. Come on, I want to show you my room."

I let her go inside first so I get a last look at the Bays.

The door is open at the end of the hall. The room has windows on two sides, one overlooking each bay. The bathroom is almost as big as my bedroom. There's plenty of room for Becca to maneuver her chair.

"Be right out." She closes the door behind her. "Make yourself at home," echoes off the tile.

I choose the window looking over Elliot Bay. Way up at the channel's end big pleasure boats park on this side in a fancy marina near restaurants and shops along Preston Street. Mom, Dad, and I had dinner at a fish place there on Valentine's Day. I got invited because we haven't spent much time as a family lately. They talked about their twenty-eight years together. Some stuff I didn't know, like how Mom went back to school after four miscarriages, thinking she'd never have a kid. Then I showed up and stuck.

That night, when Mom talked about how a woman needs an education and independence, Dad got quiet, then switched the subject to me and school. Sometimes I wish they'd had more kids to spread around the attention I get. A big brother or sister might understand what's going on with them these days. I sure don't.

I scan the warehouse and shacks lined up along the old fishing wharf across the Bay. The *Linnie Jean* is lost in the distance among the rows of boats and rigging. Dad took me down there a few months ago and went on about our family's three-generation history fishing the bays. He calls Grandpa one of the last holdouts. Frankly, the place stunk and was so rundown I don't know how we lasted one generation as fishermen.

The toilet's flush brings me back to the room. It's neat and simple, easy for Becca to move in. Above the bedside table hangs a frame full of snapshots. In one, six girls cluster behind Midge. Becca's wearing her toothpaste ad smile. In another she's in the middle lane of a swimming pool, half a length ahead of the other swimmers, head turned to one side, taking a breath, her opposite arm clearing the water. I smile at the photo of her behind a bocce court end line, the red ball frozen forever mid-air beyond her fingertips. The last is a formal shot. A boy in a dark blue tuxedo stands next to her under an arbor decorated in red and gold leaves on green vines. Becca's pale yellow dress hugs her body and just covers her knees. Pink rose buds weave through swirls of hair gathered on top of her head. She's not in Midge, but a light frame chair, low back, with wheels that slant slightly in at the top. The center of the wheels are solid discs painted with Anime girls flying over a mountain waterfall. Becca grins like she just won the lotto. I lean in to look closer.

"That was our school's Fall Fantasy dance last year."

I point to the guy as she stops next to me. "Boyfriend?"

"No, a good friend since 5th grade. We were still dancing when the band quit at midnight."

"You dance?"

"You kidding?" She toggles the switch, moving her chair back and forth in tight, controlled movements, humming a Latin tune. "Samba's my favorite." She twirls in a circle. "I out-danced everybody that night." She points to the wheelchair in the picture. "Clearly, I had the advantage."

I lift a round, silver medal, attached to a dark green and white-striped ribbon from the bedside lampshade.

New York City Jr. Paralympic Trials Silver Medal-100 meter Freestyle. "Wow. You won this?"

Becca sighs, moves away from me, and parks next to an armchair at the desk on casters. "Time for the wheelchair talk," she says, positioning her hands on the second chair and swinging up from her seat. I want to look away, embarrassed for what I said and for staring at her awkward, painful-looking movements. She drops into the chair and uses her hands to pull her legs in place.

"I'm really sorry," I say. "I'm so dumb."

"Not dumb, just ignorant, like a lot of people." Her usually breezy tone cuts a cool grey line in the air between us.

"Sorry," I say.

"Stop saying that. Number one, I'm a person. Same as before the accident. I like staying busy and testing my limits. Instead of legs I use a wheelchair to get me around. The chairs are an extension of me, of my body, but they aren't me. Got it?"

"Okay. But it's kind of amazing."

Becca frowns.

"I mean you do much more than anyone I know," I say. "Especially me."

"You think that's because I can and you can't? My guess is you haven't tried yet, or you're good at things I'm not."

I put the medal back. *A few photography awards. Big deal.*

"I've got a lecture for people who get down on themselves. Want to hear it?"

"No thanks. Forget what I said before." I swallow hard and drop to the bed, fumbling through materials in the packet from this morning's training.

"Done." Becca rolls the desk on wheels toward her and opens her laptop.

I run a sleeve across my eyes when she's not looking, then hand her the Center's brochure to change the subject. "They have an adopt-a-turtle program. You want to go in together on Sunny?"

She glances over the page. "Hey, my kind of parenting. No diapers."

Mrs. Calderman raps on the door. "You two better get moving if we're going to get Elizabeth home on time."

"We have to drop off adoption papers for Sunny on the way," Becca says, moving herself back to Midge. This time it doesn't look so hard. I'm beginning to get the picture about who has what limits.

We leave Mrs. Calderman parked in the shade cast by the Center's main building. Maria and Barbara are talking to a couple of visitors in the atrium when we come through the main doors.

Barbara looks over. "Elizabeth," she says. "I want to talk to you. Come to my office."

"How was the CPR training?" she says, picking up the folder of photos I gave her last week.

"Great." Becca says before I can answer. "I learned how to tell people what to do in an emergency and they learned how to listen to me."

Oh, brother.

"I'll bet," Barbara says, smiling as she spreads the pictures across a small table. "These could sell in our gift shop. Would you like to be our first featured junior artist?"

"Really?"

"We'll pay you 60% of the sale price and decide together what Center project to fund with the balance."

Becca scatters through the photo pile, grinning.

Barbara retrieves the headshot of Sunny with the hook in her mouth. "We'd like this as the centerpiece for our fall fundraising campaign."

Becca grabs my arm. "You know what this means?"

I shake my head.

"You'll be famous—even rich."

Barbara laughs. "You never know. If your parents agree our proposal is fair, we can have prints matted and ready for the shop in a week."

I want to do a Becca samba spin. "I'm sure they'll say yes. I know my Mom will."

Becca pulls my arm again. "We're not here just about you, remember." She gives the brochure and twenty dollar bill her mom loaned us to Barbara. "We want to adopt Sunny."

"I can't think of better foster parents," Barbara says.

During the ride across town, Becca chatters at her mom about Barbara's idea for selling my photos. Her mom nods and says, "That's nice," and "wonderful" a few times, not seeming to mind Becca's excitement. Neither do I, since it's for me.

At the corner of Cooper and Preston streets, I argue them out of dropping me off at home. Luckily, the Cooper Street houses within sight have good paint and more than spit holding up their gateposts.

I wave as they drive off, then head down the block. It's been a great day. I'm not worried about Becca anymore, now that I understand her. I can't win a swimming competition or do the samba, but she's not "first featured junior artist," either.

Humming, I scoop the Gulf Courier up from the walk and flip it open. The headline rips the tune from my throat.

CHAPTER EIGHT

I COLLAPSE ONTO THE wooden porch step and drop all but the first section, reading past the first-page headline:

DEVELOPMENT PROPOSED FOR
WAYWARD LANDING

The Port Winston County Commissioners will hold a public meeting Thursday, at 7 p.m., to discuss Tortuga Sands, Pioneer Development Corporation's proposed 200 acre project, including county park land. In an unprecedented move, the developer seeks permission to build single and multi-family homes, a shopping center, water theme park, and a 250 slip marina in Pelican Bay. If approved, the project would remove the last, publicly held natural area within the county's jurisdiction.

I wad the page into a ball. "They can't!"

"Whoa," Dad says, coming through the front door. "What's got you in a snit?"

"They're going to destroy Sunny's beach, that's what." I beeline the ball at him.

"Who is?"

"Some stupid development company." I point to the crumpled paper in his hand. "It's in there."

He sits next to me. He frowns, lips moving to the words on the page.

"Well?" I say. "See what I mean?"

"Doesn't look good," he says.

"I have to call Becca." Dad jackknifes his knees sideways as I lunge past him. The screen door slams behind me.

"Hey! Your night to make supper."

I sprint through the living room, grabbing the banister knob on my way upstairs. "I know. Five minutes."

Two shakes and a week's worth of collected stuff pours out of my pack onto the bed. I unearth the cell phone from under today's CPR folder and a bag of crushed potato chips.

Becca answers on the first ring.

"Do you get the Courier?" I say.

"Yes, why?"

"Obviously, you haven't read tonight's front page."

"No. I've been reading about turtle conservation in Italy and Africa."

"Forget that. A humongous development is going to wipe out the Landing."

"Seriously?"

"Would I make it up?" I pace the floor around the wildflower pattern rug Grandma hooked for me a long time ago. The last four months I've worn an invisible track in the floor around its border.

"I'm surprised we didn't hear about it from Maria," Becca says.

"She's about turtles, not development."

"Sounds like they're linked in this one." Becca's fingers snap near the receiver. "I've got it."

"What."

"My dad's job is business marketing. Come over tomorrow and we'll pick his brain for ideas on how to convince the Commission to deny the project."

"Noon?"

"Perfect."

A small tornado of dishes rattles in the kitchen, Dad's signal I'm pushing my luck. "Gotta go."

I wink at Sunny's photo on my way downstairs. "Not to worry. We're on it."

Becca opens the door to the condo. "I read the article. I can't tell if naming the development Tortuga Sands after a turtle shows this Pioneer outfit is oblivious or just nasty."

"How about both?"

She points to two plates mounded with salad. "Mom made us lunch. I'm starved."

"Did you talk to your dad?" I say, swirling dressing over the greens.

"No. He and my Mom got home late from a dinner party last night. Now they're golfing." She locks her fork under the lettuce and puts the plate in her lap. "Wait until you taste this."

"It was nice of her to make us lunch." My Mom was always too busy to cook for my friends. "Have a good time," she'd say on her way to graduate school seminars or to make a story assignment deadline.

I squeeze into the chair against the patio wall and breathe in the sweet smell of the Gulf. My fork uncovers snow peas, chicken chunks, and pasta spirals hiding among the lettuce. A spice in the dressing—ginger, I think—tingles my tongue. This even beats the Chinese chicken salad at the Blue Moon—the one decent restaurant in town Dad and I can afford every few weeks.

"I could make this if I had the dressing recipe." Note—convince Dad to upgrade our shopping list.

A clump of noodles jiggles on Becca's fork as she taps the air. "The company's website only says, 'Tortuga Sands—Information coming soon.' All you have to do with my Dad is lay out the whole turtle angle."

I almost choke on a piece of bell pepper. "What? Why me? I don't even know him."

"Because you found Sunny. That'll give you weight with him."

"What if I screw things up? Start babbling or something?"

"Relax," she says, "he's a mush ball. Okay, background on Pioneer. According to the website the company built the three hotels downtown. You know, the ones that light up at night like Las Vegas wannabes."

I nod. I've only seen Las Vegas on TV but know exactly which hotels she means.

"And four blocks of old town redevelopment, Three Graces mall—which is pretty cool—four condo towers, a couple of big office complexes, and a lot of the custom homes around here and somewhere out in the county along the Gulf. The website suggests contacting the office for a full project list. I say we skip that. Bottom line—we're up against big bucks."

"The custom homes in the county must be Mansionland."

"Oh my God, you're kidding. There's something called Mansionland?"

"No, I named it that. Pioneer's already got a huge stretch of beach and dunes for sale next to the Landing. The whole line of beach from Mansionland to Pelican Bay will be under buildings if the plan gets approved." I put down my fork and stare at the beautiful salad.

Voices float out from the living room.

"Finally," Becca says.

Her parents sit on opposite ends of the sofa. Mrs. Calderman smiles like she's glad to see us.

"I thought you'd never get back," Becca says, parking between her mom and an empty swivel chair.

Mr. Calderman looks unhappy that Becca interrupted whatever he was talking about. Small, deep-set wrinkles crease the corners of his eyes, making him look ten years older than Becca's mom. His grey-streaked, brown hair is so carefully cut I bet he doesn't have to comb it in the morning. His clothes look like they just came from the cleaners, instead of a sweaty round of golf.

"Dad. Elizabeth and I need to talk to you."

His face softens as he looks at me. "Nice to meet you, Elizabeth." He points to the swivel chair. "Please, have a seat."

My toe clips the wheelchair tire and I plop onto the chair, sending it rocking back and forth. "Whoops."

Mr. Calderman straightens his shoulders. His smile tightens. I'm glad I can't read minds.

"What's up, girls?" he says.

"Listen to this," Becca says, leaning forward. "Go ahead, Elizabeth."

Her dad stretches an arm across the sofa back. I shift forward in the chair and try to get comfortable. My mind, not my butt.

"There's a county park," I say, "five miles from downtown, called Wayward Landing, where sea turtles—Kemp's ridleys—come ashore to nest every year, April through August. A week ago I found an injured turtle laying her eggs. Becca probably told you she and I are volunteering at the Marine Center down the street. They take care of turtles and protect their nests. Maria, the head biologist, said Sunny, the one I found, nested at the Landing last summer, too. She has a satellite transmitter so they can . . . uh . . ."

Mr. Calderman's smile dissolves. Becca circles the air with her hand, like a coach signaling a player. "Shift it out of turtle gear."

Her mom raises an eyebrow. "Elizabeth is telling the story." Becca rolls her eyes and nods permission for me to continue.

"Pioneer Development wants to cover up the Landing with a gigantic building project. Becca thinks you could help us come up with some ideas on how to block the approval and save the beach for the Kemp's."

The thin river of sweat between my shoulder blades tickles my skin. Mr. Calderman stares at me. Becca's making little jerky motions with her chin like I'm supposed to say something else.

"And," she says.

My brain is as white and empty as a dry-erase board the first day of school. I lean back in the chair, my back rigid.

She should have talked to him in the first place. I look down at my knees. "Go ahead. You finish."

"And we have a top priority situation because Thursday night there's a hearing on the plan in front of the County Commissioners. We've got to be ready. You'll help us, right?"

A look passes between Becca's parents. Mr. Calderman shifts, lacing his hands together on top of his knees.

"I know about the project—"

"Yes!" Becca pulls her fist through the air. "I knew it. Bad idea, right? What do you think? We start with a media blitz through the local television station and newspapers showing the cost to turtles—"

"And I can't help you."

Becca's hand drops to her lap. "Why not?"

"Because Pioneer Development is my client. You don't remember?"

Her face reddens. "No. I never got the details."

"My team developed the presentations for the Commissioners' hearing this Thursday and I've been working on the media campaign."

Becca's mouth drops open, then closes. "Wonderful," she says.

"I don't think you have anything to worry about," he says, looking at me, like I'm supposed to believe him. "The plan will be up on Pioneer's website tomorrow. You'll see. It leaves areas open for public access and I can't imagine anyone will mind sharing the beach with the turtles."

"Seriously?" Becca says. "You really believe they'll crawl through a beach full of noisy people and traffic to lay their eggs? Mother turtles need space." Her arm flails out, knocking into the floor lamp. Her mom snags it before it falls.

"Careful," she says. Becca doesn't seem to notice.

"The president of Pioneer Development has lived here all his life," Mr. Calderman says, "so I'm sure he's considered the turtles' needs."

Becca snaps forward in her chair. "Why? Is he a turtle scientist, too?"

"Rebecca." His tone shifts from businessman selling an idea to dad-taking-control. I hope she pays attention. I didn't come over to start trouble.

"That's your logic?" Becca says. "He cares about turtles because he's lived here forever?"

I dig my poor excuse for fingernails into the chair arms as her father's expression darkens.

Becca plunges ahead. "Two private high-rise hotels, four condo blocks, houses, shops, and a water-themed thingy taking out a dedicated, public nature park. How sensitive is that? Maybe you should research the turtles and what the Center is trying to do before you continue with such a rotten project."

Crap, Becca. I'm on fire from the top of my head to my armpits.

"David." Mrs. Calderman holds up her hand as Becca's dad starts to say something.

"The Commissioners won't make a decision until all the information and alternatives are presented and discussed over a number of hearings, right?" she says, her voice low and calm.

"Of course," he says.

"Perhaps the girls should wait and see what happens during the process," she goes on. "The impacts might be mitigated or perhaps aren't as bad as they seem. Pioneer may have talked to the Marine Center and the environmental agencies already about what is best for the turtles."

Mr. Calderman nods, then eyes Becca. "Good point. Before you get too worked up, perhaps you and Elizabeth should do more research on the plan."

I wait for her to challenge him back, but she sighs and turns to me. "Okay, then. Looks like we're on our own." She reverses her chair, spins away from the couch, and rolls across the living room.

The arms of my chair seem to tighten around me as Becca disappears down the hall toward her bedroom. I glance at Mr. Calderman, who stares back, probably waiting to see if I can stand up without looking like an idiot.

"Excuse me," I say. "I better go with her."

Shut the door," Becca says, a command not a request. "Can you trust anybody these days?"

"Your dad probably doesn't know a Kemp's ridley from a box turtle. Has he even been to the Center?" I'm only defending him because he looks like his toes never once dug into sand, anywhere.

"That's not the point," she says. "He wasn't interested in listening to us." She raises an eyebrow and leans forward, mimicking her dad's expression and posture. "' . . . before you get too worked up . . . ' Right. He hasn't seen 'worked up.'"

"But maybe he's still trainable." I smile, trying to lift the mood, but Becca's not going there. "Okay, meet me at

the Center tomorrow at three-thirty to talk to Maria."
She doesn't answer. I open the door and look back.

"Bye," I say.

She looks at me for a second then turns away to the window. "See you," she says.

"Would you like a ride to the Center?" Mrs. Calderman says, as I pocket the salad dressing recipe.

"Thanks, but I've got time before the trolley gets there." Besides, walking always helps me think.

The wild grasses in the buffer along Forster Boulevard wave in the breeze, like they're cheering me on. I look up as a faint whoosh passes overhead. A white egret, neck tucked between its shoulders, legs trailing behind, sails toward a hidden landing spot along the Bay. Suddenly, I'm back in third grade. Supper's finished, Mom's in class, Dad's dragging me to a meeting, protesting a proposal to clear the woods around Picketts Pond for houses. The development never happened.

Why didn't I think of this before? Dad's got answers and it's a cinch he'll come to the meeting Thursday.

Like a little kid on a cloud of hope, I skip into the recovery area to hang out with Sunny and wait for the trolley.

I stop to see what's floating in a pool that was empty yesterday. Maddy is handwritten on the sign nearby. CHELONIA MYDAS: JUVENILE. RESCUED ELLIOT BAY JETTY, 9:00 a.m., APRIL 11, 2010.

Slightly smaller than Sunny, Maddy's shell is smothered in green algae and white barnacles. Every few strokes in her slow trail around the pool, she bumps into the side. When she meanders around the curve and faces me, I see why. A fleshy, pink polka-dot patterned growth, the size of a smushed grapefruit, covers most of the left side of her face and all of her eye. A smaller glob sticks out between her neck and right flipper and a marble-sized one hangs off her lower jaw. A sinking feeling inside me circles the pool with her. I shove my hands in my pockets and walk away toward Sunny's pool. Before I get there, the trolley horn beeps out front.

"Gotta go." I blow her a kiss. *I promise, we won't give up.*

I shoot past Maddy's pool without looking in.

CHAPTER NINE

THE GARAGE IS OPEN "Yo," I say, popping around the door, grateful Grandpa isn't here. My bike's perched upside down on the workbench. Dad stares at the spinning wheel. "Whatcha doing?"

"The chain needed tightening." He lifts the bike to the floor and rolls it over to me. "Keepin' you safe."

"Thanks." I grab the handlebars and sit on the seat. "I need a favor and your expertise."

He leans against the bench. "Not sure I've got any these days."

"You do about this. Turns out Becca's dad is working on the Tortuga Sands project."

"Doing what?"

"He's some sort of public relations genius Pioneer brought in to sell the plan to the commissioners and the public. Starting with Thursday night's hearing."

Dad shifts to rest his elbow on top of the toolbox. "Becca didn't know that's why he came down here?"

"You've got to understand. Becca rotates in her own orbit most of the time."

"Still, it seems odd."

"Why? I don't ask about your landscaping job, either. I could be interested, but—"

"But it's not like Coulter City when you helped me pick out plants and dig holes."

"You'll have your business again, someday." I search his face for a spark he's thinking about it. And about going home. He drops the wrench in the toolbox and sighs.

"So, what's the favor?"

"I must have been all dazzled by the Caldermans being big city. So stupid not to realize it first."

"What?"

"Not what, who."

"Who?"

"You figured out how to save the woods around Picketts Pond, so you can help map out a plan to stop Tortuga Sands."

He rolls the lawn mower out of the corner and uncaps the oil reservoir. "A lot of people worked together, it wasn't just me."

"Remember that rally at the court house," I say, "and the meetings you made me go to?"

"You looking for an apology?" He reaches for the engine oil on the shelf under the bench.

"Maybe." I smile at him. "No, I was thinking what you did might work here, too."

He tops off the oil in the mower, pushes it past me, and stops at the door. "Even if I wanted to get involved, I haven't got the time."

I cross my fingers behind my back. "How long can it take to lay out moves you've already got in your head?"

His grip tightens on the mower handle. He looks down at the threshold beside his feet, like he's trying to decide whether to step in or out. "Saving Picketts Pond took three long years of trying to out-think and out-talk developer money, lawyers, and experts. We won, but the process ground us down." His gaze shifts to the open window behind me. "And that was a time when your mom was around for support."

What does that mean?

"I'm here," I say, "and Becca, and the Center will take a stand, don't you think? That's a good start, isn't it?" He doesn't answer. "Okay. One meeting. How about that? Be a 'body in the chair,' a 'number on our side,' you used to say, remember?"

He raises a hand, like a policeman stopping traffic, "One meeting turns into dozens. I've got more than enough to handle with my job and keeping you and your Grandpa out of trouble." He tips the mower through the garage doorway. "Sorry, kiddo. It's just not in the cards."

I leave my bike and trail him down the drive, past the house, into the front yard, irked he lumped me in with Grandpa as a troublemaker.

"I don't get this thing between you two," I say, perching on the top porch step. "You work like a dog all week, but almost every time he squawks about going fishing on weekends, you're there. Why? You and Grandma need to figure out how to take away his boat keys."

"That's enough, young lady. What's gotten into you lately?"

"Nothing. It's just you deserve at least one day off a week. We never spend time together anymore. And watching you mow the lawn doesn't count."

He flashes me a look, his face dark, making me wish I hadn't called him out.

"I think we're done," he says. "You and Becca and the Center will do fine." He yanks the starter cord and the mower stutters and kicks over. I watch him run the first pass along the empty flowerbed. It feels crappy that nothing holds the two of us together anymore. That he can't, or won't, be there when I need him.

Monday, April 12

Maria looks up from writing in the binder.

"She still gives me the creeps." Becca shudders, parallel parking next to the desk so I have room to pass.

"Who does?" Maria says.

I plop onto the extra chair, exhausted from my first day back at school after Spring Break.

"She just met Maddy," I say.

"What's with all those smooshy-looking things on her?" Becca says.

Maria cups her coffee mug between her palms. "They are fibropapilloma tumors."

"How did she get them?" I say.

"They're caused by a herpes virus. Other stressors, like pollution or an illness, can make an outbreak worse."

Becca touches her cheek, like she's afraid the stress of looking at Maddy might sprout bumps on her skin. "They're kind of taking over her head," she says. "Will they kill her?"

"If they're on her internal organs, they eventually will," Maria says. "We'll take radiographs and perform an endoscopy." She looks at me. "Sort of like what Sunny had, only the camera threads through a slit cut near her hind flipper."

A boa constrictor feeling tightens my chest. "And?"

"If she's clear, Dr. Nguyen will remove the external tumors. She'll be released in six months if no new ones turn up."

"And if she isn't clear?" Becca says.

"Euthanasia is the only option."

The feeling moves to my throat.

Maria sets her cup down. "You guys looking for work?"

I lay Saturday's newspaper on her desk. "Did you see this about the Landing?"

Maria taps the binder in front of her. "I'm scrambling to get a presentation together for the Commission hearing."

"What are the odds they'll approve it?" Becca says.

Maria shrugs. "The last ten years development permits have been handed out like Christmas candy. But two new commissioners were elected last fall on a slower growth platform. Tortuga Sands is the first big project to come along since then. A lot will depend on how vocal people are for, or against it."

I put the paper away. If someone like Dad won't come to one meeting, there's a chance no one else will either.

"Public priorities and influences tend to swing back and forth," Maria says.

"But what about the Kemp's?"

"The turtles are protected by law," she says. "The fact nest numbers have increased on the Landing the last few years, and Sunny's come back, help, too. But there's no such thing as a done deal on either side."

Becca slips her hands under her legs, rearranging her feet, like she's trying to get more comfortable. "Let's say Pioneer set aside more of the Landing for the turtles to share, wouldn't they still nest there?"

I snap my head sideways to look at her. What is she talking about? Just yesterday she was all over her dad about how mother turtles need space and peace and quiet.

"Some will nest among people," Maria says. "But if they're disturbed, many go back to sea without laying their eggs."

Becca gazes at her lap, fingers tapping lightly on the chair arms. She looks at me. "We can't take that chance."

"Really?" I say, "What about—" Her steely glance shuts me up.

"I read the county protected the Landing as a park in perpetuity, right?" Becca says.

"It was supposed to be," Maria says.

"What's 'perpetuity?'" I say, feeling stupid. Becca and Maria agree on the word, so it must be important.

"It means forever after." Becca swings away from the desk. "Do you want help with the presentation? I've been yearbook editor since seventh grade."

Maria walks over to the worktable and fires up a desktop computer. "I'd love some help. The draft speech is written," she says, then points to a screen full of photo thumbnails. "All I need are images to dramatize the main points."

Becca sets herself up in front of the computer. "Student director for two class plays. I'm told I know my drama."

Maria laughs. "And you have a sense of humor, which will come in handy."

I drop my backpack strap onto my shoulder. Guess they don't need me since I've never been yearbook editor or drama queen. For sure, not class clown.

Someone's whistling in the hall. "What's going on in here?" Tom says, walking through the doorway.

Maria doesn't look up. "We're putting together the presentation for Thursday's Commission meeting. What are you up to?"

"I've got cleanup duty on Maddy and Sunny's begging for an afternoon snack." He winks at me. "Amazing how losing the fishing line from her gut gave her an appetite."

I'm out of the chair. "She got rid of it on her own?"

"Yep, first thing this morning. She's been chowing down squid, like a starved cat."

"Can I feed her?" Becca's not going to beat me to the draw this time. I glance at her double-clicking photos on the screen. I don't think she even knows Tom's here.

"I was hoping you'd offer," he says. "You can also do the work on Maddy, get some hands-on training."

Hands-on? Tumors, barnacles, algae . . . "I don't think . . ." I waver inside like dune grass in the breeze.

"Come on," Tom says, catching my elbow as we leave the office. "Squid for Sunny and a soda for you. My treat."

Sunny splashes wildly, eyeing the squid dangling from my hand. She butts her chin against the wall of the pool and looks at me—our first for sure eye contact. Mouth half-open, she snatches the squid when it hits the water, then comes back for more.

"That's enough for now," Tom says. "We don't want to give her a different kind of belly ache."

I eye the soda machine in the corner by the supply locker.

"Bring that." He points to the bait bucket and hands me a dollar in quarters.

Maddy hangs at the surface of her pool, flippers barely moving. I gulp down a fizzy mouthful of lime drink. "Why's her back end sticking out of the water?"

"She's called a floater," Tom says, "or in the official, scientific parlance of some turtle-care workers, a bubble butt."

A thin spray of soda sputters past my lips.

"I know, cute, huh? Something's lodged in her lower intestine and gas has built up behind it making her back end float." He dangles a leaf of romaine lettuce in front of Maddy's nose and good eye. When she swims slowly toward the food, Tom pulls it a foot under the water. She tries to swim after it, but only sinks a couple of inches before popping back up.

"All the algae and barnacles mean she's been on the surface a long time. Poor kid's dehydrated and emaciated, too."

I burp. Soda fumes sting my throat and nose. "Can you help her?"

"With her bubble butt? Sure. That's time and laxatives, worst case, surgery. The tumors are another issue."

"Maria told me." Maddy's graceful front flippers are the only surface not under attack. Euthanasia. Such a pretty word for something so awful. "I don't get why their lives have to be so hard."

"Me either," Tom says, "but we do what we can. Let's get her into the wading pool."

My stomach churns in spite of the soda. "I don't want to touch the tumors."

He hands me a pair of heavy latex gloves. "They're not her best feature, are they?"

I roll my eyes. "No kidding."

He grabs Maddy behind her front flippers and pulls her to the pool's edge. As he lifts her front end, I grab the back of her shell. She's lighter than I expect and, unlike Sunny, doesn't pull a flapping fit over being picked up.

The wading pool is filled with three inches of water. Tom folds a towel and puts it under Maddy's neck and chin, then hands me a sturdy scrubbing brush and a sponge.

"She's been in fresh water over twenty-four hours, so most of the barnacles should come off. Rub in circles, and be careful they don't tear your gloves. We don't want you getting an infection."

Oh great, now we're talking me getting sick. I finish the soda, sit next to the pool, and stare at a barnacle so I don't have to look at the tumors.

Put the brush in the water and scrub.

Maddy doesn't seem to mind the brush backrub. I squeeze water over her shell and bit-by-bit the algae and barnacles slide into the water around her. A mottled pattern of creams and browns shines, like a polished pebble, in the open spaces. After a few minutes, eyelids droopy, her chin sinks onto the towel.

"Poor baby."

An hour later Maddy gleams like a brand new turtle, just out of the box, if you can look past the tumors. Tom shuts off the hose and puts down a wading pool he's finished cleaning. He tickles the top of Maddy's head. She opens her good eye. "Elizabeth is great at TLC, huh, girl?"

I stare at the ceiling while Tom takes a blood sample.

"You did very well today." He plugs the blood-filled glass tube with a rubber stopper. "Think you might be ready to watch a surgery soon?"

My chest tightens. "That might be pushing my luck."

"You handled Sunny's crisis at the beach like a pro. A lot of adults would have panicked around a hurt animal."

Little does he know. "Then I guess it's a good thing I'm not an adult."

Tom laughs. "Something to be said for that." We carry Maddy between us back to her pool. "Want the good news?"

"What?"

"Dr. Nguyen says another few days and Sunny can be released."

Maddy splashes to the water as I accidentally drop my side, surprising Tom into letting go too soon. The drop was only a couple of inches and she swims slowly away like she didn't notice.

"Already?"

"She's a strong, healthy turtle and now that she is eating and lively, it's time for her to go home. Her next set of eggs won't get laid if she's in here."

"Seems so sudden is all. What about the cuts from the fishing line?"

Tom takes off his gloves. "They're healing up and the stitches come out tomorrow. She's had a full course of antibiotics and her blood work is back to normal. She'll be fine. Want to give her one more squid before you go home?"

"Sure." I stow the brush and sponge in the bucket. I could use another soda.

Wednesday, April 14

The afternoon sun glints off a white fishing boat slipping through the calm sea past Wayward Landing. Volunteers stand near the water's edge ready to carry Sunny into the Gulf. Turtle releases are usually in the morning, but Maria waited so I could come after school. I sit in the pickup bed. Sunny slides her right front flipper, up and back, along the inside of her blue tub.

"You're ready, right?" I whisper. Her head bobs above the rim of the tub, probably smelling the air and her freedom, not answering me.

I search the parking lot across the beach for the Calderman's van. It's not there, even though I left Becca a message to meet us here at four.

A cameraman and reporter from the television station stand in front of Maria near the truck. "Will the Center oppose Tortuga Sands?" the reporter says.

"The Commissioners gave us equal time for a presentation tomorrow night," Maria says. "I'm sure you will be there. Right now we have to get this turtle in the water."

Sunny hasn't moved her left flipper the whole time I've been sitting here. It still looks pretty ugly, but Dr. Nguyen gave her the all clear. Tom attached a new transmitter this morning, so she'll be beeping at the stars for another year or two.

I scratch her head as Tom drops the tailgate.

"The world's waiting," he says. "Let's go."

Four of us carry our flapping prize into the water. The deeper we get, the faster Sunny swats the air. Waves roll above our knees.

"Let her down," Tom says. She touches the water. We let go. A half-dozen strokes power her below the surface where she disappears.

My eyes burn. *Be good. Bring us more babies.*

CHAPTER TEN

Thursday, April 15

MY FINGERS SHAKE, PULLING up the zipper tab on my denim skirt. I left three more messages for Becca—what time is she going to get to the hearing, what's she wearing, is she nervous yet? She hasn't called back.

I think about her speech. What a brilliant idea—her idea, of course—to give half the Center's presentation from a kid's perspective. We practiced together two hours over Skype the other night. Took me forever to get to sleep. Her words kept rolling over and over in my head.

I pick through the shirts on the bed a third time. Maria asked if I wanted to be part of the presentation. I told her my C in public speaking means we're better off if I keep my mouth shut.

My curls fight back as I pull and poke them with the wet brush.

Warm out. Wear sandals. Six-thirty. Yipes. I slip on a yellow and blue checked shirt and run for the stairs.

"Dad!"

The wide street in front of the County building is lined with parked cars. He stops to let me out.

"Why go all the way home just to come back in an hour?" I say.

"You better hustle before you're late and I block traffic."

I check the side mirror. No cars are behind us. "I don't want to go by myself."

"Becca and the Center folks are here, right? Isn't Maria giving a talk?"

"Yes, but I have no idea what's up with Becca. Please, Dad, for old times' sake? Those times I was there for you?" I hate resorting to guilt trips, but I'm out of ideas. The dash clock reads six-fifty. I clench the door handle.

Come on.

"I don't want to get—"A car beeps behind us.

"Please," I beg. "A little father-daughter time?"

He shifts the truck into first gear. "Alright. Look for a parking place."

The commission room is full of bright lights and conversation. People sit in rows or cluster in little groups in the aisles. Maria and other Center volunteers fill the first row on the right-hand side of the room. Barbara talks to a woman with an official-looking nametag pinned to her blouse. The woman touches Barbara's arm, then sits in the chair on the end of the Commissioners' platform. The nameplate in front of her reads Valerie O'Connor. Barbara takes the empty chair beside Maria.

Dad and I find two empty seats on the aisle halfway down. There's no sign of Becca, but her dad stands with a group down front. They smile and chat with each other. The only woman says something that makes them laugh. I wish someone on their side looked worried.

Mr. Calderman sweeps a look across the growing crowd, the room almost full. I wonder if he's good enough to size up the opposition. My heart thumps. What if all these people support Pioneer's plan? Voices mingle into a drone, the bright lights shimmer off the blonde wall behind the platform.

Deja vu.

Dad got stuck taking me with him to another City Council meeting about the development proposed for Picketts Pond. "Suits," he called the developer's group. The talking seemed to go on forever, the voices sounding the same, except the people who cried or got angry at the Council. They scared me. When I begged Dad to come in with me a few minutes ago, he stared, jaw tight, like he was remembering that past.

I run my arm through his, linking us together. He winks. I lay my head on his shoulder aching to feel better, regretting we're here.

Four commissioners—three men and a woman in the lead—march out from a door behind the platform and take their seats facing the crowd. The sign in front of the woman says Lucille Avery, Chairman. The clock on the sidewall reads six-fifty-nine.

I glance behind us. *Where in the holy heck is Becca?*

Dad looks at me. "Are you going to speak?"

"No. I wouldn't know what to say."

"Tell them about Sunny, about how important the beach is to her."

"Becca and Maria have that covered."

"But you saved her and that carries weight."

Like it did with Becca's Dad. "I can't."

Chairman Avery drops the gavel three times, each hit making a sharp clack.

"The Port Winston County Commissioners' meeting will come to order," she says. "First item on the agenda is the Pioneer Development, Inc. proposal regarding Wayward Landing beach and Pelican Bay. There will be two formal presentations—the first by Pioneer consultant, Mr. David Calderman, then we'll hear from Ms. Sanchez of the Port Winston Marine Science Center. When they are finished, I will open the floor to anyone wishing to make a comment for, or against, the project, or has something for us to consider when making our decision."

I look behind us. Still no Becca.

The chairman motions to the "Suits" section. "Mr. Wilkes, would you please introduce your company and project?"

Wilkes? I don't know the man who struts to the podium, but his smirk is emblazoned in my brain. He's definitely related to Julia.

Dad tenses under my arm.

"What?" I whisper.

He shakes his head. "Nothing." His gaze shifts to the chair in front of him as the Tortuga Sands plan map lights up the wall on our side of the room. He mumbles and shifts in his seat.

Most of the map is covered with geometric shapes representing buildings, parking lots, and landscaping. The only "sand" not under a square, circle or rectangle is a narrow sliver running along the water. All but the first row of dunes closest to the Gulf has been paper bulldozed away. The green line running next to Pelican Bay isn't a wetland marsh anymore, it's lawn. Close as I can tell, one of the dark grey "parking lot" rectangles shows Sunny's nesting site could end up someday under a travel trailer or VW bug.

"For the record," Chairman Avery says, her tone like a swatch of velvet, "please state your name and affiliation."

"Madam Chairman, Commissioners." Mr. Wilkes turns to the audience. "Members of the public," he purrs. He faces front again. "My name is Larry Wilkes. I am owner and President of Pioneer Development, a local firm, which has successfully supported the city of Port Winston's community and growing economy for twenty-five years. We hope the County Commissioners will continue this legacy through our newest venture."

Half the commissioners look like baby rabbits caught in a cobra's trance. All except Chairman Avery, who gives Mr. Wilkes a nod and big smile. Commissioner O'Connor looks detached, like she's watching the weather channel.

Dad sighs.

"Before we get to the project," Wilkes says, "I want to welcome our two newly-elected Commissioners, Ms. O'Connor and Mr. Montoya. I hope to assure you Tortuga Sands is an example of positive growth. The sort you can stand behind."

Suck-up.

"We all recognize Port Winston's historic fishing industry is no longer competitive in the world market," Wilkes says, "but Winston County is poised to shine—to lead the rest of the Texas Gulf coast in recreation, business, and fine coastal living."

Dad's voice is low, angry. "Got your phone with you?"

"Why?" I whisper.

"Call me when it's over. I'm sorry." He leaves his seat. Before I can object, the door at the top of the aisle closes silently behind him.

How could he do this to me? I look at Wilkes, then drop my chin to stare at the chair in front of me, heart pounding.

"The proposal before you . . . " He goes on and on, explaining.

"Hold on, Larry." Chairman Avery sighs after what seems like forever. Clutching the neck of her desk mic, she scowls and points in my direction.

I slide lower in the chair. *What have I done? She's mad 'cause Dad walked out while Mr. Wilkes was talking? That was paragraphs ago.*

"Listen here, young lady," the Chairman says. Heads turn. I tense, then relax, when I realize people are looking beyond me. "You can't stay there."

Three rows back Becca sits in the aisle. She looks almost celestial in tight black Capri pants and a dark grey, scoop-necked top printed with silhouettes of birds, flying off a rippling pond. Mini rhinestones, like water drops, cascade off their wings. Every time she breathes, pinpoints of light flash around the room.

Oh, my Lord.

"There's room in the back," says Chairman Creep.

Uh, oh.

Becca raises her seat to its full height. Mrs. Calderman, sitting in the chair beside her, lays a hand on her shoulder and whispers. Becca frowns and whispers back before a light press on the thumb control rolls her, not backwards, but down the aisle. She moves past Maria to the end of the front row and stops near the wall. Looking straight at Wilkes, she lowers her chair, then folds her hands in her lap. The Chairman blinks twice, leans toward the microphone, mouth open, then sits back and nods at good ol' Larry.

"The proposal," he says, "would give the county its first four-star hotel, upscale condominium units, marina and, most exciting, a theme park, thus accommodating the Commission's long-held mandate to maintain Wayward Landing for public use."

Becca looks toward the map on the wall, even though she's too close to see anything but a blur. Knowing her, she memorized every inch of that drawing days ago. I bet she was too busy pulling everything together to call me back. I can forgive her that.

"In fact," Wilkes goes on, "in the last few days we decided to make the beach set-aside larger to provide more open space. And to recognize the chance more sea turtles will see Wayward Landing as a destination location."

He smiles at his joke, as if Kemp's ridleys travel to lay their eggs at the Landing, like families take vacations to Disneyworld.

What a jerk.

"No reason we can't all live together."

I look at the Commissioners, but can't tell how they're taking his pitch.

"Now, I'd like to introduce our project consultant, David Calderman, who will continue the presentation."

Becca's dad walks to the podium. Reaching to adjust the mic, he looks at Becca and slightly shakes his head. I doubt anyone noticed except Becca and me.

What's that about?

Becca looks at the papers in her lap, the confidence when she came down the aisle seems to fade like a sunset.

Mr. Calderman's voice is full and soothing as he describes the benefits of the project. No firm, irritated father voice telling Becca and me to do our homework about the plan. Wait until he finds out how seriously she took his challenge. I settle deeper in my chair and try not to worry.

Becca doesn't look up once while her dad talks. Every so often she closes her eyes and takes a deep breath, probably practicing her speech. The cheat sheets have disappeared from her lap. A good sign. Working herself into a groove, like before a swim meet. I wish Dad were here to see how brilliant she'll be.

Becca leans over and says something to Maria then, chin up, gaze straight ahead, she makes for the side aisle with Maria behind her. Almost before I realize what's happening, she's out the door, just like Dad.

What . . . she's on any minute.

Mine aren't the only eyes watching. Her dad stopped mid-sentence when she started up the aisle. His gaze settles on Mrs. Calderman as she follows Becca out. A momentary lull, then, like nothing happened, he finishes his thoughts and thanks the Commission. Wilkes walks to the podium. My pulse tweaks. I turn to look up the aisle and about smack foreheads with Maria, squatting beside my chair.

"Come with me," she whispers.

Becca sits with her back to us in the hallway outside the doors. Her mom's taking the stairs down to the building's main entrance.

I step around so I can talk to Becca's face, not the back of her head. "What's going on?" I say.

"You've got to do the presentation," she says.

"What? Why? We practiced. You're great. You're perfect."

"Will you do it or not?" Her eyes remain focused on the elevator doors across the room.

My armpits stick to my sides. "But—"

Fragments of Wilkes's speech drift through the speakers in the other room.

" . . . something for everyone . . . Tortuga Sands gives . . ."

Maria puts her arm around my shoulder. "We've only got a minute. Becca says you know the presentation inside and out."

"I'm terrible at public speaking. Becca-a." I instantly regret the whine in my voice.

"I have to go." She reaches the elevator and pushes the down button. The room expands around me then disappears—*this wasn't the plan . . . isn't what we prepared. She can't bail.* The elevator opens and she rolls inside without a glance back.

Maria turns me to face her. "It doesn't matter who gives the presentation. Becca was right, the Commission needs to hear from your generation, to know what you value. It's in her speech and in your heart."

Wilkes's speech flows through the door. "More county revenue, taxes . . . needed funds. Turn an underused beach into a dreamland."

I step forward. Maria takes my hand and squeezes it as we push through the doors. The sight of Dad's empty chair scares me for a second.

"Thank you, Mr. Calderman. Mr. Wilkes." says Chairman Avery. She's glowing, obviously pleased. She looks at Maria's vacant chair. "Ms. Sanchez, where'd you go?" she says, ruffling the edge of her note pad, like a school principal caressing a stack of blank detention slips. Maria leads us forward to the bottom of the aisle. She lets me loose and walks to the podium. I stand beside the first row, butt muscles tight, knees locked together, praying to stay upright until I can hang onto the podium. Out of the corner of my eye, I catch Barbara walking quickly up the far aisle.

What is it with my side disappearing?

"Madam Chairman, Commissioners. My name is Maria Sanchez. I am staff biologist for the Port Winston Marine Science Center. We begin our segment a bit unconventionally. One of our teen volunteers, Elizabeth Barker—granddaughter of one of the fishermen Mr. Wilkes referred to earlier—will present the first segment."

She steps back from the podium and moves to her laptop to start our slides. She smiles at me, eyes bright. I force my feet across the floor, not believing she mentioned Grandpa, and trying to forget how many people are in the room.

Chairwoman Avery picks at a cuticle. "Introduce yourself for the record," she says.

My mouth feels as dry as an undressed baked potato. "My name is Elizabeth Barker." My voice cracks on "ark." I try clearing my throat, but petrified doesn't produce spit.

A Center volunteer walks to the podium and hands me a bottle of water.

"You'll do fine," she whispers.

The cap feels like it's glued on. No matter how I twist, it doesn't move. My hands shake. I twist hard once more and it breaks loose. A gigantic blop of water lands on the top of the podium. I take a long drink, swiping my arm across the puddle, sending a small shower of water beads to the floor.

"Sorry," I brush my shirtfront for good measure. "I get very nervous speaking in front of a crowd." I adjust the mic up and smile lamely at the Commissioners. "If I faint, work around me." Public Speaking Lesson 1: make them laugh, they'll love you.

The room is dead quiet. I imagine the hundreds of pairs of eyeballs scanning my back, including Mr. Calderman's. With Becca gone, it seems like the cat's in the bag for his side. Her speech has also jettisoned from my now empty mind.

Chairman Avery sinks her forehead into her hand. On the end of the platform, the oldest commissioner writes something on his note pad. The other two men stare blankly back at me. Only Ms. O'Connor's face is alive. Her eyebrows lift and her shoulders arch slightly forward, like she's willing me, nicely, to get on with it.

I nod to Maria, remembering what she said in the hall. The lights dim. A color slide—not a fancy watercolor map—glides onto the blank wall across the room. A monarch butterfly face perches over the center of a flower.

Sunlight dances across the tiny hexagons of its eyes. A gentle whistle from someone in the back corner of the room strengthens my knees. The photo is mine. I took it at Pelican Bay.

"I'm here to talk about generations," I say, surprised my voice sounds calm. I focus on the photo. "In fourth grade I learned how every year thousands of Monarchs fly from Canada to Mexico—crossing many states, including Texas—to breed in one forest. Their offspring have to fly all the way back. Many die going each direction." I point at the screen, thrilled my hand is steady. "To a Monarch, that simple plant is a fast food restaurant—a critical refueling station. If Tortuga Sands gets built, the next generation of monarchs passing by Wayward Landing will go hungry. Why? Because the spot in this photo will be squished under a condo."

The wall turns black, then bright with the next slide— Sunny's stubby tail hangs over the eggs in her nest. I take another drink of water to buy thinking time.

"The picture tells the generation story. Sunny likes Wayward Landing." My mind suddenly spins off to a beach, but not this beach. *Drink. Don't panic.* I slurp and swallow. "I'm new here and until last month, when my path crossed Sunny's, if given the chance to leave Port Winston, well . . . my family's been here for generations but I wasn't born here." I lose the thread to anywhere. A balloon of fear pops in my chest, whatever I learned in public speaking, or from Becca, is gone.

I can't do this.

Look at Sunny.

I stare at the gooey pile of eggs and Sunny's fat tail and smile, remembering the tags on her flipper Tom showed me the first day.

"Twelve years ago," I say, warmth flowing through my arms, "Sunny was released as a hatchling from Wayward Landing. So, just like Mr. Wilkes, she is a native of Port Winston. That gives her, and all her offspring, the right to claim Wayward Landing and Pelican Bay home base. When Mother Nature told Sunny it was time to lay eggs, she followed her nose and her internal compass back there." I stop and count to three, letting the "what next?" question sit in the room. Public Speaking Lesson 2.

"Twenty years ago the citizens of Port Winston convinced the Commissioners to protect the Landing and Pelican Bay for nature. And for people, because people need nature. Not for five years or twenty, or fifty, but in perpetuity." I love that word. Councilwoman O'Connor flashes me a sly thumbs up.

Wide-angle photos light up the screen. Downtown Port Winston, as if from the back of a sea turtle floating in Ghost Crab Bay. Buildings and streets, cars and trucks, boats and docks, and people fill every inch. The next slide is a turtle's view from the Gulf of the Landing. Miles of beach and plant-covered dunes. Then photos I took before I found Sunny. A heron's view of the tidal marsh, a lizard hiding under driftwood, and mouse tracks in the mudflat. The screen goes black, then my picture of tire tracks crossed by Sunny's tracks lights the room.

"Sunny was hurt when she came in to nest. I don't know for sure, but if Wayward Landing was filled with houses and people, she might have stayed in the Gulf and died from hunger or infection. Thousands of generations of the Kemp's ridleys would have been lost with her."

The last slide is a people's-eye view of hundreds of baby turtles swimming for the first time in the surf. The thank you list has "Elizabeth Barker" as "Photographer." I'm glad the lights stay out for what I have to say next. I clear my throat. "Sunny was released yesterday and is out there doing her part. We ask you to do yours, think generations, and keep the Landing untouched. Thank you."

I pick up the water bottle. Nothing else rustles in the room.

Make that a D in public speaking.

One person claps, then two. The lights come on. More clapping. I turn and look at hands moving everywhere. I want to hide under a chair. Until I see who's standing in the back of the room, hands raised, making the biggest racket.

CHAPTER ELEVEN

D AD HOLDS OUT HIS arms. Barbara stands framed by the doorway beside him.

I rush up the aisle. "Did you see all of it?"

He clamps his hands on my shoulders. "You were terrific."

"Perfect," Barbara says.

"Thanks," I say, thrilled to hear terrific, perfect, and you in the same sentence. "I thought you went home, Dad."

"I'd just hung up from talking to your mom when I saw Becca coming out the front doors. I introduced myself and asked where you were. She muttered something about you giving a speech, then took off to a waiting van. Guess you figured out what to say." He crosses his arms, looking satisfied. "Thanks to her, I got here in time."

I'm not giving Becca credit for anything until I get an explanation.

"She looked upset," Dad says. "Did she give her presentation?"

"No, she just lit out and stuck me with the job."

Barbara cocks her head sideways.

"What?" I say. "That's the truth, isn't it?"

"Maybe she got a case of nerves," Barbara says. "When she's ready, we'll find out what happened."

Becca Calderman with a case of nerves? I don't think so.

Councilman Avery bangs the gavel, waving it in our direction. "We have to move on."

Dad hesitates. I grab his arm. "Oh, no you don't." I pull him to our seats. Maria steps to the podium to finish the Center's presentation.

"What did Mom say?" I whisper.

"I'll tell you later."

I keep my hand in his. No way he's disappearing again.

The meeting ends just before ten. I'm wiped out, but flying. Tons of people spoke for and against T.S., aka, Totally Stupid, my new name for the project. The people against it want the county to honor the park as open space. The people for the plan want jobs and businesses. Chairman Avery and that old-guy commissioner looked bored to tears the whole time Maria was talking. In the end, the Commissioners voted three to two to have another hearing before they start reviewing environmental documents.

At the car, I crawl onto the front seat and drop back against the headrest.

"So, what's with Mom?"

"She has a surprise for you when we get home."

Dad hangs his jacket on the rack by the front door.

I follow him into the kitchen and stop. Mom turns from rinsing a coffee cup.

"Hey, there." She holds out her arms to me and winks at Dad.

"You're home." I look at Dad. "Why didn't you tell me she was coming?"

"My plans were all last minute," she says. "I wasn't sure what flight I'd get out."

Settling into her hug and familiar scent, I squash the ping of resentment that she's interrupted the new closeness between Dad and me. He bumps his hip against hers, reaching to fill the water pitcher. She turns his tease into a kiss that's long enough to be embarrassing. But the part of me that's been worried about them takes a step back.

"I thought you had another week in Mexico." I sit down at the table. "Then were going to Honduras or someplace."

"Nicaragua," she says, taking the pitcher and glasses from Dad. "I wrapped up early so I made a hop to Managua to grab an interview, took a short side trip, then came home."

"Do you get to stay for awhile?"

"Looks like it, since I don't have another job offer."
She pulls a carton of mint chocolate chunk ice cream from
the freezer. Dad goes for bowls.

"I thought we could celebrate my homecoming."

Dad lays a spoon in each bowl. "And Elizabeth's speech
at the hearing. You'd be proud, Amy. The Center used a
lot of her photos tonight. They're selling some in its gift
shop." He steps over and hugs her shoulder. "Like mother, like daughter."

"You gave a speech?" Mom says. "Steven, why didn't
you tell me when I called?"

"I didn't know." He smiles at me. "Last minute change
of plans, right?"

I dig out a spoonful of ice cream. "The only reason I
got up there was because Becca crapped out just before
she was supposed to go on. Barbara thinks she had stage
fright, but we practiced and practiced until she had it solid. Even I knew it cold."

"Good thing," Mom says.

Dad breaks a vanilla wafer over his bowl. "There must
have been fifty people who spoke out against the project,
but a lot more seemed to agree the county needs it."

"If I'd have stuck to Becca's speech, instead of getting
wrapped up in my own story, the vote would have been
different."

"Don't go there," Dad says. "I warned you these are
never one-meeting deals. The fight over Picketts Pond
looked lost a half-dozen times." He lays his hand across

mine. "Main thing is, you stepped up tonight and did your best. You earned the applause."

"Yeah, that felt awesome, but you being there was better."

As I squirt soap on the sponge to wash our bowls, I think of Becca. For the first time since the elevator doors closed, I feel uneasy about what made her leave.

"I'll do those later," Mom says, steering me back to the table. "I brought you a present." A newspaper wrapped bundle held together with jute twine sits on the table in front of my chair. The headline in Spanish lays across a fold.

"What is it?" I squeeze the bottom of the package, trying to guess. Mom doesn't hand out presents for any old reason.

"Something I found outside Managua." She leans forward on her elbows. "Come on, open it. Then this." She slides over an envelope.

I pull the tail of the bow, free the knot, and fold back the layers of paper. The dark teal-colored neck and brown stippled shoulder of a vase appear. I lift it from the wrapping. A foot tall, the surface swims with green sea grasses and brown turtles, carved in relief with carefully etched details on the shell and flippers. Two turtles swim at the water's surface, two dive toward the bottom. They look like Greens, like Maddy, only healthy.

"It's beautiful," I say. "You're the best."

"I thought you'd like it."

Dad reaches for it as I open the envelope. A photograph of a young man slides out. He's standing beside a wooden table under a woven cloth awning of colorful geometric designs. The table is covered with pottery, each different and decorated with birds, animals, amphibians, or reptiles: orange and green parrots, yellow sunfish, or green snakes and frogs. There's even a monkey or two. The man holds my vase, his mouth open, caught speaking the second Mom snapped the shutter.

"Who's this?"

"His name is Jaime Estavo and he's a potter in San Juan de Oriente, a village where artists have made pottery for 3,000 years. I told him about you and Sunny, and he's honored you will own his work."

"He is?"

"As a kid, he saw villagers on the coast load trucks with sacks full of turtle eggs. He watched them butcher the mothers for meat. It made him sad for a long time. Then he decided making pottery in the ancient ways might give him hope."

"How?" I say, toying with the twine and trying not to think of turtles being murdered, even for food.

"He hopes people who hear his story and see his work will act to protect species they care about."

Dad hands me back the vase. "That's a great idea. What was he saying when you took the picture?"

"Turn it over," Mom says.

On the back she's written, 'Tell Elizabeth this vase is our bond and a talisman of strength in her fight for the turtles.'

I put the vase on my desk under Sunny's picture. She'll like the company, feel their vibes as she swims the bays. It's after eleven, but I know Becca never goes to bed before midnight. If I don't find out what's going on, I won't sleep. I fluff my pillows and settle against the headboard before punching in her number.

Wait. Why am I calling her, instead of letting her call me? Her outgoing message comes on in one ring.

"Becca be busy, leave a message."

I hang up. *Who's she talking to at this hour?*

Maybe she's upset. Maybe called her best friend back home.

But I'm her best friend here.

I slide further down on the pillows. The first month after I left Coulter City, Teresa and I talked every day, missing each other like heck. Then she stopped calling so often. Every time I called her the conversation always shifted to the new group she hangs out with and to Brad. Now we're down to texting once every few weeks. She's moved on. Why not, since it looks like there's slim chance I'm moving back. Becca's going home in June to a life she barely left. I set the phone on the bedside table and go to the computer to check for an e-mail. I shouldn't care who she talks to, but it bugs me that right now it isn't me.

A note from Tom sits alone in my In-box.

Hey,
Maria sent me a text about your impromptu speech. Way to go! FYI, Maddy's blockage cleared so she's on for surgery Saturday afternoon to remove the tumors. Dr. Nguyen will start at 1:00 with the endoscopies to make sure her insides are clear. He says you're welcome to watch. Night, superstar!

Saturday, April 17

"You're too much." I watch Maddy dive to the bottom of her pool, pull her flippers hard, and rise to the top. Over and over, up and under, like she's thrilled her rear end's not stuck in the air. I came early to be with her, relax a little before the surgery, if she and I get that far.

"What hit that one?" I startle at the voice behind my left shoulder.

A boy about my age, brown hair, dressed in jean shorts and a red T-shirt, gawks at Maddy. A girl walks up next to him and looks in, adjusting the beach towel knot at her hip. She leans against the pool's edge, watching Maddy scrape along the side.

"Those are fibropapilloma tumors," I say, pointing at the bulges on Maddy's skin.

"Not going to get many dates looking like that," he says.

The girl rolls her eyes.

"You should have seen her before I scrubbed off the barnacles and algae," I say. "She looked like a Chia pet in bloom."

"I should remember, but why is she called a Green?" the girl says.

"They're vegetarian. The seagrasses and algae they eat turn their fat green. People used to make a fancy soup out of them."

The boy scrunches his nose. "Green fat? Yu-uck."

"Where's the turtle named Sunny?" the girl says.

"Back in the Bay."

"That's good, I guess. The docent told us the story about the girl who found her."

"You're talking to her." The familiar voice spins me around. My back to the door, I didn't see Becca come outside. She stops next to me. We're almost eye level. I tense, anxious, then angry.

"I wouldn't have stood up to three guys over anything," Becca says.

The boy looks at me and grins. "You must be a little nuts. Hi, I'm Berto and this is my sister, Shawna."

"Elizabeth."

Becca leans out beyond me to shake his hand. "I'm Elizabeth's friend, Becca."

Friend? I stare at her. *Un-freaking-believable.* She looks back at me, but I turn away, not willing to get sucked in again.

"I dropped off Maria's books and she said you were out here." Becca says. I look back and she cocks her head toward the door. "I thought you might be up for bocce practice."

Bocce? I glare at her with a look I hope says, *Really? That's your answer?*

"Thanks," I say, "I've got other plans." Which is true. Maddy's surgery, but that's not for over an hour. I watch Becca's ever-present I've-got-it-together bubble fade into an anxious gaze. The same look I saw Thursday night right after her father gave her a nod from the podium.

"Bocce." Berto props his hip against the pool. "I'd love to see how you play. What do you think, Sis?"

Shawna raises an eyebrow. "Whatever. You're driving."

Becca looks at her lap for a second before catching my eye again. I keep my face neutral. Her move. "Great," she says. "Let's go."

I feel the sting, let down she didn't make clear she wanted us to be alone. Berto at her side, laughing at something she says, they pass through the automatic doors into the building.

"You're coming with us, right?" Shawna looks at me, her tone pleading.

I can't hang out with Becca like nothing's happened. "I thought I'd chill here and try to work up the nerve to watch Maddy's surgery."

"You're so lucky." Shawna walks around the pool, following Maddy's bumpy trip.

"Lucky? More like queasy."

"Not me," she says. "I've wanted to be a vet ever since our cat, Pickles, had six kittens under the Christmas tree. On top of the robe and slippers my Mom gave me. I took it as a sign."

"If you want, I could ask Tom to let you watch, too. I could use some support."

"You'd do that? What time? I'm stuck to Berto's schedule. Which may be extended, since he has Becca to entertain. Or cut short if she sees through, I mean, decides not to put up with him."

She's a run-on talker, like me, when she gets excited. "Becca holds her own."

"Come on, you need a distraction from worrying about Maddy."

She's right. Considering Becca's being weird, the chance to make a new friend couldn't hurt.

Shawna and I walk out to the beach. Becca skims across the sand in the distance, waving toward a spot for the bocce court.

"I don't remember seeing you at school," Shawna says. "I'm a sophomore."

"Freshman. We moved here in January."

"It must be hard, dropping into the middle of the year."

"I'm not doing such a great job adjusting."

"How come?"

"Got off on the wrong foot somehow, and one girl's always giving me a hard time."

"Who?"

"Julia Wilkes."

Shawna laughs. "Don't worry about Julia. She's stuck on herself because her dad's such a big shot around here. Her boyfriend, Pete—he graduated last year—is the only reason she has any friends. He has a line on getting booze, other stuff, too, I hear. The powers at school banned him from campus in January after he beat up a kid."

"He's one of the guys who came after Sunny and me. Got mad, I guess, because I ignored his trying to pick me up."

She shakes her head. "Sounds like him. Piece of work, that guy. He scares me, but Julia must get off on the rough type."

I stare at the sand, thinking about the bruise on Julia's face. If I'd known about Pete that day at the Landing, I wouldn't have had the nerve to stay with Sunny.

"Hey you two, step it up." Berto juggles the pallino and a red ball between hands. "Becca's going to help improve my technique."

She eyes Berto. "You didn't say you play."

"Didn't say I didn't." He grins and winks at Shawna and me. "I said I want to see how you play. Want to go one-on-one?"

Becca stares at him, like she's trying to figure out what he's up to. "Sure." She flips him a quarter.

Berto kisses the coin for luck and flips it in the air. "Heads." It lands in the sand, head up, between them. He squints, grinding his toes into the sand at the throw line and leaning forward. His ball sails easily through the air and lands, with barely a roll, an inch away from the pallino.

Becca laughs. "You little Texas con man." She swings toward the line. "Move over, the Manhattan Master is taking you out."

Berto steps back, opens up a space. "Care to bet on that? Cost you a soda if I win."

"You're on." Becca's dead on aim smacks Berto's ball a good foot past where he'd parked it by the pallino.

He bends to pick up a ball, half hiding his surprise. "Not bad, not bad," he says.

"The 'outside' man goes next," Becca says with a smirk, "that's you."

Stepping to the line, a long breath whistles between his teeth as his low toss knocks away Becca's blue ball, his red one stops next to the pallino.

"Yes! Mr. Outside Man just moved inside."

Becca wriggles the chair at the line, like she's adjusting her footing. I bob back and forth, thinking I ought to be in her camp, but would rather see Berto knock the snot out of her.

"Hold onto your wallet, gambling man," Becca says. "You haven't won yet."

"She's mean, this big city girl," Berto says. "Wants to take away a poor boy's lunch money."

Becca lowers her arm beside the chair. All of us stand quiet. She sets her gaze where she wants the ball to go. Four warm-up swings and the release. The ball arcs through the air and drops. With a crack, it hits Berto's, blasting the red sphere clear out of the end zone.

"Whoa." Berto's mouth drops open. Becca stares at the court, like even she is awed by the shot. "I give," he says.

"Thank you, thank you." Becca bows and wheels away from the line. "Am I ever thirsty."

Berto and Becca seem to forget Shawna and I exist as we head to the refreshment stand. I can see why Becca might like him. Besides being quick and a tease, he's cute with dark eyes, tussled hair, a slightly crooked smile, and teeth that have never seen or needed braces.

"You've got a terrific eye for the game," he says, as we wait in line to order drinks. "Where'd you learn?"

"From a couple of seventy-year-old Italian hot shots. How about you?"

"From our Nonno."

"Your grandfather. Figures." she says. "You're Italian."

"Half. He and Nonna came from Italy after World War II."

"Berto's Italian?"

"Alberto. It means 'noble.'" Shawna groans. "What?" he says. "My outstanding character was evident from birth." He digs his wallet out of the back pocket of his shorts and looks down at Becca. "Any player as good as you deserves more than a lousy soda. How about we go somewhere for lunch?"

Becca hesitates maybe a nano-second. "Why not? My mom will give us a ride."

"I've got a car," Berto says, "we can all go."

"Can't," Becca says, pointing to her chair. "I need a ramp and van for Midge."

"There's a little deli we can walk to in half an hour. They make great fish tacos. What do you think?"

"Perfect," Becca says.

I brought a lunch and can't afford to buy one, even if I wanted to. Despite being a little over it, I'm still tweaked at Becca.

"You guys go," Shawna pipes up, saving me before I have to dream up an excuse. "I want to hang out with Elizabeth and hopefully watch Maddy's surgery." She looks at me. "If that's okay with you, that we don't go with them, I mean."

"It's great." *I knew I liked you.*

Shawna holds out her hand to Berto. "Drinks, please."

He drags a ten-dollar bill from his wallet. "Three o'clock at the parking lot."

Not a word from Becca as they head down the sidewalk along Forster Blvd.

"I wonder what that's about?" Shawna points toward a table and umbrella not far from us. The sign fluttering on the edge of the umbrella says, "Save Wayward Landing." A man sits in a beach chair between two surfboards, stuck upright in the sand. The banner stretched over his head reads, Top-to-Bottom Surf and Dive Club. The young woman, talking to the guy at the table, waves a clipboard like she wants to deck him.

CHAPTER TWELVE

"THEY'RE GOING TO PUT a development on a nesting beach?" The woman says, just short of a screech. "That's outrageous."

Denim shorts and aqua blue T-shirt hug a body Mom would call one-meal-a-day thin. Frayed pieces of camo cloth, stitched catawampus, cover the baseball cap shoved low on her forehead. The logo on her shirt is a swimming sea turtle under: *Loggerhead Nesting Team ~ Greece ~ 2009.* She punches the air with the clipboard. "You gotta take this issue to the streets."

Shawna and I stop at the table. I recognize the two men with the surf club by their Hawaiian-print shirts. They were at the Tortuga Sands hearing and surprised me when they spoke out against the plan—big time. The guy behind the table motions to the sign on the surfboards.

"Our main issue is public access for surfers and kayakers—in maintaining Wayward Landing as open space—"

"Exactly." She puts the clipboard down. "Look, your issue and the turtles' cross-pollinate. They fertilize the whole."

"Fertilize? What whole?"

"The ecosystem whole. The more issues we tie together—turtles, birds, plants, surfers—the more powerful the argument for saving the Landing, and the more people will get behind the cause. Get it?"

He scowls. "Noel, is it?"

"Yes," she says.

"Of course, I get it. We're here, aren't we? The beaches are our streets."

I scan the pictures of surfers and kayakers taped to the table next to a second clipboard.

"I recognize you," the man in the chair says. "Elizabeth Barker, isn't it? One heck of a speech you gave the other night for someone so young."

My face sizzles. My slightly chubby cheeks always peg me as younger. Tees me off.

His buddy laughs and offers his hand across the table. "Forgive my friend. It's been a long, long time since he was 'young.' He's right about your speech, though."

Shawna picks up a clipboard. "Am I old enough to sign?"

"You bet," he says. "Nothing official, we're collecting signatures to let the Commissioners know how the community feels."

"I have time to help collect more," Noel says.

The guy at the table looks a little wary. "As long as you remember our issue is about public access," he says, "not about turtle habitat."

"Whatever stops this assault on the Landing," Noel says, "is all the same to me."

He hands her a stack of petitions. "Can you work a shift next Saturday outside Kroger's grocery?"

"No problem."

"I'll help, too." I'm volunteering again, before I can stop. I love Noel's 'cross-pollinate, fertilizing in the streets,' or whatever she said. "Shawna, you want to come?"

"I can't. We've got family stuff."

Noel double folds the petitions and squeegees them and my phone number into her back pocket. "I'll call you with a time," she says. "Great meeting you guys."

Tom's rummaging through papers at his desk when Shawna and I show up. Dr. Nguyen and three assistants, wearing scrubs, gloves, and masks are already in surgery huddled around the operating table. A happy tickle runs through me. I grab Shawna's arm.

"He's operating."

She looks puzzled. "Isn't he supposed to be?"

"He wouldn't operate if the endoscopy showed tumors inside her. That means Maddy's okay, right, Tom?"

He snaps papers onto his clipboard. "That's not Maddy."

"What?"

"The boy there at the window and his dad were fishing and found a loggerhead half-dead at the surface. He brought it in about forty-five minutes ago."

"What happened to it?" Shawna steps sideways, straining to see.

"Shark got the left front flipper close to the shoulder."

I waver, bumping Shawna.

She steadies me. "You okay?"

I swallow and nod.

She looks at Tom. "Can I watch?"

"Sure, just don't be a distraction."

"What about Maddy's endoscopy?" I say, afraid to ask.

"Won't be long. Dr. Nguyen has to remove the bone remnant at the shoulder joint and stitch up the raw edges and that's that."

"Tom." I lean on the edge of his desk. "Skip the details."

"Okay," he says. "I have to get the recovery pools ready." He stops at the door and looks back. "Nice meeting you, Shawna. Keep Elizabeth off the floor."

"Very funny," I say.

The guy at the window glances at Shawna and me. Hands thrust deep in his pockets, feathery wisps of brown hair poke out from under his ball cap. The logo stitched across the front says, *Samson's Fish Hatchery.*

I follow Shawna to the window. She stops and I end up next to him. "Price Lungren, right?" she says.

He nods.

"I'm Shawna Lucio." She points at me. "Meet Elizabeth Barker. You're both turtle angels."

He looks puzzled. "Hi." His voice is mid-range deep
and sort of distant, like he's shy. Then again, maybe he's
just not that interested in us or feeling angelic.

Quit staring. He'll think you're a weirdo.

I shift my attention to the surgery ten feet away. Dr.
Nguyen turns sideways, clearing my view to the turtle and
the crimson-colored hole where the flipper used to be. A
bone shard drops, with a muted clink, into a bowl on the
instrument tray. My legs fold. My shoulder bumps something as I fall.

A low groan burbles in my throat.

"She's not out." Price's voice floats above me.

Whatever I'm on doesn't feel like the floor. I stretch
my legs, delaying the moment I have to admit being a
complete loser. Peeking through my lashes, I see Price
staring at my half-closed eyes.

I wonder what he's thinking.

That your head's in his lap.

I wriggle away from him and stand.

"You all right?" he says, getting up off his shins.

"Fine." I wobble like a top winding down. He grabs for
my arm, but I tuck it tight to my side and shift my feet so
I don't fall. "Blood's still getting to my head."

Shawna's at the window, ignoring us, shuffling on her
toes and craning her neck.

Price checks me out longer than a casual look, then adjusts his hat. "I've gotta get going. Sure you'll be okay?"

"Yep."

A glimmer darts through his eyes. "You might want a chair if you're gonna hang around this window."

"Right. Good idea. Thanks for the tip—and the catch."

"No problem. See ya, Shawna."

"Bye, Price," she says without looking.

I wait until his back is turned, then watch his red and yellow plaid shirt disappear into the hall. A new combination of excitement and confusion scuttles through me, like a ghost crab looking for its burrow.

Shawna glances over her shoulder. "Are you going to watch them work on Maddy?"

"Oh, sure," I say, shaking out my legs to speed up the blood flow. "Not after that performance."

"You can lean on me. Look." She points to the turtle in surgery. "See the vet's making stitches, like hemming a pair of pants. Does that make it easier?"

I inch next to her, clamping my teeth together as Dr. Nguyen pokes a hole with the curved needle. The black thread slides through the fabric of the turtle's skin. It's too much. "Um, no." I clomp over to Tom's desk and drop into the empty chair.

Five minutes later, she looks to her right. "That was so cool—where? Ah, poor kid." She sounds like a mom soothing an owie. "It's safe now, all done."

"How's it going?" Tom says, coming through the doors.

"That was fabulous," Shawna says, like she just stepped off her first Ferris wheel ride.

He looks at me. "And you?"

"I maybe fainted—a little. It was embarrassing. If there hadn't been blood . . . no, I'd better skip it. Maddy doesn't need me." I fiddle the water bottle cap between my fingers. "She might not have surgery, anyway."

"If you watch the endoscopy first," Tom says, "you might get more comfortable." He smiles, no doubt trying to make me feel better, like Shawna with her seamstress angle. "She won't feel a thing and you'll get to watch movies of her insides."

"Which is so cool," Shawna chimes in.

"And why, exactly, is my watching her movies or surgery so important?"

"It's not," Tom says. "Just good to get over being squeamish."

I shake my head. "Let's face it, I'm not cut out for this medical stuff."

Tom slaps the table. Shawna and I jump. "I've got a terrific idea," he says. "You had no trouble that day at the Landing playing documentarian for Sunny because you were focused on getting the photos."

"What's that got to do with now?"

"We could add a endoscopy video to our website. If you take the footage, and it's good enough, we'll YouTube it. The footage might help raise donations. What do you think?"

It's weird, but behind a camera I always feel in control. He's nailed it.

"Promise no blood?"

"A tiny drop, but I really don't think you'll notice."

"I'll try."

"Terrific." He claps me on the shoulder.

Tom lays out the rest of the plan for the shoot. Shawna's bummed it doesn't include her being in the surgery room.

"You're the one who ought to do this," I tell her when Tom walks off to get the video camera.

"Hey, I've got the stomach for being a vet and you've got the eye for showing the world how important we are." She smiles. "Cross-pollination, right? "

"Right."

"You are my eyes in there," she says, "so be sure to ask good questions."

"Like?"

"You don't have to be specific. Something like, 'What are you doing now? What will you do next? How will this help the turtle?' Darn, I wish there were room in there for me."

"Me, too."

Three techs carry Maddy to the surgery room. She's beautiful and I'm proud. If it weren't for the tumors, she'd look normal. Her front flippers slap up and back against her shell. Tom approves Shawna's interview idea. Dr. Nguyen shows me where to stand so I won't be in the way but still have clear views of the action. I pull on my surgical mask, grip the camera, and zoom in as the needle slides into a vein on the open side of Maddy's neck. A respirator covers her nose and mouth and a tech holds the breathing tubes, waiting for the medicine to work. Two minutes later, he nods that Maddy's asleep. The monitors whoosh and wheeze the sound of blood pumping through her heart and air flowing in and out of her lungs. I focus on the small cut Dr. Nguyen makes in Maddy's skin. In slides a camera small as a laser beam. The monitor glows with lights and darks, solids and spaces. The camera stops moving and light sweeps slowly over a pale pink bulge. Blood vessels run over the surface. I glance up. Shawna's at the window, smiling. I swallow, breathe quietly, and hope the microphone doesn't pick up my pounding heart.

"So, Dr. Nguyen," I say, "what are we seeing here?"

"Thanks for a great day," Shawna says. We watch Berto and Becca head toward us on Forster. "I'm so glad Maddy is okay and they're going to use your video."

"Me, too. Tom's idea got me over a hurdle." Dr. Nguyen searched Maddy thoroughly inside and didn't find tumors. And I didn't feel sick once.

Becca parks next to Shawna and me while Berto retrieves his car from the lot.

"Your brother is seriously fun," she says, watching Berto turn past a row of cars.

"Glad you approve," Shawna says. "He's got stiff competition for once."

Berto pulls to the curb in a long, black station wagon that must be forty years old. It has whitewall tires, red seats, and a matching red dash.

"What kind of car is that?" Becca says, her voice tipping up, all excited.

"Chrysler Imperial, 1965," Berto says through the open passenger window. "It was our Nonna's, now it's the Junior class nerd-mobile."

"No kidding," Becca says.

Shawna slides into the front seat and looks at me. "See you at school."

"Okay. No, wait, tomorrow morning the Center's sponsoring a beach cleanup and barbeque at Highland. Want to come?"

"I'll be there."

I watch the wide rear end of the Chrysler shrink in the distance as silence settles between Becca and me.

Guess I have to start this. I ball my fists behind my back to steady my breathing. "Why didn't you tell me before the meeting what was going on?"

She glances toward the building. "You said you hate public speaking. I didn't want to freak you out unnecessarily." She picks an invisible crumb off her shirt. "Anyway, what's the big deal? Maria said you did great. Applause and everything." She looks at me for the first time. "Maybe I did you a favor."

"So, what then? You just went to show off your outfit?"

Becca raises her dark glasses, squints, and drops them back on her nose. I've seen that move before—from Julia on the beach when Becca out-classed her.

"I had every intention of going through with the presentation," she says. "And make a note—how you dress can sway an audience to your side."

Public Speaking Lesson Three, I suppose. I never got that far.

"On second thought," she says, "your heart-on-a-gingham-sleeve thing probably was right for down here."

"You weren't there to see what was on my sleeve. At least I don't act all high and mighty and treat you like some sort of underling."

She rolls her eyes and sighs. "This is so not about you. Leaving was one of the hardest things I've done, and you weren't involved in my decision, at all. I didn't need that complication."

"Really? You suck me into your 'follow me, I'll take care of everything' game, shove your job on me, and now act like I'm some sort of burden?"

"Hold it—"

"You're the one who said to treat you normal. Where I come from normal means friends stick together against outside stuff, even when they're mad at each other, which we aren't. At least we weren't, but maybe that's something else you don't think I need to know. You big city girls must grow up with way different ideas about friendship than us hicks."

Becca shifts in the chair, her eyes glisten. "I never called you a hick. I made a decision, gave Dad my word I'd back off." She turns her head away and moves Midge toward the sidewalk. "I've got to go."

"Hey." I knew her dad was behind this. "Wait up." Wilkes too, probably.

She squares her shoulders and speeds up.

"Becca, come on." I catch up and jog next to her. She doesn't stop or look at me. "You don't have to give it up completely."

"Too late."

I swing around, hustle past and stop in her path. "Will you hold up a sec?" Thankfully, she does. "Your dad has no right to force you out. You won't let him, I know you."

She glares at me. "Quit acting like you know stuff you don't." Her voice snaps the air between us. "Where I come from friends know when not to push."

She jams her hand against the control lever, pivots around me and takes of. The singing sound of Midge's motor fades. Angry tears blur their form as I watch her race toward Primrose Circle. I whip around and head back to the Center.

Along the water's edge, my gaze skims over sand flea holes. I look back across the grasses at the row of condos in the distance.

Go ahead and rot up there for all I care.

Becca's right about one thing. She did me one favor Thursday night. Feels like she just did me another.

CHAPTER THIRTEEN

Sunday, April 18

"MOM, COME ON. I call out the back door. She's in the garage, scrounging up the ground cloth for under the tent she and Dad are using on their "date"— a picnic and overnight at a campground an hour north. I'm twenty minutes late to get to Highland for the beach clean-up. It's only six blocks. I should've walked.

"Found it." She barges through the door, sounding all cheerful, and dusting off her hands. "I'll wash up and we can go."

"Well, hurry please." I sound harsh. Leftovers from my fight with Becca yesterday. I grab my water bottle from the freezer and sweep the car keys off the table.

The lot at Highland Beach is full and cars are parked along Preston Street. Highland's a man-made beach along Ghost Crab Bay. Dad says bays don't have beaches, they have mudflats. The city figured it's hard to sell tourists on the idea of sunbathing on a mudflat, so they dredge and haul in sand every year from the shipping channel. Maria says the garbage we're collecting comes from as far away as Mexico, even farther.

The local TV van aims its satellite dish to the southern sky. I wonder if its beeps talk to Sunny's. I've watched her on the tracking map. Except for a blip inside the Bay early yesterday, she's mostly been hanging not far from the Landing, waiting for the egg timer to go off in her brain, telling her it's time to build her next nest.

"Grandma or Grandpa will pick you up at two, right?" Dad says.

"Yeah, I know." I shut the door harder than I mean. "Have a good time." I hurry to the beach, scanning the crowd for Berto and Shawna. I spot them and Noel in a group near the lunch territory that's staked out with towels, ice chests, and beach umbrellas.

"Hi, guys, sorry I'm late."

"We figured you overslept," Shawna says.

"You know parents. Impossible to get them going first thing in the morning."

"I called Becca last night to see if she was coming," Berto says, "but she and her mom are off to New York this afternoon."

"For good?" I say.

"No, but she didn't say how long. Appointments or something. She didn't seem to want to talk about it."

Guess that's it, then.

Noel starts jogging in place. "See you Saturday at Kroger's." She takes off toward a crowd of college kids.

"Okay," I call after her, my energy bouncing up a notch.

Maria steps into the pickup bed and raises the mic on the portable system.

"Welcome, everyone, to our biggest turnout ever. Fifty-three adults, ten kids, and twelve teenagers." A woman nearby blasts out one of those fingers-between-the-teeth, ear-splitting whistles.

"You all have these." Maria holds a bag and gloves over her head. "Grab a partner, if you want one, and let's spread the group across the beach. Remember, don't pick up dangerous objects—no sharp glass or, heaven forbid, syringes or needles. Let one of us know if you find something like that and we'll handle it. The high winds last night brought in a lot of trash, so work the sea wall at Preston Street hard. The folks with Top-to-Bottom Surf and Dive Club will collect underwater trash close to shore."

They get a round of applause.

"At noon we'll stop for lunch and fun, so let's get going."

Kids whoop around me, and Whistle Woman lets loose again as the crowd breaks up.

Shawna drops in beside me as I start down the beach. We chatter about school while picking up mostly plastic: bags, bottles, and packaging pieces in all sizes.

"Over here." I head for a well-used fire pit. Shawna follows. Most of what's there is burned wood, cigarette butts, soda and beer cans. Half-buried in the sand are torn paper bags with hamburger wrappers from a nearby fast-food restaurant.

"Man." I shake the sand out of a French fry carton. "Do people think this stuff just dissolves?"

It takes us two hours to pick our way along the wall. At eleven thirty, Shawna drops to the sand. "I need a break." She drinks from the water bottle Tom gave her on his last pass, loading up full bags in his truck.

"Me, too." I drop, hot and sticky, onto a clean patch of sand and run my drippy-cold water bottle around my forehead, breathing in the cool air.

Trash pickers, and people out for a day at the water, mill up and down, stepping out of the way of passing cars and trucks. I still can't get used to traffic on the beach. Three of the five kayaks are back on land and a couple of divers help Tom toss their full mesh bags onto the blue stack in his pickup. I lie back, arms under my head, and stare at the sky. Last night's storm scrubbed it bright blue. The smell of moisture in the breeze and heat rising off the sand make it feel like summer could show up tomorrow. I close my eyes and listen to cars rattling by on the street behind us.

"Look out there," Shawna says.

I sit up, shading my eyes in the direction she points. A crowd's collected at the surf's edge.

"Looks like they've found something more interesting than a pile of fishing line." She scrambles to her feet. I struggle up and plod across the sand after her, fighting the urge to veer off toward the smell of barbecuing hamburgers.

Through a gap in the bodies, I spot Maria kneeling near the surf line. The circle is too tight and I'm too far away to make out what's in front of her. Kemp's ridleys don't nest on Highland. And if it were a nesting turtle, Maria would make people let it through.

Dry sand flips up my ankles as I broad jump a wide sweep of dried seaweed.

"Excuse me." I squeeze between a kid and his mom. "Coming through." I drop next to Maria. It is a Kemp's, nose to knee with her. The jolt across my chest is like a sledgehammer. Open scar, left front flipper.

Sunny.

Satellite transmitter is gone. White flesh. Deep gashes across her back. Skin laid open on top of her head.

"Is it dead?" the kid whispers.

"Yes." Maria looks at me. A gentle touch on my arm. "Boat propeller. I'm so sorry."

I barely hear her. I stare at the sand, numb. Voices buzz above me, like a hive of warning bees. Tom crouches next to her. I hear a whispered, "Okay." They lift Sunny, like when we rescued her. Like when we released her at Wayward Landing. Only now, her flippers hang, like oars at rest.

This isn't happening. Her radar blipped just yesterday.

The crowd moves aside to let them pass.

I seize Maria's arm. She stumbles. I burrow my body in next to her, grabbing Sunny's shell. "Where are you taking her?"

Maria bumps into me every other step. "To the Center where we can dispose of her properly."

"Dispose of." The phrase jams me to a stop. "Blue bag her onto the heap like the rest of the garbage?"

Maria and Tom stop. "Would you feel better if you came with us to say our last goodbyes?"

I wheel around, shoving against the small parade of people straggling behind us.

"Let me through."

But the crowd isn't holding me in. I run, steering toward open sand.

What good was saving her if she was only going to die?

"What's wrong?" Volunteer Bud's voice scatters off the breeze as I fly through the parking lot.

Up Cooper Street, my feet burn, pounding the pavement. At the end of our driveway I slam the gate open against the fence, run to the big oak, and fall under it.

"Elizabeth." Grandpa's voice snaps near me.

I tense. *How long have I been here?* I breathe twice to clear my head before rolling over.

He looks down on me from the edge of the patio.

"They told me at the beach you'd run off, upset over some turtle. What's the matter with you?"

I stare past him. *Go away.*

"You still fussin' over those things?"

I tuck my legs, scoot back and lean against the tree, hands flat behind me pressed onto the bark. "That 'thing' was Sunny." My voice rattles on the edge of anger. Grandpa's attention on my face doesn't waver. Maybe he hasn't heard or doesn't remember who Sunny is. I try again. "The turtle I saved got killed by a boat propeller." I steel myself for the next dismissal.

"Life toughening you up is all. Plenty more turtles out there you can worry over, if that's what you want."

I glare at his stoic expression, remembering his comment the day I found Sunny.

"'Plenty of turtles, alive or dead,' is all this is to you, isn't it?" My voice rises and chest swells with a mix of power and fear. "You'll never understand."

His eyes laser into mine. "You assume a lot about what I do or don't understand." He walks toward the gate. "I told your folks I'd collect you, so gather your things. I want to get home."

"You go on." I push the unspoken line he's made, with no one here to back me up. "I'll ride my bike over later."

He lights a cigarette. The cloud of smoke surrounds his face, making him cough. Hand on the gate latch he stops and turns back.

"Your folks ain't given permission for you to bicycle any place. You're supposed to go with me."

"But Dad and Mom let me ride to your house a bunch of times."

His eyes warn. "Last time I'm tellin' you. Get your things."

Upstairs, I cram my pajamas and clothes into my backpack. Sunny seems to watch me from the photographs on the wall as I stomp from the bathroom with my toothbrush. The quiet turtle shapes swim around Jaime's vase on the desk. I squeeze my eyes closed, ashamed to look.

I'm sorry, but I can't do anymore. I won't. You're dead and if Maddy grows more tumors—

The truck horn blares from the driveway. I walk out of my room, down the stairs, and lock the front door behind me, steeled for a long, silent ride.

Grandma looks up from trimming the hydrangea bush by the front porch when we pull into their driveway. Grandpa gets out and walks through the back yard gate without saying a word.

She shifts her gaze from him to me. "Hi," she says, snipping two cabbage-sized, long-stemmed blooms, adding them to the woven basket in her hand. "Did you have fun?"

I drop my backpack and sit on the porch step, the concrete a cool relief against the backs of my bare, sweaty thighs. "Sunny got killed by a boat."

Grandma sits beside me. "Oh, no. No. Poor darlin', you must feel awful."

Mostly I'm angry, thinking how Sunny hadn't moved her left flipper one time in the tub before we let her go. "They released her too early. If she were stronger she could have dived away from the boat's propeller." I pick up a hydrangea bloom. An ant crawls out onto my palm. I almost crush it without thinking. A soft honey smell drifts off the flower and the little black body seems to follow it, peering over the rim of my finger. I slide a petal under the ant and watch it disappear into the purple and blue folds.

Grandma pats my hand. "I'm sure it's hard to tell about such things. My guess is those folks know what they're doing, but I understand you being mad, about not being sure." She picks up the basket. "Let's us get some lemonade. I made Missouri Melt-Away cookies in honor of you staying over."

I avoid looking at Grandpa as we pass through the living room on the way to the kitchen. He's perched in his chair, like a sailor scanning for trouble from the crow's nest. I haven't got any trouble left to give.

I don't want to leave the bedroom when Grandma calls me at six for supper. Two hours counting patterns of yellow rosebuds in the wallpaper hasn't added up to a new idea. I've argued and reasoned with myself, and made my decision. I swing off the bed.

From the living room I hear the reporter's voice on the portable television in the kitchen.

". . . there was speculation within the group opposed to the Tortuga Sands development that this mother sea turtle, as a second year nester, was important to saving Wayward Landing. With her passing, these hopes may have dimmed.

Mike Jefferson reporting from Highland Beach."

"One damn turtle or two dozen," Grandpa says, "nobody going to stop Larry."

"Hush," Grandma says. "Elizabeth will be down any minute. She's upset already, don't go making it worse."

"It's okay, Grandma." I walk toward the counter to pick up the basket of rolls for the table. "Grandpa's right. We don't have a chance."

CHAPTER FOURTEEN

Monday, April 19

GRANDPA LEFT FOR THE boat early this morning to do some repair work. He wouldn't like it, but Grandma says I need a day off. I hardly slept worrying how to tell everyone at the Center I'm quitting, but after my fit and running away yesterday they may not care. Grandma thinks working in the garden is better for fixing my mind than brooding at a desk all day at school. She says weeding is good for the soul.

The deep oak smell of the soil beneath the snap pea vines makes me miss the garden Dad and I built back home. I probe under the leaves, curl my fingers around the neck of a dandelion root, and rip it loose.

Grandma's dead-heading flowers two beds over. "Carry in the broccoli before the heat gets it, will you?" she says.

I wash up in hose water and tote the metal bowl of broccoli heads past the buzzing dryer on the back porch.

"You want me to put the laundry away?" I call to her.

"Please. Everything goes upstairs."

First thing to hit me when I open their closet door is the smell of rose petals from the sachet she's hung inside. I smile, thinking about Grandpa walking through a dock full of fishermen, his shirt smelling like a florist shop.

I slip the last blouse onto a hanger and shove open a space for it on the rod. A faint light shines from the other end of the darkened shelf—the white mystery box. I know three things about my Uncle Roy. He's dead, his life story fits into one cardboard box, and Dad doesn't want to talk about him. The nerves in my fingertips tingle.

What if he's in there? I've heard some people can't let go of their loved ones and keep their ashes in a jar on the mantle. Not with their clothes, though. Grandma's not weird.

The letters, "R-O-Y," are carefully scripted in black along the side of the box top. A gold line underneath catches and bounces back a tiny spark of light to the doorway. I stare at the box, my mind swimming.

What if Uncle Roy did something terrible, like robbed a bank—got killed in a shootout.

Not likely.

Overdosed?

Possible. You could find out.

I lean out of the closet. The only sound in the house is the argument in my head. *Whatever's in there is none of my business.*

Is, too. He's family, and this may be your only chance. Look quick, put it back, and no one will know.

I listen one more time for movement downstairs, then squeeze between the clothes and the wall to pull down the box. I shake it twice. The insides slide—no rattling that might be dusty bits.

Cross-legged on the bed, I wiggle the lid off a neat pile of papers, carefully bundled with tissue and a black, grosgrain ribbon, the kind Mom used on my ponytail in second grade. I pull one end of the ribbon, ignoring the part of me saying not to, and lay open the tissue. On top is a high school senior photo of Dad like the one in our family album. He's smiling, probably looking forward to getting out of here after graduation.

I flip the photo over, "Roy—September 1984," is written in Grandma's handwriting. I stare at it, turn it to the front, then over again, trying to make sense of what I'm seeing.

Why would Grandma write Roy on the back of Dad's photo?

"They're twins?"

I throw the lid over the box, ready to dive for the closet if anyone heard and investigates. Fifteen seconds. Nothing. I ease the lid off again.

Under the photo is a stack of Roy's report cards. A, A+, A+, A, class after class. I flip through the cards. Every semester, the same.

I'm related to a genius. I set aside a separate white box and lift the thin tissue underneath. Watercolors, beautiful, precise paintings. Of buildings mostly. Some I recognize—houses in the historic part of Port Winston—others are sleek, modern homes, apartments, or office towers in settings I've never seen. Every one is signed R.B. in the right corner. Just like the painting of this house hanging down the hall.

Larger pen and ink drawings underneath the paintings are folded in half, twice. I open three and spread them out on the bed cover. They look like the ones in the Tortuga Sands proposal. Geometric shapes for buildings, double lines for streets, and squirrely-edged circles for the trees and bushes. Other drawings are like the watercolors—full buildings—apartments and businesses, surrounded by paths and landscaping drawn with careful detail. Like you're standing inside the picture ready to walk through the front door or stroll down the shady walk on a hot summer day. Attached to the front of each page is an Advanced Drafting grading sheet. "Outstanding," or "Innovative design," or "Excellent. Imaginative use of materials, light and space," repeats in similar words across all. I didn't even know Uncle Roy and I'm pumped with pride.

Shuffling back through the pages, I stop at several drawings. Hotels and apartment towers. A row of stores.

Something feels familiar. The background isn't any place in Port Winston. Not downtown or out where Becca lives because that wasn't built then. I must be imagining things.

No, I'm not. The buildings come straight from Pioneer's presentation Thursday and are definitely in the plan. "Innovative, Imaginative." Larry Wilkes used the exact same words to describe the Tortuga Sands designs.

Impossible. But Uncle Roy's initials are in the right-hand corner of each one and the grading sheets are signed by the drafting teacher and dated in Uncle Roy's senior year. Next to the teacher's signature is A++.

Larry Wilkes stole Uncle Roy's work, but how? And when?

Who cares about that. He's not getting away with it. Wait until I tell—

"What are you doing in here?"

Grandpa's voice, like a winter wave, blasts me off the bed. The box drops, scattering papers around my feet.

He walks toward the bed, frowning, smelling of cigarettes, engine oil, and mad. I can't move, and don't dare.

"You botherin' things that don't belong to you?"

"But, Grandpa, if I hadn't—you're never going to believe what—" The words scatter from my mouth, like BBs from a rifle.

"You put that box right and get downstairs."

I swallow hard, desperate to loosen my throat. All the fight a second ago to save Uncle Roy's history squashed. "I'm sorry." I turn away from the rigid anger lines in

Grandpa's face to the soft pattern of the chenille bed-spread, looking up only when I hear his footsteps start down the stairs.

My knees shake. *He's gone to tell Grandma.*

I slide to the floor, bundle a few of the drawings into my lap and squeeze my head between my hands. Swiping away tears so they won't land on Uncle Roy's papers, I arrange things the best I remember, Uncle Roy's photo on top.

She's gonna hate me.

The box slides easily in place on the closet shelf.

Couldn't mind your own business.

I creep across the hall to the rosebud bedroom, lie back on the pillows, and let hot tears slide into my ears.

"Elizabeth," Grandma says outside the door. I bury my face in the pillow, desperate to dissolve into the mattress. Cooler air from the hall flows across my legs when the door opens. The cast iron bed frame creaks as she sits beside me. I wait for a touch, but it doesn't come. No words rustle the air. I pull my elbows in tight to my ribs.

"Stuffy in here," she says after a moment that goes on forever. "How about we go downstairs where we can breathe?"

I shake my head. Stuffy up here is better than yelled at down there by Grandpa. "I can't," I mumble against the pillowcase.

"Sure you can. You didn't do anything terrible."

You ask Grandpa about that. Should have left things alone.

"Did you steal anything?"

My nose bends against the pillow as I roll my head back and forth.

"Lie about anything? Or hurt anything—or anybody?"

I lie still.

"You did not, so no use burying your head in a bunch of feathers the rest of the day."

I turn my head, mainly 'cause it's getting hard to breathe. Her face has serious written in it, but not mad.

She pats my leg and holds out her hand to help me up. "Come on, we've got some old ground to walk." Roy's box, looking heavy as a block of white granite, lays on the end of the bed. I turn my head away.

She stands. "Bring it."

My grip on the box tightens at the top of the stairs. I start down, wishing there was some way to become invisible. Grandpa's not in his chair. I scan the back yard from the kitchen, not trusting he won't appear again out of nowhere again.

"Grandpa's mad at me."

"Don't worry about that. I gave him plenty of errands to keep him gone awhile."

I set the box on the table, grateful whatever she has planned won't include answering to him.

She moves the colander of broccoli heads next to the cutting block, leans her hip against the counter, and points the paring knife toward the box. "Did you finish?"

"Not everything."

"Go ahead then." She sets to work, cutting the big broccoli heads into little ones.

I lay the things I've looked at and Uncle Roy's graduation picture on the table. A small white box holds snapshots of Dad and Uncle Roy growing up. I never noticed how many parts of my face look like theirs, especially our eyes, the way they slant down a little at the corners. A woman, probably Grandma, sits at the head of the dining room table, which is covered with dishes of food. I know it was taken in this house by the built-in hutch behind her. Two teenage boys sit on one side of the table. Another man, woman, and teenage boy are on the other. I'm guessing Grandpa took the picture since he's not in it. "The Gang. Christmas 1983," is all it says on the back.

In the next picture, Dad, Uncle Roy, and the same boy from the Christmas picture, wear tool belts and stand, side-by-side, in this driveway in front of a building almost as run down as the.garage at our rental house.

"Spring 1984," Grandma's written. "The boys help James with garage renovation."

The last picture is Roy and a man who looks a lot like Dad does now. Arm draped over Roy's shoulder, he smiles like a lottery winner. Roy cradles a silver and pale red-sided fish in his hands. In the background are the dock and the *Linnie Jean*.

"Big drum fish and a brand new boat—two happy men. Roy and James, May 14, 1984."

Despite the evidence between my fingers, I can't believe Grandpa was once so different.

I put the pictures away. Two toys poke out from under the corner of some yellowed newspaper clippings in the big box. One is a Lego piece, I bet because Uncle Roy liked buildings. The other is a deep blue, toy car. I turn it around in my hand trying to guess why it's been put in the box.

I open the first clipping. It's dated May 15, 1984, the day after the fish and boat picture I just looked at. The headline reads:

LOCAL BOY KILLED IN MIDNIGHT COLLISION

> Last evening ended tragically when two Port Winston high school seniors turned County Rd. 25 into a drag strip. Friends of the dead boy said Larry Wilkes challenged Roy Barker to a match over who had the fastest car.
>
> According to witnesses, Wilkes and Barker took off, side-by-side, from the south end of Rd. 25. At a half-mile, Barker lost control of his vehicle at high speed, slid off the side of the road and across a shallow drainage ditch. The car rolled several times. Barker was thrown through the front windshield and killed instantly.

Grandma quietly fills a bag with broccoli pieces. I shiver, imagining what it was like for the woman at the Christmas table and the man on the dock, all those years ago, losing their son. Roy's face—that looks just like

Dad's—smiles up at me from the photo on the table. I turn it over and sit still for a minute before forcing myself to pick up the next article.

> Funeral services will be held Monday, 10 a.m., at Sacred Valley Baptist Church for Roy Kingston Barker, killed in an automobile accident Friday evening. A third generation native of Port Winston and 1984 class valedictorian, Barker was to graduate from Port Winston High School in three weeks. In March he was awarded a full scholarship to the University of Illinois at Chicago where he planned to study architecture and urban planning.
>
> Roy is survived by his parents, Mr. and Mrs. James Barker, and a brother, Steven.

And Larry Wilkes. I repack the box. Wish I'd never opened it. I walk over to Grandma and wrap my arms around her waist.

"I'm sorry."

She wipes her hands on her apron. The knife taps down onto the counter.

"Grandpa was right to be mad. I shouldn't have gotten into your things."

She turns and folds me in a hug. The soft kiss on my cheek lingers.

"I'm surprised Steven didn't tell you," she says. "That it's still so hard for him."

"They looked so much alike . . . I keep imagining Daddy lying in that field." My words choke. "If I ever lost him . . ." What was it like for Grandma and Grandpa. Not just Roy dying, but Dad a constant reminder every day. Dad must have thought about it too, even now. No wonder he's changed so much being here.

Grandma rocks us gently side to side, letting me cry, everything all mushed together. Crying for her and Grandpa, Dad and Roy, for Sunny and for me quitting.

When I'm down to snuffling, she digs in her apron pocket and hands me one of her linen hankies. "How 'bout we wrap us in some iced tea and swing?"

I wash my face and fill our glasses while she cuts two hunks of banana cake. She follows me across the garden where I set the loaded tray on the table by the swing. We sit close to each other, quiet for a few minutes. She wipes sweat from under her eyes with the corner of her apron and sips her tea.

"Roy and Larry were best friends." Voice calm, she stares past the garden down the path to the house. "Your grandpa and I were best friends with Larry's parents, Holt and Janet." She snuggles further into the cushions. I push the ground to start the swing.

"Are they in the Christmas picture with you guys?"

"Yes. We spent every Christmas dinner together. Eighteen years, until Roy died. Those three boys had so much fun. Always tussling and teasing each other. Roy and Larry had big ideas for this town, too, for their futures."

She gazes at the peach tree across the yard, its branches dotted with hard green fruit. We swing, silent. Maybe she's figuring out what she wants to talk about, and what to keep wrapped inside, like the papers, in black ribbon.

I remember Larry Wilkes's confidence in front of the Commissioners. My insides churn. I want to tell her about him using Roy's drawings, but her far-away look and relaxed smile keep me quiet. She rolls her neck, one side to the other and sighs. The smile dissolves.

"After the accident Janet didn't talk to me for a year. She thought I blamed her because Larry was her son. Truth is, neither boy was thinking that night. They went one tease too far."

I force down my first bite of cake with a gulp of tea. "How'd you get over it? I'm sorry, that was stupid. You don't ever get over something so awful. I don't know what I mean."

She restarts the slowing swing. "James has never gotten over it. Poor Holt and Janet haven't heard more than hello out of him all these years. Larry's success grinds on him. Reminds him what Roy could have done. In James's opinion, a whole lot better."

"A girl named Julia Wilkes is in my class."

"She's Larry's daughter."

"And a huge . . . snob." Grandma wouldn't like what I almost said.

"Janet says Julia's spoiled. Larry and his wife give her anything she wants and no rules. Too busy to bother, I guess. Then again, maybe Larry's scared if he presses he'll lose her, too."

"What do you mean, 'too'?"

"Roy's death hurt Larry deeply. In a way, the boy in Larry died that night. "

"I don't feel sorry for him."

"It's not feeling sorry for him. I'm sad a good boy is cemented under an unhappy, selfish man who lost his best friend."

"Grandpa looks like a different person in the old pictures," I say, ready to dump the Larry Wilkes subject. "Like he actually knew how to have a good time."

"Those were fun days." Grandma chuckles. "We danced almost every Saturday night at the Pig and Hound. James and Holt joking and carrying on about the smallest things. Janet and I'd get the giggles so bad we'd have to run for the bathroom not to embarrass ourselves with a flood."

I shift on the swing and push us again. "How come you didn't stay angry like Grandpa about Roy dying?"

"The loneliness the first year about killed me—James swamped by his anger, your dad driven off to Missouri by it, and Janet not talking to me. One day, sitting on a dune at the Landing, it came to me. James needed me to be the strong one and Janet and I needed to carry our load together."

I think about Teresa, how we'd get mad at each other, swear never to be friends again, then always come back to start over. Even though I'm done with Becca's thinking she's so special, I don't like what's hanging unfinished between us.

"One day I showed up on Janet's doorstep and told her it was all okay, that we needed to start over. We sat and talked, cried, and laughed about our boys. The loneliness and pain got smaller every time we saw each other." She takes a long drink of tea. "James took to the bays." Her voice is quiet, like she only cares if the dust motes in the sunshine hear her. "I told him his heart attack meant he had to stop fighting the past."

"You must have been really scared when he got sick."

She looks in my eyes and takes hold of my hand. "That's why I asked you all here. I needed us to be together as a family again."

We sit and talk for a long time. Turns out, opening that box was just what I needed.

"Thanks for telling me about Uncle Roy." I lean over and kiss her. "And for wanting us back."

CHAPTER FIFTEEN

I DROP MY PACK in the shopping cart. "How come you guys never told me about Uncle Roy?"

Mom stops in the middle of the soup aisle. "What brings him up?" She takes a can off the shelf and runs a finger down the ingredient label. We've stopped at Kroger's for groceries on our way home from Grandma's, but I have a non-food agenda.

"Grandma and I were talking about him," I say. "She thought Dad had told me what happened. I always figured Uncle Roy did something terrible."

Mom sets three boxes of chicken broth in the cart. "All I know is your Dad left home because he and your grandpa couldn't get along."

"Worse than now?"

"I wasn't there."

"I'm going to ask him about it." Mom's mouth draws tight. I hang onto the front of the cart to stop it. "I'm old enough to hear Dad's side of the story."

"Of course," she says. "Good luck is all. He didn't tell me anything about Roy until after we were married."

"You know they were twins?"

"Yes."

"And that Roy got a scholarship to study architecture and was killed before he graduated from high school?"

"Yes, and your father made clear whatever happened was in the past."

"But Grandma said Grandpa's heart attack is because he never got over Roy dying. The same thing could happen to Dad. He needs to talk about Uncle Roy."

"Steven isn't his father—he's healthy and doesn't smoke. And he has many of your Grandma's calmer qualities. Though I admit, moving back here has buried most of those." She rifles through the shelf of pasta bags, choosing the whole-wheat spinach spirals.

"If he keeps that stuff inside," I say, "we'll all go bonkers."

"Believe me, I've encouraged your dad to get out what's bothering him, but it's like pushing the back end of a mule."

I think about the phone conversation I overheard when she told Dad she had about reached her limit.

"Your date with Dad was good, right?"

"It was nice to get away together."

"You guys okay?" I hold my breath, waiting for the right answer. Maybe now's not the time to push Dad about Roy. With Grandpa rattling things up all the time, and Mom just getting home, everything feels shaky.

She looks at my forehead and smiles, like she knows I'll see the truth isn't in her eyes. "Sure. We're fine." I hate it when she tries to protect me.

We turn into the condiment and spice row. "Now that your assignment's over, we can settle back in together. That'll be good."

"Hmm..." She's backed away, like I've edged us into forbidden territory.

"Dad and I missed you a lot," I say, "in case he forgot to mention it."

She sighs and puts a jar of capers in the basket. "Good to know."

Tuesday, April 20

"There." Grandma twists the lid ring snuggly around the last canning jar. Her earliest tomatoes sized up fast this week in the hot weather, enough for a batch of green enchilada sauce. One-by-one, I carefully lower the pints into the water, center the pot lid, and set the timer.

"Let's sit," she says, rubbing her apron skirt around her face. "James will be in soon."

I invited myself over after school. She invited me to stay to supper. Finding out about Roy, and talking to Grandma, opened my eyes. She never gave up: not on her friends, not on Dad, not even on Grandpa. Losing Sunny still hurts but it's not the same as losing a son, or a brother, or even an uncle I never knew.

Last night I made up my mind to tell Grandma and Grandpa that Larry stole Uncle Roy's designs. Short of a herd of turtles nesting at the Landing this summer, I figure our only leverage is proving Wilkes is a thief, but I need their help to pull it off. I set the table, nervous as a cat at a dog show.

The back door bumps closed. Grandpa sets a small toolbox on the washing machine and comes into the kitchen. There's something tucked under his arm. I about drop my teeth. He's smiling. I've only seen that in the photos from Uncle Roy's box.

"Got a ways to go," he says, "but it ain't too bad. Gonna take a month of Sundays to do the hardware and rigging lines." He balances a wooden boat, the size and color of a loaf of wheat bread, between the salt and pepper shakers in the center of the kitchen table. I walk around, surveying each side. The carving is rough and some of the proportions look off. I swallow a giggle, not because the cabin slants, but because he looks so proud. No mistake, he's making the *Linnie Jean*.

"Paint will help," I say.

His smile drops. "I ain't no painter. Besides I like her plain." He opens and closes his puffy fingers and rotates his wrists. "Not as limber as they once was for detail work."

I try again. "I could give you a hand sometime."

"What time you got between school and homework?"

"James." Grandma smacks the kitchen towel on the counter, like she's dead-aimed it onto a fly. "Elizabeth made a nice offer. Frankly, I'm surprised she wants to spend time within miles of you."

She's right, but for a second seeing Grandpa's soft spot carved in that little cockeyed boat got to me. And I need his support for what's coming.

He walks to the back porch sink, grumbling. "Only meant I work better alone."

Duh. Grandma looks at me funny when I laugh out loud.

"I need to talk to you guys." I avoided bringing up my idea all through dinner, but I'm running out of time before I'm supposed to be home. Lemon pie, the brown-streaked meringue oozing gold beads of moist sugar, sits heavy on my fork and in my stomach. I don't want to bring up Uncle Roy, but there's no way around it.

I put drawings of the Tortuga Sands project from off Pioneer's website in the center of the table, laying the stack of Uncle Roy's originals beside them.

Grandma picks up one of Roy's, turns it over, and touches the grading paper on the back. "He was so clever. We haven't looked at these in years."

"Thank goodness you saved them," I say.

"What do you mean?" She puts the drawing back on the table and picks up one from the Tortuga Sands pile.

There's nothing in her face to read. I don't dare look at Grandpa's.

"I didn't want to tell you," I say, "but this is too important. Larry Wilkes is using Uncle Roy's designs in his development project for the Landing."

I go through the plans, comparing its buildings to Roy's drawings.

"What does that have to do with us?" Grandma says.

"If you tell Mr. Wilkes he can't use Uncle's Roy's work, that could stop the project."

I glance at Grandpa, relieved, and worried, he didn't jump all over me the second I mentioned Uncle Roy. He looks uninterested, but his face—same as in the drawing of him upstairs—shows he's paying attention. His jaw works overtime, and not just on pie. I pick up the wooden boat and squint at him through the pilothouse windows, looking for an ally. He stares back, pressing the side of his fork through a piece of crust.

"What makes you think we want to get involved?" he says.

I gently lower the boat, meeting his gaze straight on. "Because you know what's right and that Mr. Wilkes is wrong."

"So you say."

"What would you say if I took this boat and told the kids at school I carved it?"

"You'd be stupid, and it ain't the same."

"Why not? I'd be stealing and lying."

"But stupid cause I'm alive to say so."

"Exactly what I mean about the drawings. They don't belong to Mr. Wilkes—I mean, did he ask or offer to pay you and Grandma for the right? He could make a gazillion bucks off them and what will you get? Zip. Then there's the Landing, which doesn't belong to him, either. It's a park. Everybody's park. Wilkes can't waltz in like he owns everything, ignore reality, and get his way."

Grandpa swirls milk into his coffee. "I'd say he's made a good start."

"But you can help stop him, Grandpa. And you wouldn't have to do it alone. I'm sure that one of the new commissioners, Ms. O'Conner, probably Commissioner Montoya, too, is totally against the project. She could use this kind of ammo to bring the whole thing to a screeching halt."

Grandpa drains his cup. "What happens makes no difference one way or another in my life, much less in the grand scheme of whatever's watchin' us mere mortals down here."

"But it does matter, really, Grandpa. If we don't find more nests on the Landing to prove the turtles are using it, the drawings may be the only way to protect it."

"I figured that's what you've been circlin' around to," he says. "Answer me this. Them turtles been around how long?"

"Over a hundred million years. That's why we—"

"Then they got the know-how to find another beach if Larry manages to latch onto this one." He flinches as the boat drops from my hands onto the table.

"That's not the point." I say, sliding the boat between the shakers, relieved nothing broke. "Why are you making this so hard?"

"I ain't making nothin' hard, and I sure ain't too senile to follow your point. You want to protect the Landing and the Bay for the turtles. Fact is, I know more about the way things work around this county and in them bays than you, but you got no interest in learnin'."

I straighten in the chair, fuming. "It's not just about the turtles. You know your precious shrimp need clean water to grow up healthy. Pelican Bay's got the best water within fifty miles of here." He stuffs the last bite of pie in his mouth and stares at the piles of paper.

"What I don't get, Grandpa, is why Larry Wilkes stealing Uncle Roy's work doesn't make your blood boil. Everything else does."

His fork clangs against the plate. I've crossed one of those lines, but don't care.

"Don't go rearin' your horse at me, young lady. I keep sayin' it and you keep ignorin' what's true. You're wastin' your time. Period. Larry knows how to work the system to get what he wants."

"My heart's with you wanting to save the Landing." Grandma's been quiet, maybe letting us get it all out. "Walking up and down that beach every day for months after Roy died was the only thing that kept me sane. But Holt and Janet Wilkes are my best friends. No good can come from what you're asking." She looks at Grandpa. "I don't want them hurt again, whatever Larry's doing with Roy's drawings."

Grandpa scoots back his chair and stands. "What Linnie's sayin' is we ain't gonna step in. What I'm sayin' is your idea's a fool's effort. But seems like something's pushing you to be that fool." He picks up the boat and walks to his chair in the living room.

Grandma sighs and runs water in the dishpan.

I fold the drawings and put them in my pack. Grandpa doesn't matter, but going against Grandma will be the hardest thing I've ever done. I have no choice and have to trust she'll forgive me if it all goes wrong.

Thursday, April 22

PIONEER DEVELOPMENT, INC. I stare at my reflection in the blue-green glass entry doors. Three weeks ago this building was just another twenty-story corporate office down the street from my trolley stop to the Center. That was before Tortuga Sands, before Sunny died, and before I knew about Uncle Roy. I straighten my jean skirt and check my shirt collar. My stupid curls, for once, lie tentatively in place. No matter what Becca says about dressing to impress people, I doubt Larry Wilkes will be swayed by what I'm wearing. Only by what's in my hand.

Inside, the main lobby shines like a new nickel. Glass, marble, and chrome make light dance on every surface. The receptionist at the main desk tells me to sit, and I do. The up arrow dings on the elevator across the room. The people waiting step inside. Uncle Roy's drawings lay rolled in my lap. Grandma speaks to me out of one end — "Don't want Holt and Janet hurt"— Grandpa out of the other — "a fool's idea." I don't know who's right. Uncle Roy can't speak for himself, but I bet he wouldn't like his best friend ripping off his talent.

The receptionist hangs up the phone and directs me to the top floor. The sleek hum of the elevator motor buzzes in my ears. The door opens facing a set of frosted, double doors in tall wooden frames. I glance at the names on the wall to make sure I'm in the right place.

The company's softly lit inner office is decorated with cream-colored leather chairs and a long blue sofa. Spotlights highlight photos and drawings on the walls of the company's finished projects. No Better Homes and Gardens, Highlights, or O magazines stack up on the side tables, like in the dentist's office.

A brass plaque beside a pair of wood doors behind the receptionist is inscribed: LARRY WILKES, PRESIDENT. The doors are carved with leaping dolphins.

The receptionist glowers at me through rimless glasses. "Good afternoon," she says. "How may I help you?"

I step forward. "I'm Elizabeth Barker. I don't have an appointment, but I'd like to see Mr. Wilkes about Tortuga Sands."

"About what exactly?"

I didn't expect her to want details and I'm not a quick thinker. "I'm here to threaten your boss" probably won't get me into his office.

"I have new information that's really important to the project, but it's private." I give her my confident, but not too cocky, smile.

Eyes locked on the papers in my hand, she inspects them from under her thinly-penciled brows. Shifting to her computer, she scrolls down the screen as if checking his calendar for an excuse to keep me out. After a moment's hesitation her guardian-of-the-gate act opens a crack.

Her mistake. I smile a little wider. Just because I'm a kid doesn't mean I'm not dangerous.

She sweeps a hand toward the chairs. "I'll see if Mr. Wilkes is available." She taps lightly on the dolphin door, closing it behind her. I let out a long breath and try to keep my mind out of panic mode. Butt in the chair, not out the door, means a fifty-fifty chance of getting in. Zero if I chicken out.

I settle onto the edge of the sofa cushion the second the receptionist returns. She carries a stack of folders and a tray with what looks like lunch remains.

"Mr. Wilkes will see you when he is off the phone."

"Thank you." I press my hands against my knees to stop my legs jiggling up and down.

Fifteen minutes later, just as I'm about to forget the whole thing, something buzzes on her desk.

"This way, please, " she says, holding the door open.

"Miss Barker, how nice to see you." Larry Wilkes's controlled smile speeds my heart into over-drive. I force myself to look calm.

"That was quite an impassioned presentation you gave at the hearing." He sits down at an angle to the desk, and motions me to the chair in front. Mine is lower, but I'm tall, so he can't look down his nose at me.

I hug the roll of drawings close in my lap.

"I was surprised to see Steven the other night," he says. "Surprised he's back in town."

I stare at him and don't answer.

"Barker. He is your father, right?"

"Yes." *What dumb game are you playing? I saw you look at us twice before the hearing started.*

"Is he doing well?"

"Fine, thanks." *Cut the chatter and get on with it.*

He swivels his chair to face me straight on. The smile is gone. "So, what can I do for you?"

I stroke the drawings between my palms, which pulls his attention away from my eyes. Heat rises in my face. Suddenly, I feel uncomfortable taking an adult's time, remembering what Grandma and Grandpa said last night.

Being a kid doesn't mean I'm wrong.

I level my gaze at the bridge of his nose. If I look directly at him, my nerve will dissolve into his pale blue eyes.

"I know about you and what happened to Uncle Roy."

His eyes flicker away. He fidgets a second with his pen, then refocuses on what's in my hands.

"My secretary said you have something to tell me about the Tortuga Sands project. Certainly, Roy has no bearing on that."

"But he does," I say. I unfold the drawings and push them across the slick glass desk. "Uncle Roy did these in high school." I point to Roy's initials on the bottom of the first page and the teacher's comments and grade. "You're claiming his designs are yours, playing them up as a big part of your plan. I don't know how or when, but you stole these from Uncle Roy, from my grandparents."

Wilkes leans back in his chair, lips drawn close. "I'd be careful making such an accusation. You're obviously here on a misunderstanding."

"Not an accusation or misunderstanding. It's the truth."

He leans forward, elbows anchoring the corners of the drawings. "The truth is Roy gave me a copy of the drawings. They were part of our dream to make Port Winston something special."

"Did he sign them over to you?"

"No, he didn't have to. We were best friends, partners. I loved him like a brother and built the business so one day I'd be able to honor and memorialize, in a small way, what we lost."

This isn't what I expected, and I'm not sure whether to believe him. "But you never got to be partners. Not legally." I'm scratching in the dark, calling his bluff and hoping he won't call mine. A silence I can't figure out hovers for a second over the desk.

"No?" I say. "Then you can't prove the drawings are yours. You need permission from Grandpa and Grandma to use them, which you will not get."

"If your grandparents are concerned, they should come see me. I'd be happy to talk to them. It's been much too long, frankly."

Heat races up my neck. Fool. I stand, pull the drawings away from him and roll them up.

"They won't come, but that doesn't mean you can use Uncle Roy's work. It's not right. Not fair to them."

"Look, I understand why you're upset, but try to understand what I said about Roy. This is important to me, and to his memory."

I pivot and move away from the desk.

"Miss Barker," he says.

I reach for the door, then stop, my back to him.

"I appreciate what it took for you to come see me, especially considering the difficulties between our families and your father's role in Roy's death."

An unexpected sigh escapes my throat. I turn and face him. "What?"

"I'm sorry. You don't know this?" All I can do is stare. "Steven orchestrated the race between Roy and me that night, kept daring us. We finally gave in to shut him up. But the blame for the accident got laid on me. Everyone thought the race was my idea and rumors spread I'd bet Roy money I'd win. None of it was true, but Steven never spoke up. People believe what they want when blood is spilled and families mourn."

Stunned, I watch him pick up the phone.

"I'm sorry you came here for nothing," he says, punching in a number.

CHAPTER SIXTEEN

I LEFT WILKES'S OFFICE so rattled I missed the first floor button and ended up on the 2nd floor parking level. Grandpa's right. I am a fool and my ace just washed into a ravine the size of the Mississippi. I've been sitting three steps down in the stairwell between floors twenty minutes with no energy to get up. To go where? What's to tell? The commissioners won't care about stupid drawings. Wilkes could be right about them, and the race, or just trying to shut me up. I can't believe Dad would have done something so dangerous.

Sunlight and warm air flow through the cutout in the concrete wall below me. Ghost Crab Bay dances beyond the wharf restaurants and shops two blocks away. I unzip the pack between my feet and take out my camera, looking for my water bottle.

The door at the bottom of the stairs quietly opens and closes. The corner of the wall blocks my view and there's no sound on the stairs.

What if it's some weirdo? The street's only a floor below. Anyone could wander in, looking for privacy or a place to hide. Goosebumps cover my arms. *Don't think about who or why.*

I clutch my camera in one hand, grip the pack straps with the other, and slowly stand, ready to bolt if I hear one footstep. A slight rustling below, then everything is quiet again.

I press myself flat against the wall and inch a foot onto the step above. The door below opens and closes again. I breathe out. That was close.

"Meeting here's not safe." A woman's voice mixes hesitation with demand.

I flatten tighter against the wall.

"Meeting here is what you've got, Lucille, take it or leave it."

Larry Wilkes and Chairman Avery!

"I ate lunch in your restaurant downstairs," she says, "so my being in the building won't seem unusual. I must say, you've got a lot of nerve charging what you do for that measly shrimp salad."

"That seems petty, considering what I'm handing over."

"You brought the money?"

Money? I may be a fool, but I'm not stupid. Camera. Lens cap off. I try not to shake, turning the setting to movie mode and pressing the ON button. Low Battery flashes red in the upper corner of the screen.

Hurry up!

I slide the lens around the corner, straining to see the LCD and keep my head on this side of the wall.

At the bottom of the stairs, backs to the camera, they're lit up like Christmas by the sun through the window. Wilkes pulls a bulging, white mailer envelope from inside his coat.

"The first $5,000, as you requested," he says. "Another twenty goes in an off-shore account when we're done."

"You guarantee the other two commissioners' campaigns get the same?"

"No question. Public sympathy is building against us, thanks to the Center's presentation. We can't let it get out of hand. This project is too important to the county to watch it killed for lack of Commission votes."

"This isn't a short slam-dunk, you know." Chairman Avery's voice has a brittle edge. "If things get tight with the public or environmental agencies, the process could drag on. You might have to compromise parts of the plan."

"Lady," Wilkes says, "my backers don't pay out for compromises. Your job is to keep things moving. Once the final environmental reports and comments are in, even if they stack against the project, you three have the power to approve it over any objections. Trust me, no one in the opposition can afford to hire the legal talent it would take for a court battle. If necessary, I have lots of favors I can call in." He opens the envelope and ruffles the corner of a stack of bills. "You keep your eye on the goal or all this goes away."

Chairman Avery stuffs the envelope into the bulky leather purse draped over her shoulder. "Let's get out of here."

I spring noiselessly through the doorway at the top of the stairs and bolt across three empty spots to the first car in the row. A tight swing around the trunk, and I drop to the floor. Halfway under the car I become one with the pavement as footsteps echo off the hollow spaces and hard cement walls. A pair of tasseled, black loafers stop a few feet from the other side of the car. The shoes swivel slightly, the owner maybe looking around.

I hold my breath. The shoes pass the car and angle toward the elevator. The bell dings. The elevator door slides open, then shut. I breathe and wait for another set of footsteps, but it's quiet. I inch my way up and peek over the hood. Except for cars and trucks, the garage is empty.

A bribe on camera. Now what?

Get to the Center.

The safest way out is down the stairs to the street. I look at my phone. The trolley will be at the stop in five minutes. I circle the floor first, checking through the openings on two sides to make sure Wilkes and Chairman Avery are nowhere in sight on the streets below.

Down the stairs and out. At the end of the side avenue, I switch onto Preston St., walking toward the trolley stop a long block away. Around the corner emerge the last people in the world I want to see. Arms locked around each other's waists, Julia and Pete head toward me. The busy street on my left and a wall of plate glass shop windows on my right leave nowhere to hide. If I go back, I miss the trolley. My only hope is to keep walking and minimize the damage on the way by.

"Hey, Mizurry girl." Julia stops, daring me to go between or around them. Pete stands a few feet away. "I want to talk to you," she says.

I move left, ready to step in the street. "I'd love to chat, but I'm late for an appointment."

"Pete says you made a pass at him on the Landing." She blocks me with a side step. "Too bad Protecto Gimp's not here this time."

I flare at the nasty reference to Becca, but not the lie. I step closer into Julia's path, betting she and Pete won't take their scene public. My face reflects in her sunglasses. She leans her head back, wrinkling her nose, like I've had onions for lunch.

"He's a liar." I say. "And your dad's the one's gonna need protection."

Pete moves toward me. "Meaning what, twit?" he says.

I knock into Julia's shoulder as I step in the gutter and pick up a jog.

"Come back here," Pete yells. "We've got business!"

No way. I cross the street and hop into the waiting trolley.

They're gone when I glance out the back window. Probably ran up to her daddy's office to tell on me. I watch the clouds collected into soft white bundles over the water. Could this day get any better?

"You guys are never going to believe this." I swoop around the corner into Barbara's office, waving the camera above my head.

Maria, Barbara, and Tom sit, backs to me, around the conference table. Their attention is glued to the television in the corner. A night video shows a monstrous burst of flames, shooting up and out across the water. Firelight scatters through plumes of black smoke that disappear into the inky sky.

"Today is Earth Day," a reporter says. "But this was the scene two nights ago in the Gulf of Mexico. Fifty-two miles off the port of Venice, Louisiana the *Deepwater Horizon* exploratory drilling rig exploded and caught fire. The search by ship and helicopter continues in the oily waters for the missing crewmen."

I collapse into the chair next to Maria. The news feed switches to daylight videos taken this morning. A Coast Guard helicopter hovers several miles from the still burning rig as a second explosion rips through the air. The platform tips, exposing the silver underside. Its red, Leggo-shaped legs rise in the air, then the whole burning bundle disappears below the surface.

"The sinking *Deepwater Horizon* platform snapped its drilling line at the ocean's floor more than 5,000 feet below. Yesterday officials stated environmental impacts of the first explosion were minimal. Today reports about a leak at the ruptured wellhead range from zero to over three-hundred thousand gallons a day. The large sheen spreading across the surface of the Gulf could be remains of the rig explosion or oil rising from a mile down."

Tom rubs his hand across the back of his neck. "They better figure it out, quick."

Barbara stares silently at the television.

Maria gathers a pile of papers, her eyes angry. "It's prime breeding and birthing season out there."

The camera focuses on a large pelican, resting on an old dock post. Clear water laps the tall estuary grasses near the reporter. The pit of my stomach feels like I swallowed wrecking ball.

"The Brown Pelican, Louisiana's state bird, was only recently saved from extinction, thanks to protections under the federal Endangered Species Act. As wildlife officials watch the oil slick spread and move, they worry the pelican and many other species along the Gulf coast may suffer serious or permanent impacts. Crab, oyster, and shrimp use shallow, tidal areas to forage, lay eggs, and rear young. If the oil is not contained near the spill, the shrimp and fishing industries may be devastated for decades. For now, the cause of the accident remains under investigation."

Tom shakes his head. "Accident, my—"

"Okay, kids," Barbara says, flipping off the set. "That's enough bad news for the moment." She smiles weakly at me. "What's going on?"

It takes me a second to remember. I hold up my camera, hoping what's in it still matters. "Maybe some good news."

"We could use a dose of that," Tom says. "What have you been documenting now?"

"The ruin of Tortuga Sands, I hope." I tell them about Uncle Roy's drawings, the visit to Mr. Wilkes, and my busted plan about blabbing to the commission and the newspaper. Until my pity-party in the stairwell got interrupted by Wilkes and Commissioner Avery.

"Now that's my kind of accident," Maria says. She plugs my camera into Barbara's computer and they crowd around to watch.

"I can't believe you got them dead-to-rights," Barbara says.

They all hug me, looking relieved, then Barbara's smile drops. "You and your folks have to get the video to the District Attorney, like now, before anything happens to it."

I didn't tell Mom and Dad my plan to confront Mr. Wilkes. Dad and I would have gotten into a big argument. He'd forbid me to go, I'd ignore him, leading right where I probably am now. In trouble.

"Can we call Dad from here?" I say, wanting to be with friends in case he starts yelling. If I'm lucky, Barbara will get across how important the video is.

"Of course," she says. Dialing the number, she puts us on speakerphone.

"Hi, Dad," I say when he answers. "I'm at the Center. Barbara has something to tell you."

"Elizabeth, you've gone too far," Dad says, his face a *You're in deep dirt with me* shade of red. I grab the armrest as the pickup swings backwards out of the parking spot behind the Center. He jams the truck into first gear. "You said you were coming here right after school. What in the name of good sense were you doing at Larry's office?"

"I had to try to stop him—"

"Now the DA? Possible criminal charges? Unbelievable."

We fly down Forster Boulevard. "Dad, slow down!"

Foot off, then back on the gas, he's still speeding. "Stop Larry? From what?"

"Using Uncle Roy's drawings to take over the Landing."

"What drawings? From where?"

"You know, the box in Grandma's closet."

"I don't know. What box? You were snooping?"

"Quit hammering me with questions and slow down so I can tell you. Jeez."

"You tell me anyway," he says, but the truck eases toward the speed limit.

"The box has a collection of Uncle Roy's stuff, including his building designs from high school. They're all in Wilkes's Tortuga Sands project. FYI, because I 'snooped' I came up with my own plan, and now we're on our way to probably saving the Landing."

"This plan of yours included getting tangled up in a bribery scheme?"

"Of course not. That was an accident. I went to the Pioneer office to confront Mr. Wilkes about his using Uncle Roy's work."

"You what?"

"Grandpa and Grandma—"

"My God, Elizabeth, tell me you didn't drag Mom and Pop into this."

"I didn't drag them anywhere. They were against my idea. Grandpa said Larry would win no matter what, but look how *that's* turned out."

"I'll never hear the end of this," he mutters.

"Why are you so upset? I'd think you'd want to protect what belongs to them. What about the Landing and everyone's hard work to save it for the turtles? I thought after what you said at the hearing you cared."

"You've no idea the mess you've stirred up."

"How can stopping Tortuga Sands be a mess? You can't believe Uncle Roy would want the Landing destroyed under a bunch of buildings. His buildings!" Then it hits me. "Wait a second. This is somehow about Uncle Roy and the accident, isn't it? Well, if that's the mess you're talking about, between what's in the box and Grandma, I know all about it."

"I doubt it."

"Then tell me."

"There's nothing to tell, and talking about it won't change what happened."

"You don't know that, besides I have a right to know what's happened in my own family. I'm in the middle of it—this mess—apparently. Seems like now's a chance to stop keeping Uncle Roy a big secret and make things right."

"There's no way to make right Roy dying in a stupid accident. Look, after it happened Pop took his anger out on me—rightly so, maybe—and when I'd had enough, I left. It was painful. I put it behind me and that's where I want to keep it."

I search for what to say or ask, thinking about how long Grandpa's held onto his pain and all the picking he's done at Dad since we got here. I want to ask what he meant by "rightly so." Then again, I don't really want to hear the answer if what Wilkes said about the race turns out to be true. We stop at a red light. I shift in the seat, searching his face for the hero I used to count on. The light turns green. The truck eases forward.

"At least tell me something about Uncle Roy."

He glances at me, then back out the front window.

"I bet he was like you," I say.

We pull up to the District Attorney's office. He shuts off the engine and opens his door.

"No, he was the smart one."

My camera sits in front of the District Attorney on her desk. Without it and my stupid idea, we wouldn't be here. Her fountain pen scritches softly to a stop on the yellow legal pad.

"There," she says. "I'll have this typed up, you can sign it, and the first step will be out of the way." She's made notes of what exactly happened in the garage stairwell before, during, and after Larry Wilkes gave the money to Commissioner Avery. I'll have to swear the camera is mine, that I took the video the three of us just watched, and that it's been in my "sole possession" since. The "Chain of Custody," as she called it, is beginning to feel like a chain around my neck.

She calls over the intercom for her assistant to take away the notes for typing and my memory chip with the video as evidence.

"What happens next?" Dad's right hand squeezes the truck keys.

The DA hands me my camera. "An indictment will be filed against Mr. Wilkes and Commissioner Avery, stating they have committed a crime. They will likely turn themselves in rather than force an arrest. After booking, a judge reviews the evidence and orders the amount and condition of their bonds. That should only take a few hours. My guess is they'll be released on their own recognizance the same day."

"Meaning, they'll be free until the trial." Dad says.

"Yes, if they come up with bond money, they'll be free until the preliminary hearing."

"Will they be arrested soon?" he says.

"Not immediately. There's lots to do, but we also need to move quickly so wind of this doesn't get out to them or the two other commissioners they mentioned, but didn't name."

"I know for sure Commissioner O'Conner isn't involved," I say. "She was definitely on our side during the hearing about the Landing."

"We'll investigate her along with the others," she says. "The information trail in the case could be deeply buried. Mr. Wilkes is a powerful man with many people in his circle of influence." She looks at Dad, then at me. Her gaze holds. Nerves in my neck prickle. "You and your video are critical to this case."

She can keep saying that, but at the moment, I'd rather be a lot less special. "What do I have to do at the trial?"

"Tell the truth and answer, to the best of your knowledge, whatever questions the defendants' lawyers and I ask."

I glance over at Dad. I wish he'd take my hand like he used to when a nightmare scared me. Tell me everything's okay. That my imagination's having a field day. That this isn't real.

"The Wilkes family and ours have a long history," he says. "Elizabeth's only a kid. Can't you keep her out of court?"

The DA leans forward in her chair, hands linking together on the desk. "I appreciate that you want to protect her, but she's too close to the principal action to give her a pass."

The assistant returns with the typed notes and a CD of my photos. The DA scans through the papers, then slides them and her pen across to me. I can't pick it up. The page turns solid white as my eyes defocus. I shut them.

"You and your parents must assure me you will testify for the prosecution. I can't have you switching to the other side because of ties between the families, you're scared, or feel pressure from them. You are not to discuss the video or this case except with my staff or with me. Should anyone try to influence you in any way, contact me immediately. Witness tampering is also a crime. Understood?"

I open my eyes. For the first time Dad's looking at me. His skin is pale and every line in his face is tired. I didn't mean to end up here, but I did and I'm not scared of Wilkes or his power. I'm not worried about Grandpa being mad, I've lived through that before. I know Mom will be proud and Grandma will hopefully forgive me. The only one who matters now is Dad. I need him on my side to do this, but whatever is churning inside him may come out in an answer I don't want to live with. I'm not sure he can live with any answer.

"Dad, what are we going to do?"

I follow his gaze as it moves away from me to the old photographs of Port Winston on the wall behind the DA. One is the harbor forty years ago when it was packed with shrimping and pleasure boats. Dad was a kid, then. The other is Old Town rebuilt. I know from pictures I saw at Pioneer Development that Wilkes restored most of the buildings. The whole place now is busy and expensive.

He looks at me again. "Bribery trumps everything," he says.

I pick up the pen.

Friday, April 23

"You just got home." I drop onto the bed and watch Mom stuff a neatly folded shirt into her duffle bag. The magazine she wrote the immigration article for wants three pieces—with photos—of the oil spill and its effects. "I bet Dad's having a fit, and what about the trial?"

"Your father doesn't have fits, and the DA said nothing will happen right away. I know these last two assignments are longer than usual, but you'll get along fine." She rubs her fingers together. "Think of the fabulous pay, and I'll be your eyes on the front line for the turtles."

I've watched the news. She's headed to Venice, Louisiana, right where the confirmed, 210,000 gallon-a-day slick is supposed to hit soon. She zips her camera bags closed and shoulders the duffle. "This assignment's connected to the biggest American environmental story in fifty years. I have to go."

I'd rather they put someone I'm not so connected to on the front line.

At the airport, she and Dad exchange worried looks and long hugs until twenty minutes before her boarding call pulls her away.

"I'll be okay," she says, kissing me goodbye. "Home before you know I'm gone."

I doubt it.

Saturday, April 24

I aim my bike down the aisle of parked cars toward Kroeger's front doors. The whole signature-gathering effort feels like a waste of time since volunteers have already collected over 3,000, and now that the District Attorney has my video.

Noel's here with a homemade "Beaches for Turtles" sign on her hip. The woman she's talking to draws a little boy closer to her side. Probably thinks Noel's some sort of survivalist in her jeans, camo vest, and the matching cap I saw her in the other day.

An easel and poster board rests against the wall. The top photo on the board is Sunny laying her eggs, the hook and line visible. Underneath, hatchlings scamper across the photo toward the water.

"Hi." I store my bike behind us.

"Is the turtle all right?" the mom says, pointing at Sunny.

"She was fixed up and released." I don't mention Sunny's dead. Instead, I smile at the little boy. "In about three weeks you can come watch her babies go swimming in the Gulf, like the ones in the picture. You'd have to get up really early, though."

"Sounds like fun, huh, Joey?"

He stares at the pictures, his blonde head bobbing up and down.

Noel holds out a pen. "Would you sign our petition asking the county Commission to keep Wayward Landing a park for people and nesting turtles?" She's typed in two sentences about saving turtles under the original petition's demand about protecting surfing and kayaking.

Go Noel. Cross-pollination.

The mom signs in a curling script. "Thanks for doing this."

Noel touches her cap brim. "We're here all day. Tell your friends to come down."

"Hi," I say to the couple coming up the walk. "Want to help save our turtles from developers?" The direct approach.

The woman looks at the man, who stares straight ahead. "No thanks, not today," he says, hurrying past us into the store.

"If not today, when?" Noel mutters at their backs. "Lame."

Who needs him? We've got a video.

Noel nudges me in the ribs. "Go for it," she says. An ancient couple totters toward the handicap walk-up, their arms linked together. The man uses a cane and watches the ground. Noel nudges me again.

"What?" I whisper without moving my lips. "They've got enough to think about just walking."

"Good morning, folks," Noel says in a voice that could soften cold cheddar on stale toast. "Would you help us save the Kemp's ridley sea turtles from extinction? Just takes a second and a signature."

"I'm sorry, I didn't hear," the man says. "You want what?" Noel steps back, leaving them to me. The man gazes out from under sagging lids, his blue eyes pale and moist. The woman wears a gentle smile and looks straight at my neck, not my face. She must be blind.

"We're trying to stop a development from taking over Wayward Landing?" I say, louder. "To save it for nesting Kemp's ridley sea turtles?"

"I'm sorry?" The man turns an ear toward me, then looks down at the petition, moving his finger along the explanation on top as he reads. His wife keeps staring.

Deaf, too, maybe.

"Save the turtles, sign our petition." Noel's call makes me jump. She moves around me toward four people crossing the parking lot.

"Of course we'll help." The old woman's voice is croaky, but sure. The man cups his hand to his ear and leans toward her. "We were archaeology students in Mexico just after World War II," she says. "Pitched our honeymoon tent on the beach at Rancho Nuevo the night before an *arribada*, remember, Sweetheart?"

"I was there," he says.

"Have you heard of *arribadas?*" she says.

"Yes, ma'am, it's when all the turtles come ashore to nest at the same time." I can't believe I'm talking to people who were alive when tens of thousands of Kemp's swam in the Gulf and nested on that beach.

He pats her hand. "Darn near ran us out of our campsite."

"Our daughter hatched nine months after that trip," she says. "Where would you like me to sign?" She holds out her hand. Her husband wraps her fingers around the pen and guides it to the paper. Her shaky signature covers two lines. He signs below. Pulling his shoulders back, he flips the pen over toward me.

"Done," he says.

"Thank you so much," I say, taking the pen, my heart dancing.

He guides his wife to the door, raising the cane up and down, like a drum major leading the band inside.

"Hey," Noel says. "I thought you were gone this weekend." Three guys, tan and buff in T-shirts, shorts, and flip-flops, walk toward us. They hug Noel.

"Can you handle things for a minute?" she says.

"Sure, take your time." I watch them walk down in front of the pizzeria to talk, wishing I were interesting enough to be included.

A break in the foot traffic gives me a chance to count signatures. I finish page one and flip to the next.

"If it ain't the turtle girl scout." The bag of groceries under Buzzcut's arm bulges a snake tattoo on his bicep. Heat slices through me like I've been bit. He and Pete block the front of the table.

"I want them pictures," Pete says.

I hold up my hands. "Deleted." Truth. "Gone forever." Lie. I keep forgetting to dump my computer's trash folder.

"Better be, 'cause if they show up anywhere, I'll make sure we run into each other when there ain't no rescue patrols around."

I press my thighs against the table so he can't see my legs shake. I want to yell to Noel, but then these two would know I'm scared. I stare at Pete and smile.

"Thanks for stopping by. Save the turtles." I turn away. "Noel, could I interrupt you?"

She motions her friends to follow. Eyeing them, Pete and Buzzcut turn from the table and head for a row of cars.

"What's up?" she says. "Dude, you're shaking. What happened?"

"A couple of guys looking for trouble. Sorry if I spoiled your visit."

"No, it's clearly fine. My buds came to help with signatures."

"I could use a soda." I say. "Want anything?"

"Nope, go ahead."

Inside the store, I lock myself in the ladies room and lean against the door as the blood drains from my head to my feet.

CHAPTER SEVENTEEN

THE OIL SPILL HIT Venice yesterday. Dad's called Mom a bunch of times, but she's always busy taking pictures and interviewing residents or business owners. Last night she gave us a short report, confirming people's complaints of headaches and sore throats from the fumes they can smell but can't see. She sounded far away and exhausted when she told us not to worry. How realistic is that?

Grandpa leans against the garage doorframe in the late afternoon sun. He's going on about how the fishing bans and fat checks from the oil company are driving fishermen of all kinds into cleanup work caused by the spill.

"Hang out a big hunk of bait, a starving fish is gonna take it." The tip of his pocket knife blade digs under a fingernail. "Boat's no good tied up to the dock." He folds the knife closed, watching Dad sharpen the lawnmower blades. "Including mine, so be ready tomorrow morning when I get here."

Grandpa's been itching to skip the bays and get onto the Gulf. Catch bigger shrimp while the price is up. "Get before the gettin' gives out," he says.

Dad lowers the mower to the dirt floor, careful with the arm he wrenched a week ago hoisting potted trees on a job. "I know the drill, Pop." He rolls the mower next to me. "You do, too."

My job tomorrow is mowing the lawn, which I hate. But I will love a day of peace and quiet with them gone long before I wake up.

Saturday, May 1

The armrest on Grandpa's truck door gouges my side for the nine-hundredth time. It's four a.m. and a "change in plans." Dad's in the middle but Grandpa's driving so fast over this pot-holed, oyster shell-packed road, if we weren't wedged in, I'd be bouncing off the ceiling. Good thing Dad made me take sea-sick pills, otherwise my breakfast would be up there.

Ask me how much I do not want to be headed for a shrimp boat with these two. But last night Dad and Grandpa finally agreed on something. Dad's arm isn't 100%, so they need extra hands. Grandpa checked yesterday when he was down at the dock fueling and loading ice on the boat, but the good deckhands had already hired out. Or they don't want to work for him. Whatever, I come free.

The radio station rolls from Garth Brooks's "Friends in Low Places" to the morning news:

> "Oil continues to flow from the sheared *Deepwater Horizon* wellhead pipe. Officials admit that work to shut off the leak is like performing surgery in the dark, blindfolded. *The New York World* reported yesterday a company executive recently complained: 'We couldn't deserve this.'"

Grandpa slams his fist on the steering wheel. "Families of the dead don't deserve it neither."

We pull up behind the corrugated metal fish house next to a crumbling pile of oyster shells. I open the truck door and tumble out to the sound of growling boat engines. The air tastes like diesel and fish past the edge of going bad. I bury my nose and mouth in the crook of my arm and hesitate following Dad and Grandpa onto a wharf lit up like daytime. Grandpa stops to talk to one of the other shrimpers as Dad walks on.

Men in uniform: jeans, plaid shirts or T-shirts, white boots, and ball caps. They move along the walkways or on and off their boat decks. The largest boats run sixty feet long with cabins you might live in. These are the Gulf boats. They're not the biggest kind, but they dwarf the flat-bottomed eighteen-foot, bay-only boats. The ones that are walk-across level with the dock. The *Linnie Jean* sizes up somewhere in the middle. Built for the bays, Dad says she can manage day trips into the Gulf. Lucky me, today's the day.

I pick my way down the sloped gangway. The *Linnie Jean* gently rocks, grating her white hull against the barnacles clinging to the pilings. I think of Maddy, glad she's isn't a traveling barnacle island anymore.

Dad stuffs his pant legs into a pair of white boots and steps over the side railing. "Hand me your stuff," he says. Reaching for the lunch box, he grabs my backpack and sets it inside the pilothouse.

I put my foot on the railing to jump in.

"Stay put." Grandpa comes up beside me. He bends stiffly, but without hesitation, and steps onto the deck. "When I signal, take care of the lines," he says over his shoulder.

I look at the boat. *And which would those be?*

Cables stretch from the bow of the boat, angle over the pilothouse, past the smokestack and radio antenna to the top of a twenty-foot high, welded pipe, A-frame rigging over the stern. The frame spans the width of the *Linnie Jean*—fifteen feet across. Heavy bolts fix it to the deck on each side. A green, double-layered net falls lazily from the top into a shallow puddle on the stern deck. Cables run to winches, ropes attach to the net and tie off randomly, it seems like everywhere. The whole set-up looks like a giant spider went berserk.

The week I visited as a kid, Grandma made Grandpa take us for a ride on the bay. He tried to teach me stuff about the boat, but I wasn't interested in anything but the water and wind and the big birds. Especially, the pink ones, called Spoonies, that flew off the islands when we came near. Grandpa said I was to "stay out of the pilothouse" and not "monkey around the equipment." I followed the rules but he never asked me back. Partly, I think, because I'm a girl.

I scan the dock and boats, looking for women. There aren't any. Grandma told me about the long history of superstition among sailors and fishermen: anything female onboard—even a dog—can bring bad luck. Go figure why most of the boats have female names. Grandma said a shrimper uses a female deckhand only if he's desperate, saving money, or broke.

Dad and Grandpa lift the low wooden cover off a hole in the deck. Dad slides into the dark space behind the engine and Grandpa heads for his captain's chair in the pilothouse. Unlike the Gulf boats, this cabin is just big enough for four people to stand shoulder-to-shoulder across and two deep. The outside hasn't been painted in a while, but inside, the wooden dash, the instruments, and floor space are neat and ready for duty.

Grandpa flips on the radio and lifts the hand microphone out of its holder between the two front windows. Instead of music, through the open door and side window I hear the punch of men's voices. A mix of English, some Tex-Mex, and fishing talk that's another language altogether. Grandpa slaps the side of the radio when the sound quits, then slides the mic back in place.

I lean against the piling and wait for instructions as small waves from departing boats bump the *Linnie Jean* into the dock. I close my eyes and rotate my jaw against the headache creeping up my neck. The sounds and movement, maybe the diesel fumes, are making me nauseous and drowsy.

Grandpa bangs on the back window. "Cast-off."

My eyelids fly open. Dad's out of the hole and the cover's back in place. The engine rumbles and shimmies the dock under my feet.

I stare down at him, replaying and trying to translate the words.

"The lines!" Grandpa yells, the creases in his forehead needling together. He waves toward the wooden pilings and ropes holding the boat to the dock at her bow and stern.

I wedge my fingers between folds in the bow rope, struggling to loosen the knot.

"The shrimp'll be gone 'fore you're done fiddlin'." Grandpa's voice blasts out the door.

Wrangling the knot loose, I jerk the rope loops free of the post and scowl back at him.

"My God, girl, throw it onboard, undo the stern line, and get in."

I blanch, embarrassed who might hear him yelling at me. He ought to be more patient with someone up in the middle of the night doing him a huge favor.

I toss in the lines and step gently to the deck. Dad hands me a pair of boots that match the other fishermen's, only these aren't stained brown with engine oil and who knows what else. They're brand new, thin, and shiny white.

"Didn't want you coming to the party without your best shoes," he says.

"Thanks, I'm dancing already." I prefer sky blue or dark green, but no one asked. I stow my sneakers in my pack and slide my bare feet past the wide boot tops into the narrow foot. Instantly, the space between my toes starts to sweat.

The engine growls higher as Grandpa maneuvers the *Linnie Jean* away from the dock into the channel of Elliot Bay. I climb onto the four-foot square, wooden ice box, squeezed in center deck behind the engine lid and the winch and cables. Our mast light is so bright Dr. Nguyen could operate by it.

We cruise past spaces empty of shrimp boats that beat us out. In five minutes we near the junction of Elliot and Ghost Crab Bays. Becca's condo rises on our right. I count up the floors and corner windows. Her light's on. She's back from New York. I look away at the spread of moonlight on the water, trying not to care.

Dad unties a rope on the rigging. The net drops from the A-frame and crumples to the deck beside a V-shaped rack that holds two heavy wooden board things. They're layers of plywood stiffened with rows of two-by fours nailed to one side. A couple hundred pounds each, I remember now. Grandpa calls them doors. I watch Dad's fingers pull at the net and straighten the rope and chains, all connected to the doors.

The engine revs us into Ghost Crab Bay. Small waves curl away from our sides and water drops sparkle in our deck lights. The only wind is the forward movement of the *Linnie Jean*. It runs cool through my hair and makes my eyes water. I breathe in air cleaned of diesel fumes, air that smells of salt and whatever makes the shades of green and brown in the water surrounding us look black in the night.

Ahead of us, far across the bay, I count a dozen dots of light—probably other shrimp boats. Behind us, Port Winston is a shrinking jewel box of yellow-tinted street-lights, shop lights, and restaurant neon. The line of lights fades out at the edge of town, past the neighborhoods of lucky sleeping kids. I climb down and make my way to the engine box and sit on the floor. Leaning against the lid, I hug my knees. A faint heat in the wood warms my back. I pull my shirt collar close around my neck and stare at the neat pile of green net laying in the stern. Eyes closed, I drift away to the soothing rumble beneath me.

Sunlight, but not the sun, inches past the horizon, streaking the deep blue sky with soft oranges and pinks. The enormous waters spread in every direction, as far as I can see. While I cruised dreamland in a nap, we slipped from the bay into the Gulf. Gulls trail close over our wake and the boat rolls, bow to stern. The water isn't calm anymore. Dad gives me a hand up and I totter across the deck to get my camera from the pilothouse. I want to catch the sunrise and the birds. I splay my feet wide, lean against the center rigging, and zoom in on a seagull back-lit against a cloud swollen grey at the bottom with moisture.

One look at the camera's LCD screen and my stomach follows the wave that rolls under us. I drop to my knees, grip the rail, and throw up over the side. Twice. Eyes closed, my head hangs in the spray. A hand touches my shoulder. I sit back and open my eyes, afraid to move too far too fast. Dad hands me a wet rag and water bottle. I wipe my face and rinse my mouth, then slump back against the side.

"Breathe slowly." He takes my camera and leaves me to my misery.

The gulls behind us call, hover, drop, and switch dance with each other back and forth over the wake. The boat rises and dips. I throw my head between my knees and try to stop feeling like a low-speed mixer set on pulse. My stomach rolls again. The Gulf gets another gift.

Grandpa talks back and forth with someone on the radio, but I can't hear the words over the engine. I stare at my knees so I don't have to focus on anything moving. Finally, the *Linnie Jean* slows to a crawl. I look up as Grandpa drops a bucket on a rope into the Gulf and reels it in. He sucks a handful of water from it into his mouth, holding it a moment before spitting it overboard.

What kind of weirdness is that?

"Got shrimp," he calls over the water, talking more to the Gulf than to Dad—for sure, not to me. He glances at the sky then walks to the stern.

I hoist myself up along the main frame to get ready for whatever job they've drug me out for. Suddenly the band across my stomach tightens.

Nobody's driving!

I look through the cabin window at the wheel, expecting to see it rocking and rolling, but a grungy piece of rope ties it off to the dash. Shrimper's autopilot.

Dad cinches off the bottom of the net to form a sack where the shrimp will end up. He kicks it into the water where it floats out, tugging folds of netting off the deck as the *Linnie Jean* moves forward. A round metal grate sewn into the throat of the net hits the starboard rail and stands up on its edge. I recognize it from the model of a shrimp trawler at the Center. It's the TED. I hope Maria's right that these things really work—most of the time. I'll die if we haul in a dead turtle.

The mouth of the net drops in after the TED. The sound as it fills with water is like wind rushing through pine trees. The sudden weight on the net yanks and rattles the wooden doors in their rack. Grandpa kicks the pile of chain over the stern and walks back to the cabin, his face hard on business. The boat lowers in the water as we speed up.

Dad starts the winch running double cables over a pulley. The heavy doors lift out of their rack, then rattle and jolt to a stop five feet above the deck. I hold my breath.

Grandpa pushes the *Linnie Jean* faster. Dad unlocks the winch. Cable rolls off the spool, sending the doors crashing to the water beyond the stern. They ride the surface on edge, the water pressing them further and further apart, spreading the mouth of the net into a giant yawn. The gulls swarm and cry. Dad releases more cable and the doors and net vanish. I breathe out. Staring at the stiff wires from the A-frame that pierce the dark water of the wake behind us, I wish any turtles away.

"What are you looking for?" Dad says watching me rummage in my backpack in the corner of the pilothouse.

"I thought I'd read while we wait."

"You must feel better," he says.

"I think so. How long does this part take?"

"We'll check in an hour to see if Dad's taster's found us shrimp.

"Slurping Gulf water tells him that?"

"Some think that when salinity changes shrimp bunch and move together. You tasted something you're betting on, right Pop?"

Grandpa shrugs.

"Okay, whatever," I say. I'm just glad they didn't make me drink it. "Do I have a job today, by the way?"

"You start at the bottom, culling, like everyone else," Grandpa says.

"What's that?" I ignore the tone reminding me I have a place and better know it.

"A drag always catches more than shrimp," Dad says, heading off Grandpa's answer.

"I know," I say, "it's called by-catch. Becca's read all about how it's a big deal. How shrimping kills a bunch of other sea life."

Grandpa shakes his head. "Environmentalist, sports fishermen, and government know-nothing propaganda— aka Bull."

"But the government reports have proof," I say.

"Then they must be followin' the worst shrimp boats in the world. No good shrimper drags where there ain't shrimp." He squints an eye in my direction. "If I was gonna throw away time and money catchin' fish, I'd own oil land and buy me a big sport fishing boat. Then I wouldn't have to worry about makin' a living, I could just fish and tell shrimpers how to run their business."

"Grandpa, the environmental groups' research says the same as the government's."

"I don't care about any of them. If most of what comes up in that sack ain't shrimp, I'm a lousy shrimper, got bad luck, or am just plain lazy-stupid. And damn right I ought to lose my license, my boat, and be tied to a rocking chair in an old-folks home someplace in Wisconsin."

"But what about the thousands of turtles that die—"

"Stop," Dad says. "Forty years people have been at each other's throats over this. We've got a long day out here together, so there's no sense you two starting an argument." He looks at me. "Your main concern is turtles."

"Yeah, but—"

"You saw the TED, so whether Pop likes it or not, he's doing right by the law."

Grandpa snorts and looks out the front window.

"Moving on to the basics of culling," Dad says, "which is separating out the shrimp." He looks between Grandpa and me. "From whatever else, large or small, good or bad, that comes up in the net." He points out the back window to the plastic laundry baskets hooked to the icebox. "You'll put the shrimp in those, rinse them off, then I'll empty them into one side of the ice box and you shovel ice on them from the other.

"Sounds pretty simple," I say.

Grandpa shoots me a glare. "Hardest damn work you'll ever do."

"Leave her alone, Pop." Dad walks out of the cabin and I grab my pack and follow. His sticking up for me feels good. We sit on the ice box, back to back, me facing the stern.

"Look at those silly birds," I pull my camera out of my pack. A double row of silent gulls perch, wing-to-wing, down the sloping cables stuck through the wake. A Brown Pelican sits at the bottom of each line, like a stopper keeping the smaller birds from sliding into the water. A lone gull swings in. There's haggling at the head of the line, then everyone settles in place and quits talking. I snap a picture. We are all lookouts.

The warm air feels charged. I tip my head back against Dad and trace the hills and valleys of the dark clouds piled up in the distant sky. I breathe in the power of traveling on open water—the freedom, and the fear, of moving away from familiar things toward ways I don't know. I'm glad I'm going there with him.

Grandpa reams me for trying to help Dad untie the sack when it comes over at the end of the first drag. I figured the wind's picked up, Dad's arm is hurt, I'm here, and how much can Grandpa do, anyhow. He orders me off to the side and Dad yanks the knot loose. The sack opens and a gush of shrimp and other sea stuff drop to the deck, spreading around and beyond their boots. Becca was right about by-catch, there's plenty of it, but Grandpa's face lights up like Christmas because the pile is mostly shrimp. It takes only a minute for Dad to retie the sack and kick it over for a second drag.

Cigarette clamped in his teeth, Grandpa shoves a short stool to the edge of the pile of wriggling, jumping, and dead-still creatures. "Sit," he says. Shrimp pop and leap, some several feet in the air. Small fish buckle and flap, blue crabs scurry away from the pile, the few spider crabs unfold their long legs, feeling their way around plops of transparent jellyfish and bits of seagrass.

"Ahhh!" I kick out my boot hard, hurling the crab on my toe over the railing.

"Watch what you're doin'," Grandpa says. "Crab can punch through that boot quick as anything."

I'm shaking.

"Give her a chance," Dad says, handing me a pair of gloves. Grandpa lowers himself onto a second stool across from me. "Pop, what are you doing?"

"Tend the wheel," Grandpa says, waving him off. He looks me in the eye after Dad's gone. "Listen here, girl. It ain't your right to work the net and it ain't my job teachin' you to cull shrimp. But we got no time for your daddy's pussy-footin' around your feelin's." He shoves a heel against a dead sting ray, moving it out from the pile. "First off, rays got tail stingers and all crabs got parts that stick or pinch." He picks up a shrimp and points to its head. "See that barb? It'll nail you good. End up with hands lookin' like mine—or worse—you're not careful." He swings me a laundry basket. "Shrimp in here. Shove aside the trash and keep movin'."

I tighten with anger. How can he call these animals trash?

"Told me once you know how to work," he says, "so get to it."

His big hands fly over the pile, tossing shrimp in his basket and pushing aside what isn't. One eye squeezes shut against the cigarette smoke rising above his lips. He never looks up.

My stomach churns as the boat tops one wave after another. I hold my breath, grab the tails of two shrimp, and drop them in my basket. I toss a few live fish into the Gulf, praying they'll survive once they're back in the water. A beautiful, six-inch bat ray glistens at the edge of the pile. Already dead, its black eyes stare at nothing. I leave it, pick and toss a dozen shrimp, then carefully scoop its body into my hand and toss it overboard.

I'm sorry. Two gulls dive for it midair and miss.

The gulls mass, their cries are deafening. Grandpa sweeps a broad board across part of the pile he's picked through, adding to the discards. I duck as birds swarm the stern for the cast-offs. Grandpa slaps at one bold enough to try to steal a shrimp that missed the basket.

In what seems like hours, but is only twenty minutes, we're done. Shrimp fill his basket an inch from the top but only cover the bottom of mine. I shake the cramps out of my hands and wait for criticism. He struggles to his feet and leaves without a word for the pilothouse.

Dad grabs a shovel and hands me the bucket on the rope. He heaves part of the discard pile over the side.

"How did it go?" he says.

"Check my basket and you tell me."

He combines the baskets. "Seventy-five pounds of shrimp out of about a hundred total catch. Excellent drag, I'd say."

To him, but I can't get the ray out of my mind. I toss and retrieve the deck bucket from the Gulf and splash water over the shrimp. When Dad raises the lid on the ice box to dump the basket, the smell of long-gone shrimp rushes from the hole. I move to the rail and brace myself against the now familiar feeling. But the deep twinge passes.

Good pills, good pills.

Dad helps, sloshing buckets of water across the deck, then shoving off the last bits. When we're done, he hands me a wet rag and a bar of soap. I scrub shrimp slime off my gloves in the bucket, then work the cloth and soap all over my hands. The gritty, industrial-strength lather burns where a couple of shrimp managed to stab me. I rinse in the clean water he offers and collapse against the pilothouse, my shoulders and neck tense from the work and being under Grandpa's watch.

Dad props himself on the wall next to me. "You did a good job."

"Thanks." I shake extra water off my hands. "How can you stand doing this? We got a lot of shrimp, but those poor fish and other things—it's disgusting."

"Look on the bright side." he says. "We make the birds happy." A few more pelicans have joined the seagulls. At least they're not squawkers. He points off the side. "Those guys love a free meal."

Dark grey dorsal fins and backs of bottlenose dolphins rise and fall through the water beside the boat like carousel horses riding side-by-side, taking turns, up and down. I want to touch one but they're too far away.

"Greedy as gulls," Dad says, "but a lot cuter." He's trying to make me feel better, convince me this by-catch thing's really like Grandpa says. No big deal.

I dig out my camera and take pictures of the dolphins. Dad hands me a sandwich and bag of chips. I'm not hungry, but set myself against the engine box and let the heat and rumble work my back again. A seagull lights on the ice box and cocks an eye toward my sandwich.

"Guess again, buster."

He pecks around the top of the box, like he's trying to figure out how to get inside, then squawks and flies off over the pilothouse.

"Comin' sooner . . ." is all I hear for sure. We're on our third drag, but even before opening my eyes, I know everything around us has changed. The sun's completely gone, swallowed behind dark grey clouds . . . thunderheads. The wind's up, making the boat rock and roll harder in the waves and through the swells. I scramble off the floor, hanging on to the rigging arms as I stumble my way into the pilothouse.

"Pop, be reasonable," Dad says. "We're treading a fine line now, much less once it starts raining."

"The shrimp are here. Could be a quick squall. Ten more minutes are all we need."

"No. Second-guessing the storm is too dangerous, especially with Elizabeth here. We quit now."

"What's going on?" I say, moving close to Dad.

"The storm speed's faster than they predicted," he says. "We're pulling the net and going home."

Grandpa stares out the front windows, looking like a kid on a time-out. Dad doesn't wait for an answer. He's out the door with me at his heels. The winch grinds. I watch the spool fill with dripping cable. The bow of the boat bounces through a wave. The engine throttles back.

I grab the rigging arms to keep my balance as a nasty taste fills my mouth. Should have let the gull have the sandwich.

It seems forever before the wooden doors break the surface. The winch lines haul them over the stern. A gust swings them above the rack. Dad stops the winch, lets them calm, then slowly lowers them in place. I glance back at the cabin. Grandpa's locked, face forward, keeping the boat steady, taking the waves.

Dad works the sack up along the port side of the boat. A line, one end threaded through blocks and pulleys in the rigging, runs to the winch. The other end, fixed with giant hooks, sails from his hand, catching the net above the sack. He starts the winch. The sack rises until it hangs and swings, like a lazy pendulum, three feet off the deck. I watch Dad struggle to steady the bulging bag. My stomach threatens, but I'm too scared to look away. The rigging groans, the rest of the net bobs on the waves. A swell lifts the boat higher than the one before, pitching Dad and the sack toward the low railing.

"Dad!" My hip catches the corner of the ice box, twisting me sideways as I lurch for the rope. I run it under my arm, working my way along the deck to the sack.

"No," he yells, regaining his footing and scrambling toward me.

A sharp tug razors the rope against my shirt and skin.

"Let go." Grandpa's order bursts past my ear. I hold tight, not caring if he bans me from the planet for life.

I lean hard on the rope. The boat rises. The sack bumps my shoulder, knocking me into Grandpa. He drops against the deck behind me.

"Pop?" Dad calls out, struggling to steady the sack. I tighten my grip, pulling opposite to him, not daring to turn around.

Grandpa doesn't answer.

The sack stills enough for me to drop the rope and step away. Dad yanks the release cord and the catch spreads onto the deck. I turn and look for Grandpa. He's in the pilothouse bent over the wheel, his back rising and falling in heavy breaths. He reaches for the throttle.

If I hadn't been so stubborn, been in the way, he wouldn't have fallen.

He lays a hand on the dash. The boat rolls.

Hands shaking, I pull my gloves free from my back pockets. I sit on the deck, eyes glazing over at the wriggling mass, and start to cull.

Dad raises the rest of the net out of the water and piles it on the deck. Water runs everywhere. I'm soaked.

"Son, take the wheel," Grandpa calls to Dad.

"No, Pop, you're in no condition to be out here."

"I cull quicker 'n you, now do as I say."

Dad gives in and walks past Grandpa to the cabin. Grandpa kicks the stool in place and sits down. He looks ragged, his skin is grey, and the deep line between his eyebrows is pulled taut. For once he isn't telling me what to do. All the same, I wish he'd say something. I'm tired and more than scared. I grab for shrimp to a rhythm—

one, two, one, two, trying not to think or notice the gulls arguing and demanding all around us.

Grandpa turns sideways on his stool, grabs the stern rail, and buckles forward.

"Grandpa?" I reach out, but he turns his head away.

"I'm all right. He runs his hand back and forth on the rail a few times. "Rain's comin'." He starts picking shrimp again, but half speed.

I finish culling my side with a basket that's half full this time. Another clean drag, as Dad called it, but cutting the drag short means we didn't get as much as the first two runs. Grandpa leans his elbows on his knees, breathing heavy. My jaw clamps as tight as a lid on one of Grandma's canning jars.

Only a small pile of shrimp lies in front of him, but he sits, blank-faced, like he's never seen a shrimp in his life, much less knows what to do with it.

"Want me to finish?"

He nods. I watch him stand, his legs stiff as they carry him into the pilothouse. I finish the pile as the first fat raindrops splash onto the deck.

I slide to the floor in the corner of the pilothouse, out of the wind and spray. Grandpa glances at the sky behind us and pushes the throttle farther forward. The darkest clouds are almost overhead and the sky in every direction is gray-black.

"Put this on." Dad hands me one of two life jackets, his already cinched tight around him. He hands the other to Grandpa, who drops it to the floor.

I slip my sweatshirt on first, then the vest and pull up my hood to dry my hair. Grandpa looks at me, then turns back as the bow rides up a wave. Spray blankets the side windows. I pull my arms in tight around my knees and close my eyes.

Would it have killed you to say thanks?

CHAPTER EIGHTEEN

VOICES CHATTER BACK AND FORTH through the radio speaker, then stop. Grandpa swears. I'm standing pressed into the corner between the side window and the closed cabin door, tired of having my butt banged against the floor each time we hit a bigger wave. Quick pops of light appear and disappear on the water far behind us.

"Dad, I think someone's out there." I'd feel better knowing we're not alone.

He squints through the door windows, but the lights are gone. Shrugging, he turns back to say something to Grandpa. The bow of the *Linnie Jean* breaks over a wave. Hugging my shoulders and sweet-talking my stomach, I try not to panic.

A bright flash, then a thunder crack vibrates the doors. Lightening flickers on, off, on, like a giant light bulb about to explode. I don't have to count the seconds between. The storm's wrapped around us.

"Dad, how long 'til we get home?"

"Another hour." His voice is strained and loud over the engine.

I close my eyes imagining another hour of rain, waves, and a space the size of a big closet that smells like an ashtray.

Beam me up.

"Pop!" Dad's voice is sharp. Grandpa's slumped sideways. I grab his arm as he starts sliding off the chair. He leans into Dad. We lower him quickly to the floor, but there's barely enough room for us to fit. The boat slams sideways into a wave and leans left. Dad jumps for the wheel.

"Grandpa!" I yell, kneeling by his head. He doesn't answer. I press my fingers against the artery in his neck. No pulse. Mouth wide, eyes wild, beads of sweat glisten across his pale forehead. The rise of his chest disappears. He's stopped breathing. "Grandpa!" I shake his shoulders hard. Nothing.

Dad steadies the boat as we ride up a wave, then dip down the other side. The sky flashes white from another lightening hit.

He's going to die. We're all going to die.

Shut up and think.

The clock above the front window gleams in the next scatter of lightening. Thunder rumbles through the boat.

"Dad, I'm starting CPR."

I tip Grandpa's head back, pulling his chin up to look inside his mouth. There's not enough light to see past his front teeth. I don't want to do this.

"Rescuer One." Becca's CPR training voice pings through my brain, like a tennis ball off a racket. "No guts, no glory."

I breathe deep and run my fingers around the inside of Grandpa's mouth.

Clear. I wipe my hand on my jeans and lean close, listening for breath. The bitter stink of cigarettes fills my nose. I gag, shake my head, and sit up. Hands above his breastbone, I shove all my weight onto his chest to start the compressions.

"Mayday. Mayday," Dad calls into the mic. The boat slows. "This is shrimp trawler *Linnie Jean,* the *Linnie Jean.* I say again, *Linnie Jean.* Tango, X-ray 1451. Three people aboard. Sixty-seven year-old male, probable heart attack. CPR in progress. Request immediate assistance." Dad gives our relative location and describes the boat. "Over," he says.

"Push hard. One, two, three." Becca's call and rhythm drum inside my head.

"Mayday. Mayday," Dad calls into the mic again. "This is the shrimp trawler, *Linnie Jean.* Again, I say the *Linnie Jean.* Tango, X-ray 1451." He gives our position once more. "Over."

The radio's silence and the pressure cramping my shoulders make my head pound. I check the clock. Ninety seconds since Grandpa stopped breathing.

Dad slams his hand against the radio speaker. "Damn junk. Coast Guard should've answered by now."

I keep my count—twenty-six, twenty-seven—thirty. Check breathing. Grandpa's chest isn't rising. My temples throb as I lock my elbows again. Thirty pushes and my arms turn to putty.

"Dad," my throat spouts a loud squeak. "Can you take over with your arm?"

"Handling the wheel's no easier. Keep trying."

"I can't get his chest down far enough."

He looks between Grandpa, the front window, and back. "Tell me what to do."

"Lock your hands together, like this." I thread my fingers, one hand on top of the other. "Here on his chest, then push, hard, twice a second to thirty, then check his breathing."

He swivels off the chair and hands me the mic. I take his place and wrap the wheel's circle in my forearms, locking my hands and the mic together at the top. The wheel tugs one way, then the other, but I tighten my arms, blocking it from turning too far.

"Take the waves at a slight angle," he says. "Keep the compass needle northeast."

Dad drops beside Grandpa and starts the compressions. I brace my boots on the chair rails and lean my chest against the wheel—weight against motion. I steer through a wave and glance back. Dad hisses through the pushes on Grandpa's chest.

"Deeper." I turn back to the front. "Two inches down or it's no good." I hear a snap behind me and pray it's not Grandpa's rib. I look again. Dad's up on his knees pushing with everything he's got, lips moving, counting.

"Good!"

I stare out the front window. A red light glows misty on our port side bow, a green one on starboard. Every light on the boat blazes, but it's raining so hard I don't know who'll see them. My thumb rests next to the mic's talk button.

I check the clock. Three minutes. Technically, Grandpa's dead. Even if he starts breathing, he could have brain damage.

I raise the mic to repeat Dad's Mayday call and a man's voice crackles through the speaker.

"*Linnie Jean*, this is trawler *Heart's Desire*, Tango X-ray 1643 on Channel 16. Switch and answer Channel 38. Over."

My heart pops. "Dad, what do I do?"

He keeps pumping, breathing heavy. "Press the up arrow under the display until you get to 38 and wait. He'll call you from there. Wait for him to say, 'over', then answer." Dad pushes and watches. I lean harder on the wheel. It bucks when I reach for the radio. I hang on tight and find the channel, my finger on the mic button.

"Keep your finger off the button unless you're talking," Dad snaps. "It's not an open line like a phone." Sweat drips off his jaw. He checks Grandpa's breathing. I steer through another wave and wait, arms locked tight around the wheel, one hand holding the mic close to my lips.

"*Linnie Jean*, this is *Heart's Desire* on Channel 38, do y'all read me? Over."

My thumb slips past the button, but I lift it back on and press. "*Heart's Desire*, this is *Linnie Jean*, uh, over?" My voice cracked so I'm not sure he heard me. I let go of the button and inhale through my nose to calm down.

"*Linnie Jean*, this is *Heart's Desire*, I read you." The man's voice is steady and so clear he could be standing next to me. "Give me your situation. Over."

"My Grandpa's had a heart attack. He isn't breathing. Dad's doing CPR, but his arm's hurt, too, so I don't know how long we can hold out, and the Coast Guard won't answer our call. Over." It all comes sputtering out at once. I snap my thumb off the button and look at Dad.

"Steady, gal," the voice says. "The *Payday* and I are with you. Your radio's been cuttin' in and out, so I'll relay your information to the Coast Guard. Over."

I twist my head around. Lights on two boats behind us are getting closer and brighter. I hold down the mic button. "I see you. Over." I'm yelling.

"Elizabeth," Dad calls through a pant. "He's breathing."

"Dad, you did it!"

"*We* did it!"

I lean down and he hugs my neck with one arm. I almost fall on him as we roll hard against a wave.

"The wheel," he yells.

Heart racing, I wrap myself back in place, barely steadying the roll.

"*Linnie Jean*, this is *Heart's Desire*. Everything all right? Over."

My hand shakes so hard I can hardly find the button. We take the next wave more smoothly.

"Repeat, *Linnie Jean*—"

"We're here, we're here. He's breathing." I'm laughing, staring at the spray flying around us, like fizz out of a soda can.

Wait. He didn't hear if you talk at the same time.

The radio is quiet. He must be keeping the air clear for me. I push the button.

"*Heart's Desire*, sorry. Grandpa's breathing. Over." I sit up straighter and watch a smaller wave ride toward the side of the bow. The radio is silent. One minute, then two click by. I look behind us. The lights of the boats are still there. Dad isn't next to Grandpa. He's on deck in the rain.

The speaker crackles.

"*Linnie Jean*, this is *Heart's Desire*. We transmitted your information to the Coast Guard. A medevac crew's flying a patient to Port Winston Memorial and will let us know when they're headed our way. Meantime, you slow down a little more, I'll make your ride a whole lot smoother. Over."

Dad fights his way through the doorway, hugging a blanket and tarp he pulled from a box on the deck. He's half soaked.

"*Heart's Desire* wants to catch up," I say. He takes over the wheel. I take the pile and almost drop it on Grandpa, my arm strength near gone. He kicks me Grandpa's abandoned life preserver.

Dad raises the mic. "*Heart's Desire, Payday*, this is Steven Barker. Thanks for sticking with us."

I lift Grandpa's head and slip under the life preserver. The blanket reeks of every smell from every trip since Grandpa bought the boat. I lay it over him and tuck under the edges. The tarp on top will hold in body heat. I bend my ear over his open mouth, listening and happy for every cigarette-smelly breath against my cheek. I touch the salt and pepper-colored nubs of his crew cut hair.

Maybe we'll get another chance, huh, Grandpa?

I stand in the starboard corner of the pilothouse watching the lights of *Heart's Desire* ride up along side. She's a Gulf boat. Her bow sits high in the water. As she passes, despite the rain, I see a white-haired, bearded man in the cabin. He waves and presses a thumbs up against his window. I wave back at him, pressing my smiling face against our window.

The *Heart's Desire* runs out past us, slicing through the wave ahead. Her stern moves in line with our bow. The *Linnie Jean* calms and settles into the center of the wake. Behind us a boat, I assume is the *Payday*, rides the end of ours. We're a shrimp boat sandwich.

Dad's got the radio on Channel 38 waiting for *Heart's Desire* to relay exactly when the Coast Guard helicopter will get here. I sit on the floor next to Grandpa. His eyes are closed, his breathing still shallow. I press my fingers onto his neck. The pulse is weak and I lose it every few beats. But his face is relaxed, the lines that usually broadcast his anger and impatience are gone. He just looks like an old man asleep under a two-day beard. I think about Grandma's drawing in their upstairs hallway, the photos in Uncle Roy's box, and try to imagine the man beside me, young and happy. I can almost see that guy in this face. Almost. I wish I'd known him then.

"*Linnie Jean*, this is Coast Guard cutter *Admiral Carter* on Channel 38. We have your location. Please go to Channel 22a and transmit your condition. Over."

I fly off the floor, grabbing the back of the chair. "They must be close." I bounce up and down like I'm standing on hot sand. Dad waves at the air for me to stop.

"Coast Guard cutter *Admiral Carter*, this is *Linnie Jean* transferring to 22a. Over." He dials in the channel. I try to stand still so I don't bug him, but all this slow, formal back and forth on the radio makes me crazy.

"Coast Guard cutter, *Admiral Carter*, this is *Linnie Jean* on Channel 22a. We have sixty-seven year-old, male heart attack victim, breathing and unconscious." Dad looks back at me. "Pulse weak and unsteady." I nod. "Over."

The radio's quiet. I grab Dad's arm, sure the radio's gone out again. I zero in on the clock, counting the seconds.

"Where'd they go? What if the radio—"

"*Linnie Jean,* Coast Guard cutter *Admiral Carter.* Roger. Have cleared you as priority. Chopper en route. Estimate reaching you six, repeat six minutes. Over."

"Roger, *Admiral Carter.* We're in good company 'til you get here. Over."

I hug Dad around his shoulders. He pats my arm. Then my knees give out. I drop to the floor and lie on my back next to Grandpa. Our arms touch— sweatshirt against tarp. I stare up at the ceiling and, for the first time, notice it's painted pale blue. A puffy white cloud floats on it directly above Grandpa's chair. Hot tears roll down my cheeks. I recognize the artist.

We'll get him home, Grandma.

I hear the deep thump and thrumming a minute before the helicopter drops through the rain cloud. Sixty feet up, it hovers like a giant orange and white dragonfly. The wind from the blades whips the water near us into a circle of white, foamy spray. A person in a flight suit, life jacket, and helmet crouches in the open side doorway.

"*Linnie Jean,* this is Coast Guard medevac, *Hawkeye.* Over"

"*Hawkeye,* this is the *Linnie Jean.* Over," Dad says.

"*Linnie Jean,* hold your position. We're sending someone down. Over."

"Roger, *Hawkeye.*" Dad slows the engine. "Keep her steady," he says to me. The door snaps shut behind him as he walks out on deck. I take the chair and hold the wheel tight locked in behind the *Heart's Desire*. The *Payday*'s dropped farther behind, but I can still see her lights.

Dad waves when the crewman in the helicopter doorway leans out on a line. I snatch a look and watch his smooth fall toward the deck. He makes a perfect two-point landing on our stern and unclips the line from his harness. Dad leads him to the pilothouse. When he walks through the doors I see "he" is a she.

She crouches near Grandpa's head. "Mr. Barker, can you hear me?" Our gazes meet when I take my eyes off the water to glance at her.

"Your grandfather?" she says. I nod. "Don't worry, we'll take good care of him."

I can't answer. Not just because of the lump clogging my throat. She assumes he and I are close. I'm not sure what we are anymore. I turn frontways to look at the *Heart's Desire* and try to block the voice in my head saying this may be the last time I see Grandpa alive.

The helicopter lowers a shallow basket made of metal bars. They lift Grandpa, blanket, and tarp onto the cushions inside, buckling straps tight over his chest, middle, and legs. Squeezing around the deck gear, they carry him to the stern and hook up the lines to the helicopter that will take him away. She steps onto rails beneath the basket and hooks herself to the lines. At her signal, she and Grandpa rise off the deck, gliding through the rain toward the open door above.

I feel the whup, whoop, whup of the blades in my chest. A gust of wind catches and rocks the slender basket, sending a flash of panic through me. But a few more seconds and Grandpa rests inside the belly of the orange and white bug. An orange flight suit moves across the space and the door shuts. The pitch of the blades rises, pulling the chopper into the softening gray rain. I listen to the fading sound. The pilothouse feels strangely empty.

Dad nudges me off the chair. He wraps my shoulder with the arm of his soppy sweatshirt. We stay locked together, both steering and silent.

CHAPTER NINETEEN

THE STORM MOVES THROUGH and rain slows to a drizzle by the time we dock the boat. Dad walks out of the pilothouse to call Grandma, the cell phone signal back. I take his place in the captain's chair and rest my forehead on the wheel, lost in the still-rumbling engine.

"Mom, we're at the dock," I hear Dad say, his voice controlled. "Pop's had another heart attack—no, the Coast Guard took him to Memorial a little over an hour ago—I don't know, he was unconscious. Thank God Elizabeth took the CPR class—yes, she's all right. We'll get to the hospital as soon as we can."

I don't want to think about the hospital, about what's coming next. Not like I've gone all mushy about Grandpa, but I'm scared.

Dad motions me out of the chair. "Come on kiddo, tie us up. We've got shrimp to unload."

Jell-O-legged, I climb over the side of the boat onto the dock. Twisting and looping wet rope with stiff fingers, I tie some sort of mess around the pilings. Dad shuts down the engine and hauls himself and our gear out of the boat. He redoes my knots without a word.

"Steven." It's the voice of the *Heart's Desire.* We turn around and, sure enough, walking toward us is the bearded face that smiled at me through the pilothouse window. "You might not remember me," he says, reaching for Dad's hand.

"It's been a long time, Mr. Wilkes," Dad says.

Holt Wilkes? Grandpa's old friend. Larry Wilkes's father. I look at Dad but there's no sign he's thinking what I'm thinking—that we're helping send Holt's son to jail.

Six men, crew from other shrimp boats, walk past us, but a man Dad's age and another guy stop beside Mr. Wilkes. I blush. "This is Ben Lungren, owner of the *Payday*," Holt says, "and his boy, Price."

I sneak a look at Price. His calm eyes and slight smile show more confidence, less distance than that day at the Center. Since landing in his lap, I've watched him at school. I think the sunburn on his slightly upturned nose is new and beyond cute.

"This is my daughter, Elizabeth," Dad says. The smell of stale seawater and fish wafts off his shirt.

Mr. Wilkes shakes my hand. "Quite the deckhand. Handlin' the boat, the radio, and knowin' CPR. I imagine James is real proud of you."

"Proud" isn't in Grandpa's vocabulary, leastways not towards me. Not after he finds out what I've promised the DA.

"Thank you. I hope so," I say.

Price smiles bigger at me. I drop my gaze to count nail heads in the dock planks, hoping I don't smell like Dad.

"I hate to think what might have happened without your help," Dad says.

"We were in the right place at the right time. Now, go on." Mr. Wilkes shoos us like we're cats underfoot. "Y'all skedaddle to the hospital. We'll take care of your catch."

Dad motions toward the Gulf. "You've done more than enough. Helping us out there is one thing, but this is Elizabeth's and my work."

Is he nuts? These guys are golden and, personally, I'm never flipping another shrimp, not even if they paid me.

"There should be men at the fish house looking to earn a few extra bucks," Dad says. "We'll be fine."

"Son, listen to me," Mr. Wilkes says, "your daddy and I took care of each other before all the mess over Roy. Since he's not here to argue, you'd do me a great favor in lettin' me finish up."

Dad sighs and looks over at me.

I seriously frown back at him. No way he's winning this one.

"Okay. Thank you," he says, "all of you."

At the end of the dock, on our way to the truck, I look back at the *Linnie Jean* and watch Mr. Wilkes and the Lungrens scoop iced shrimp out of the box. Price's smile hovers in front of me like a warm coat; Mr. Wilkes's kind words take some sting out of Grandpa's criticism. He can stay mean, if he wants, but I want Holt Wilkes as my friend, forever.

We drive out the long, muddy gray lane, Dad managing to miss most of the potholes Grandpa hit this morning coming in. There's one crater I can't dodge. Once Larry's arrested and I testify, the good stuff today—my budding chance at a life—will go missing.

You can't get too comfortable in emergency room chairs. I guess we're supposed to suffer extra while we wait for someone to bring us good or bad news. I fold my leg under my knee and pick at the plastic tip on my shoelace. Grandma's been here two hours already. She looks wiped out.

Dad tries twice to get the nurse at the desk to cough up some info on Grandpa, but all she'll say is, "The doctor will talk to you when she's finished the examination."

He sits back down between Grandma and me and squeezes his hands between his knees.

"The old fool," she says into the quiet room. Before we agree with her, a woman in a white doctor's coat comes through the swinging door marked HOSPITAL PERSONNEL ONLY.

"Mrs. Barker?"

Grandma nods.

"I'm Dr. Bishop."

Dad moves so she can sit next to Grandma. The doctor shakes her hand and doesn't let go.

"Your husband's in stable condition and resting, but his heart sustained serious damage."

Grandma's eyes tear. "My granddaughter and son gave him CPR."

Dr. Bishop looks at Dad and me. I look away, afraid I'll go past being teary.

"That most certainly saved his life," she says. "The next twenty-four to forty-eight hours are critical in knowing whether he can maintain a normal heart beat. We'll be able to evaluate more options then."

"May we see him?" Grandma says, wiping her eyes.

"Certainly. He's been conscious, briefly, a couple of times, but he's under sedation so he'll probably sleep a lot. I'll see him tomorrow morning on my rounds."

She squeezes Grandma's hand. Her look seems to say, "Try to have courage." If anyone can, it's Grandma. She's had a lot of practice.

The intensive care ward is low-lit and quiet except for the soft noise of equipment tracking how patients are holding up. Dad and I walk together, following Grandma to the curtains separating Grandpa from the other patients. I peek through the gap. His eyes are closed. See-through plastic bags of clear liquid hang on a pole next to the bed. The ventilator over his nose and mouth reminds me of the one the vet techs used on Maddy.

I step through the curtains and stand beside Dad. Shrunken under the white blanket, Grandpa looks even older than when he lay unconscious on the boat deck. It's hard to imagine a few hours ago he was driving the boat, sorting shrimp, giving orders, and making me mad, as usual. If only I hadn't . . .

Grandma strokes his hand on top of the covers. "James." She clears the crackle from her throat. "It's Linnie."

He blinks and halfway opens his eyes.

"Old fool." She kisses him on the forehead. "We're all here."

He squints and stares into her face.

"The doctor said Elizabeth knowing CPR saved your life."

He keeps eyeing Grandma like he's trying to figure out what she said, or who she is. He looks at me, frowns, and closes his eyes.

I study the polished linoleum floor, trying not to cry. Dad squeezes his arm around me, but I twist out and walk away.

I hate when you're coming out of a dream. That place when you aren't quite sure which side of sleep you're on. I'm back on the deck of the *Linnie Jean*, trying to scoop a propeller-wounded, teenage-sized Kemp's into the deck bucket. Becca's driving and trying to get Maria on the radio. "Hello," she calls over the engine noise. There's no answer. "Hello," she tries again, only this time she sounds like a man. It's a gentle voice. God maybe, come to help me save the turtle.

"Hello. Elizabeth?"

The hard floor under my hip reminds me where I am. The lumpy backpack under my chin is wet with drool. I shade my eyes from the ceiling lights. Holt Wilkes stands over me, ball cap in one hand.

"Oh, hi." My voice croaks and I groan, struggling twice to sit. Every muscle attached to every bone aches.

"Poor kid." He leans down and cradles me around the back to help me stand. "Where are your folks?"

"Dad's out getting Chinese food. Grandma's in with Grandpa." I don't mention Mom. Dad called to let her know what's going on. He said she didn't need to come home until we know more. Besides, Mr. Wilkes might feel like Grandpa about her kind of job. I don't need more of that opinion.

I drop onto the molded plastic chair closest to me. The setting sun through the plate glass window darkens the trees into silhouettes. The clock over the nurse's station says eight p.m. I've been curled up in the corner, asleep, over an hour.

Mr. Wilkes holds out a fat white envelope. "We did good. The shrimp price is still up and not many boats were out because of the storm. Put this somewhere safe for your daddy."

"Sure." I zip the money in my backpack and yawn.

Mr. Wilkes sits next to me. "How's your Grandpa?"

"I think the doctor said he's pretty bad."

"He's a stubborn, tough old man." He stares at the wall opposite us. "More stubborn pride than good sense sometimes. After his first heart attack, he started treatin' the world like he did after Roy died."

"You and Grandpa were really good friends before the accident."

He rubs one hand over the other. Brown age spots mix with patches of skin dried by too much salt water and wind. I realize mine are tight from the same thing. He fingers a bandage on his right thumb.

"The saddest day of my life was when Roy died. Not just losin' Roy, who was like my own, or your Grandpa as my best friend. It was watchin' the gentle part of him die and none of us able to help him." He shakes his head. "He loved his boy so much."

"Grandpa shouldn't have quit talking to you. It wasn't fair." Especially if Dad was a big part of what happened, I want to say, but don't, still not convinced it's true.

"I was plenty angry about how he blamed Larry," he says. "But James lost more, and he couldn't let go. Some people only see life in black and white, I guess. Got no eye for the middle. Lucky for me and my wife that Linnie forgives in color." He looks at me. "Your daddy's an honorable man, comin' back here to live. Your grandma understands what a sacrifice y'all have made."

"Grandpa doesn't seem to want us here. He sure doesn't like me much."

"Don't you believe that for a minute." Calluses scratch lightly over my knuckles as he takes my hand. "James is a lot of things and he protects his insides, but he loves his family. He's just lost most ways of showin' it. If he didn't care, he'd ignore you. I know."

I stare at the darkened spot in the carpet under my feet where lots of people have rubbed their shoes wondering and worrying about people they love, even people they're not so sure about.

"Linnie says you got spunk and fire like James," he says, "but sweetness, too. You show that old man you're not givin' up on him and I bet you bring him 'round." He smiles at me, but there's sadness in his eyes. "I'd give six gold buttons off my best suit, and then some, for a granddaughter like you."

I can't see through the blur of tears. "What if Grandpa doesn't make it?" There, I said it.

He holds out a white handkerchief. "Sweet girl, we're all goin' to die someday. I wish James hadn't done so much to get himself there ahead of schedule." I blow my nose. "Main thing is, whenever James leaves this world, he knows you cared for him as much as he allowed." Mr. Wilkes pats my hand. "I admit showin' him might not be easy."

If I even get a chance to try.

Dad walks through the door, takeout bags from the Blue Moon clutched in his hands.

Mr. Wilkes stands. "Good evenin', Steven."

Dad sets the bags on the table in front of me. "It's good of you to come by."

"Just came to give y'all your money and see how James is doin'. I've been gettin' to know your Elizabeth." He smiles at me and winks. "Fine young lady."

"Yes, she is," Dad says, his look turns soft, like he's moved off somewhere.

I unload cartons, paper plates, and utensils from the bags. An hour ago I couldn't have cared less about food, now I'm ready to inhale the whole pint of sweet and sour chicken.

"I best be goin'." Mr. Wilkes puts on his cap.

"Look," Dad says, "there's something coming up you should. . . Elizabeth and I aren't really supposed to—"

He's going to tell him about the bribe and me! "Uh, Dad, dinner's getting cold."

His gaze wavers to me, then focuses on Holt. "Right. Can we offer you something to eat?"

"No, thanks. It's late and Janet's home waitin'."

"I'll tell Mom you came by. Thanks for this," Dad says when I hand him the money envelope.

Mr. Wilkes nods. "You call the house if there's anything you need."

I trail him into the hall. "I think you should see Grandpa."

"Now's not a good time."

"But, what you said. I think it goes for you, too. It's important."

I take his hand, ready to pull him like a reluctant puppy on a leash. To my surprise, he only hesitates a second.

We push through the double doors into the intensive care ward.

Grandma sits on the straight-backed chair next to the bed, flipping the pages of a magazine. Grandpa's eyes are closed.

"Grandma," I whisper through the gap in the curtains. "You two have a visitor."

"Holt," she says, looking past me. They give each other a long hug. "Bless you for being there today."

"Good thing one of us bought a new radio in the last twenty years." He grins and walks to the end of the bed to look down at Grandpa. Grandma Linnie follows and Mr. Wilkes takes her hand. What looks like years of sads and sorrys cross his face.

CHAPTER TWENTY

Wednesday, May 5

MARIA STARES AT THE computer screen. "Hi," she says, but doesn't look up, even when I sit and prop my elbows on the edge of her desk. An Internet slideshow about the oil spill parades across the screen. A Brown Pelican under a thick layer of oil stares at the camera. The caption says it's dead and pictures show offshore and marsh waters suffocating under a rainbow-colored slick of oil. Every day in science class the teacher gives us updates. The impacts from the spill get worse, and all I can do is listen and worry about Mom. It's made me hate third period.

In silence, Maria and I watch the photo stream of animals, birds, and fish already dead, or fighting to survive. She reaches for a folder on the desk marked "Oiled Bird Protocol" and drops it in her briefcase. My heart jumps.

"Oiled birds?" I say. "I thought the slick wasn't close to here."

"It isn't."

"Then what's with the folder?"

"I'm taking a decontamination trailer to one of the wildlife refuges in Louisiana tomorrow to help clean birds before they're sent to rehab facilities."

"I want to go!" Reaching for my cell phone, I punch in Dad's number. "Mom's there somewhere. And I could help with the birds." Dad's message comes on.

"Whoa, hang on," Maria says. "You can't just drop in on your Mom's work. To say nothing of leaving when your grandfather is so ill—or skipping school."

I turn off the phone. "You'll only be gone a couple of days, right? It could be a field trip. I'll study on the way so I won't get behind."

She shuts the laptop and slides it into her briefcase with the bird folder. "Oil and the dispersants are danger-ous materials," she says, walking around the desk. "No one would allow you to be exposed to these pollutants, including me. Besides, working with the birds requires special training."

The early television news starts in a Louisiana marsh. A dozen hermit crabs struggle out of oiled water onto oiled grasses. For all I know, Mom's standing outside the frame, taking notes or pictures. Two days ago she was in the Gulf on a shrimp boat, photographing fishermen set-ting out booms along the edge of the spill. Maria groans and clicks off the TV.

My throat narrows. "Mom's doing her part writing articles, and you save birds. I feel so useless. Grandma and Dad don't need me. They never ask me to sit with Grandpa, even though all he does is sleep most of the time. I want to help with something, please."

Maria's face hardens a second. "Frankly, I'm surprised at you." She rests a hip against the edge of her desk. "I don't know your family, Elizabeth, but I bet you're wrong about not being needed. Especially since your Mom can't be here. Maybe you should be the one reaching out."

I stare at the black TV screen, not knowing what to reach for, and afraid what might get handed back.

"There's plenty for you to do around here," she says. "You're one of our lead volunteers. Give tours, help feed, show kids the turtles. I promise to be back before Sunny's eggs hatch. Then we'll celebrate."

"We can't release hatchlings. What if the Gulf's not safe for years?"

"We have no choice."

I stare, mouth open in disbelief. "Why not?"

"Kemp's are too aggressive to keep together, and our facility isn't large enough to house that many turtles separately."

I grab up my pack and stand. "They're just babies."

"I don't like it either. The truth is the adult females are more important for species survival and they're in the greatest danger."

I drop back into the chair. "How could anything be in more danger than a two-inch hatchling? What if they reach the oil, or it gets to them?"

"They'll probably die. Since we're not near the oil, they've got time to hang in the sargassum and float. The adults swim from here after nesting season to feed in the shallow water off Louisiana. They're heading straight into the oil and dispersants. If we lose those breeders, we lose generations of Kemp's."

The generations thing again.

"All we can do is hope that won't happen," she says.

"I think this 'hope' thing is over-rated."

Maria squats in front of the chair. Her face is full of grief, but the stubborn resolve I've seen before is there, too. "I don't have an answer, Elizabeth. It's a one-turtle-at-a-time job. One nest, one egg, one release after another."

I can't look at her.

"Some days, when I get really discouraged, I challenge myself. Can I find one reason, one idea to keep me going? So far I have, but sometimes, like now, it seems impossible." She twists her head to look up into my face. "I know how you feel. It might help to remember a bunch of people years ago challenged themselves to bring the Kemp's ridley back from the edge of extinction. We may have to do it again, that's all."

Something a lot closer to home feels like it's walking toward that edge.

She smiles gently and picks up her briefcase. "I'll keep Barbara posted on the cleanup. Now, do something for the birds; help me pack the trailer."

Tuesday, May 7

I walk by the hospital rooms of other sick people, imaging what's wrong with them, wondering whether they're like Grandpa, or worse. He's been under intensive care a week. His heartbeat keeps going screwy and a couple of times the doctors had to shock it out of giving up altogether. Dad and I moved in with Grandma, temporarily, so she won't be alone. I've wrestled with what Maria and Holt said about family and Grandpa. Last night I made a decision.

I slip into the quiet unit and peek around his curtain. Grandma gets up from the chair.

"He's sleeping," she says. Her eyelids droop and there are dark circles above her cheeks. Sometimes I hear rummaging noises from their bedroom in the middle of the night, or smell the next day's meals cooking in the kitchen. She doesn't sleep much.

"The nurse comes in every hour to check on him," she says. "Tell them if you need anything." She hugs me. "Sure you'll be all right?"

I step away. "I'll be fine. Dad will be here in awhile— you go on."

She bends and kisses Grandpa's forehead. "I'm going home now, James," she says, like he can hear her, "but I'll be back to kiss you goodnight. Elizabeth's here. You be nice to her." Then she's gone.

What if he wakes up and doesn't want me here? Saturday, when we first saw him, Grandpa looked at me once. I felt like a stain on the curtain. Dad said Grandpa probably didn't realize any of us were there.

I sink into the chair and look at the weathered lines in Grandpa's face, his pale lips, and the puffy folds under his lower lids. His breathing is shallow. I slip off my sandals, rest my heels on the corner of the mattress, and shut my eyes, matching one breath for every two of his.

I'm glad there's no television in here that's always on, like in the regular rooms. I don't want to hear about the oil—the hundreds of thousands of gallons a day still spewing into the Gulf. Or the government employees who took favors from oil companies: vacations, parties, and other free stuff, then approved bad drilling plans. It all seems like a bigger version of Larry Wilkes buying votes for Tortuga Sands, and I'm sick of it.

Grandpa's heart beeps a steady call from the monitor in the corner. I concentrate on the blips, trying to shut out the blathering in my head, or get it to change subjects. Grandma said he's been awake and talking some, but he sleeps a lot. A couple of days ago, when I peeked in and watched him drift between awake and asleep, he may have smiled at me—maybe.

"What you doin' here?" His voice is weak but clear.

I jerk to attention, sweeping my feet to the floor, heart thumping, like when he caught me with Uncle Roy's box.

I look at him. He scowls back. I sit higher in the chair, clamping my thumbs between my thighs and the seat.

"Hi, Grandpa. How are you feeling?"

"Better 'n some. You?"

The chair under me is cold and hard no matter which way I squirm. Truth is I feel rotten. Then, I'm not lying in a hospital with my heart doing a major two-step every few days. I grope for something to talk about: Shrimping? The oil spill? I mention those, he'd probably work himself into another heart attack. I could talk about Larry Wilkes, but considering how he feels about him, better not.

"Not much going on, Grandpa. Same stuff."

"Mmm."

"I'm staying with Grandma nights. So don't worry about her."

"Never have. Strong woman. Better than I deserve."

I slide the chair closer to the head of the bed. Grandma's got to be a safe subject.

"She thinks a lot of you, too," I say. "We've been talking about when you were younger, before Roy—" I stop, but the words are out.

He turns his head toward the curtain across the room. His fingers close, then open flat against the bed covers.

"I'm sorry, Grandpa. I shouldn't have mentioned him."

He turns back, fumbling for the control that adjusts the head of the bed. Frustration knots up his forehead when he can't find it. He jabs his thumb in the air, signaling for me to raise him up.

He looks into my eyes, not opposing me for once, but I can tell something's on his mind. The corners of his mouth drop a little when he opens it to speak.

"Look," he says. "I ain't been just lying here sleepin'. Linnie and I been talking about lots of things, includin' them days." He rolls his eyes up toward the ceiling, swallowing hard, then points to the glass of water on the bedside table. I grab it, careful not to slosh any on the floor, and ease the straw to his lips. He nods when he's had enough.

"What happened to Roy wasn't right," he says, "and what I did wasn't either. Took me near dyin' to see it."

My throat cinches, my eyes feel salt-burned.

"I had two good sons. Your daddy deserved better, then and now. I told him I'm sorry for drivin' him away after the accident. He did a dumb thing pushin' those boys to race, but Larry and Roy showed even fewer brains listenin' to him."

My heart sinks. What Larry said is right and Grandpa always knew. Poor Dad, feeling responsible all these years for what happened and for Grandpa's anger. No wonder he never wanted to talk about Roy or growing up here.

"Linnie, Janet and Holt deserved better, too." He rolls his head slowly against the pillow, then lies still.

"It's okay, Grandpa."

His eyes close and just when I figure he's going to sleep, they open, first searching, then zeroing in on me. He reaches for my hand and I give it to him. This is the first time we've ever touched. He loses strength and our hands sink to the bed.

"I been real hard on you, Elizabeth."

Tears of relief gather and spill down my face. "It's okay."

"No, it ain't." His voice is urgent, his eyes pull me to them. "Roy's spirit is in you along with your daddy's strength. He had to have plenty to come back here." He looks at the ceiling, breathing hard.

He motions for more water. His voice is thin from so much talk. Fear rises through my chest. I need to hear him out, but what's the cost?

"Grandpa, please stop, you'll get too tired."

He rolls his head, no, on the pillow and hands me back the cup. "I ain't got much time left. You're the last one."

His words swirl inside me. I lay my head against the bed, but the sudden touch of his hand sits me back up.

I pull tissues from the box on the bedside table and wipe my eyes.

"You know I don't take to your momma goin' away from her family like she does."

"Grandpa, she—"

"But she's a fine woman—smart—and seems good to you and Steven in her own way."

He stops again. His chest heaves. I raise the glass, but he waves it away. His head lifts off the pillow. "I hear you caught Larry givin' out bribes."

"Nobody is supposed to know."

"Think I'm a gossip?"

"No."

"His getting caught will be good for this place and for Larry. He'll suffer, but I take no pleasure in it."

"What about his folks and Grandma. What if the whole mess between the families starts all over again?"

"Larry's parents ain't dumb about their son. They're strong, forgiving folks. Linnie and them are good souls hatched in the same nest. You're doing what's right and I believe they'll understand."

"I hope so."

He asks for water and pulls in a long gulp. I pray it won't go down the wrong pipe and choke him. He's breathing heavier, quicker now.

"About them turtles," he says, his voice low and raspy. I cringe, sure he's going to take away whatever he just gave.

"I spoke firm against what you are doing 'cause I saw no good in 'em. When you wanted to go after Larry to save the beach, I said you were foolish, remember?"

I nod. How could I forget?

"The oil spill, all the destruction and stupidity, has made me kin in your fight. May take years, but what's happening is gonna hurt what shrimp are left, our fish, too." He wheezes. His gaze hardens. "And they'll lie about it until it's too late."

"Grandpa, please rest."

"Your brave part's a gift, you hear me?"

I nod, twisting a knob of blanket between my fists.

He shuts his eyes, groans lightly, and lies quiet so long his voice startles me when he speaks again. "Keep tellin' the truth." He fumbles again for my hand. I slide it into his and he squeezes. His eyes open and burrow into mine. "I'm proud of my girl."

He turns his head away and closes his eyes. I lay my forehead on top of our hands and let the tears loose. When I finally lift my head, a smear of Dad and Holt stands at the edge of the curtain.

CHAPTER
TWENTY-ONE

Saturday, May 15

I T'S ALMOST DAWN. The breeze pushes back the
moist heat from the rising sun. Holt and Dad stand in
the wheelhouse of the *Linnie Jean* as we ride miles
out, beyond Ghost Crab Bay into the Gulf. The gulls
floating above our trail join the ride out of habit and hope.

I thought I'd be scared watching Grandpa die, but I
wasn't. Maybe it was what he said, how we ended, that
quieted me inside. All I know is, as he slipped further
away, I traveled closer.

He slept that afternoon after we talked. Holt stayed
with me while Dad went to fetch Grandma. As we sat
around the bed, she and Dad talked about the good times
when he and Uncle Roy were kids, when Grandpa, though
never short of opinions, was happy. Every so often she

leaned close, repeating things, like she wanted him to know we were there and okay. That our memory of him was going to be okay, too. I told them he was proud of me. And that's the Grandpa I'm going to remember. I hope he heard me. Over eighteen hours I listened to his breaths come less often, each one shallower than the one before, until there weren't any left in him.

A Laughing Gull calls above the boat. I watch it glide in the air a dozen yards off the stern. Grandpa was right. Larry and the three commissioners were arrested Monday. Grandma and Dad went to see Holt and Janet the next day, to tell them about my being partly responsible. They already knew from Larry. Dad looked sad when he came home, but he was relieved, too. Yesterday Holt helped him scrub up the *Linnie Jean* for today.

I wish Mom were here. I told her what Grandpa said, about her being a fine woman. She was surprised and said it helped knowing. Dad meant it when he told her she didn't have to be here today. I can't believe how he's changed since Grandpa died. I let him know, too. He said Grandpa's forgiving him made everything else okay. Mom's doing important work and he's making changes so things will be better for all of us. I want details, but he's not telling.

Janet Wilkes and Grandma sit in deck chairs and I've claimed my spot on top of the icebox, legs slung around two corners. A worn picnic hamper sits next to Grandma's flower basket. Last night I harvested almost all the hydrangea blossoms. They were Grandpa's favorite. I bet the red-violet and blue petals reminded him of the eastern sky at sunrise, the greens the color of sargassum grass and water outside our wake. There are even touches of grey and pink—the colors of his beloved shrimp.

Grandma cradles the polished salt-rock urn holding Grandpa's ashes. For the first time in weeks her face looks calm. I expect she's at peace believing Grandpa finally is, too.

The engine slows, dropping the wake to thin, flat ribbons. The men come out of the wheelhouse. Dad helps Grandma to her feet. Holt takes Janet's hand, Dad takes mine, and we make a semi-circle around Grandma at the rail. She looks toward the rising sun, then down at Grandpa.

"We've brought you home, Love." She gently pats the top of the urn and rubs a finger slowly down one side. A quick smile flashes across her lips as she glances first at Holt then the open water and long horizon. "This old sea took care of us a good, long time."

The deep engine rumble under my feet makes me imagine all the days Grandpa set and pulled his nets, facing the good and bad times the bays and Gulf lay in front of him and the *Linnie Jean*.

"Time for you to go hunt your shrimp and swim with Elizabeth's turtles," Grandma says. "We'll do what we can for things up here and try not to miss you too much."

She presses the urn under her chin, whispering last goodbyes. When she nods, Dad twists off the tight lid and wraps his arm around her as she bends close to the water.

A stream of white dust and small bits, like oyster gravel, flows onto the surface. I drop handfuls of hydrangeas over the side of the boat. Flowers and dust fold together at the tip of our wake. Grandma releases the urn when it's empty, to sink to the bottom and slowly dissolve.

Holt cuts the engine and we sit, rocking in the silence. The first full rays of morning sun warm the tightness in my chest. A dozen gulls gather and circle, calling for a meal. Grandma looks at them and smiles.

"You're right," she says. "Time for breakfast."

The *Linnie Jean* grumbles into gear for the slow ride home. Janet unloads the picnic basket onto the tablecloth I've spread over the icebox. Last night I helped Grandma make blueberry streusel muffins and fry up thick bacon. This morning she hard-boiled eggs and wrapped them in towels to keep them warm. She packed real dishes—china plates and her grandmother's, my great, great grandmother's, silver forks and spoons. Last thing out of the basket are the embroidered napkins she'd never found a reason to use. She winks at me when I hand her one with her plate. Janet takes the lid off her fruit salad and Dad opens the thermos of dark, steaming coffee. I take a muffin and a bottle of juice and walk to the edge of the pilothouse, prop against the wall, and watch the rise and dip of dolphins off the port side.

I ice the punch and arrange cookies around a glass tray. Our calm time together on the boat is gone. Any minute people will be lining up in the driveway and coming in the back gate. Grandpa didn't want a service or fuss, but Grandma caved into calls from people wanting to see her and Dad. I'm with Grandpa on this one. From inside the back porch I watch Grandma talk with Dad under the big umbrella. They can be social, if they want. My plan is to hang in the shadows.

The first group strolls into the yard, some carry containers and trays of food or drinks. Grandma hugs them all. They shake Dad's hand, happy to see him. Many are his age. I bet they knew him from school.

Grandma looks toward the porch as Becca and her parents stop inside the gate.

What? She's been back weeks, but no call, text, or e-mail. Why's she showing up today of all days?

Mr. Calderman chats with Grandma and Dad a good minute while a line forms behind him. Becca spots me and waves. Everyone looks toward the house.

"Elizabeth, Becca's here," Dad says.

I don't stop the screen door from banging on my way down the steps.

Becca turns out of the reception line. "I hope it's okay we came," she says.

"I'm surprised you'd want to."

"Not one of my best surprises, I guess."

Mr. Calderman joins Becca. "We're so sorry for your loss."

Mrs. Calderman takes his arm. "How's your grand-mother bearing up?" Their shared look is so serious you'd think someone in their family died, too.

"She's all right." I don't know what else to say.

"Now's not the time to talk about the Landing," Mr. Calderman says, "but I apologize for not listening and for getting between you and Becca."

I nod, not knowing what that last part means.

Becca gives me one of her head flips and rolls down the walkway between the raised beds and the fence.

"Excuse me," I say to her folks and reluctantly tag along behind her. She parks in front of the swing, her back to the house.

I settle onto the pillows in the shade of the canopy.

"I'm not good at apologies." She looks beyond me for a second. "But I owe you a big one. And an explanation, if you're up for it."

"Perhaps you can make it short. I'm supposed to keep an eye on the food table."

Becca touches the control lever on her chair, like she's going to take off, but slides her hand into her lap instead.

I push my sandal toe against the ground to start the swing. "You finally going to tell me why you ditched the hearing?"

Her jaw muscles tense. "Dad asked me not to give the presentation," she says. "He thought my trying to kill the project would make him look bad to his client and the Commission. Especially since we don't live here." She runs her hands along the arms of her chair. The swing slows under me.

I stare at her. "You bailed so he could look good? And since when do the turtles just belong to Texans?"

Her eyes flash. "For your information, my Dad and I ended up in a huge fight that afternoon. He left for the hearing not knowing what I'd do."

"Then why did you cop out?" I kick the ground hard, accidentally sending the swing inches from her knees. She flinches.

"Stop it!"

My feet skid against the ground, wrangling the bulky swing under control.

"When my Dad looked at me from the podium, I knew I couldn't go through with it." She stares at the ground between my feet. "It just happened and then afterwards, well . . . I couldn't stand being around you and not . . ."

She doesn't finish.

"Really?" I shove myself off the swing. "You came to my Grandpa's gathering to tell me you couldn't stand me?" I start toward the house.

"Wait. That's not what I said."

People are watching us. A few whisper to each other.

Slowing down so I won't embarrass Grandma, I turn around and almost fall into Becca's chair. I shove my hands in my skirt pockets.

"Whatever it is, say it. I want to be with my family."

"I want to say I'm really am sorry. For what happened, how I handled it, and about your grandfather."

I can tell she means it, but the whole thing still hurts.

She works up a limp smile. "I've got family, too, you know."

"I know. Your point?"

She narrows her eyebrows. "Should I go?"

I sit on the wide rim of the raised bed. "I guess not. No."

"Three years ago," she says, "I shut down when the doctors told me I'd never walk again. For a year my parents tried everything to get me out of my funk. But I'd decided to give up. You know what happens when I make a decision."

"Unfortunately."

"I was miserable. Kids at school ignored me or got off on calling me ugly names. I lost all my friends. My crappy attitude was so much fun to be around, after all."

I think about the crappy attitude I've perfected about school. Being alone's easy if you work at it hard enough.

"My Mom and Dad took turns hauling me to a rehab clinic every week for nine months. Each trip was four hours driving and five hours rehab and counseling. I had a hundred resentments against the accident, the therapists, kids at school, and my parents trying to help." She stops and swallows, her eyes liquid. "The moods they put up with. The times I dumped on them when I couldn't deal." She sweeps the trail of tears from her cheeks. "If it weren't for my folks, I'd be curled up in my closet, sucking my thumb. Everything I've accomplished since the accident depended on their constant support. If it seems like a lame excuse to you, I'm sorry, but I couldn't—no didn't—want to disappoint my Dad."

Two months ago, my Dad asked me to be patient with Grandpa, to cut him slack when I was spitting mad at him. Even though I hated doing it, Dad needed me to.

"Okay, I get that, but why shut me out?"

"When I left the hearing, I'd failed—the Center, you, mostly the promise to myself I made in rehab to be the best. I wanted to explain things the day we met Berto and Shawna, but I didn't know what to say. You're so all about the turtles and the Center. It was a blast being part of that, belonging to something so important. Quitting, being sidelined, threw me back to feeling like I did after the accident. I asked my Mom to take me home to the clinic to sort things out. It wasn't quick. I'm so sorry I hurt you."

I stare at the ground between my feet, silently sorting and sifting. In some ways, it feels like I never knew her at all. In others like she never left, but we need to start over.

"We could have done other things together," I say. She looks puzzled, like the idea never crossed her mind. "I'm not all about turtles. I'd love to hear about New York, your friends. Learn samba. My wardrobe stinks, right? We could have window-shopped at the mall in case my photos sell and I can afford to upgrade my style."

Becca laughs. "Nah, I like your style. Not that I'd ever turn down a shopping trip." She fingers the petals of the red and yellow striped dahlia beside her. "My parents and I have been watching the news about the oil spill. I told

Dad I'm going back to work with the turtles—if it's okay with you."

"You don't need my permission."

Her face goes all sparkler bright, like the day I told her about Sunny. "Good, because Berto and I hatched the most brilliant plan."

"You've been seeing Berto?"

Doubt flashes across her face. Maybe she's sorry for bringing him up. "He texted and called while I was gone, made me laugh when I didn't want to. We'd talk about the spill, too, about how all the information on the web about the damage was huge and mostly geared to adults."

"You're surprised?"

"No, frustrated. So, we're designing a website—by kids, for kids. Berto's structuring the site and I've been up all hours finding graphics and data links."

I knew she was up to something the morning Dad, Grandpa, and I rode past on the *Linnie Jean* and I saw her light on.

"We'll post info on the spill to get the site started. Have a place for kids directly affected to blog what's going on with them, their families, and communities. That way, they can take it over. Make it local. We're looking into support networks. My rehab counselor lined up a group of therapists along the Gulf to post general advice based on what kids blog."

"That is so perfect. My mom is there. She could send you photos or maybe you could interview her."

Becca beams. "Great idea! We're linking to sea turtle conservation and rescue programs all over the world. Even kids who don't live near an ocean can post what they're doing to help turtles. Or send support to kids and families in trouble at the Gulf."

"So much for the sidelines," I say. "I'm glad you and Berto are having a good time." I can't help feel a tiny bit jealous.

"Yeah, he's fun." She smiles and twists her hair up off her neck. "And a great kisser."

"Uh, good. That's nice." Becca shows off her figure, and even though it was clear at the bocce game they liked each other, I never figured her with a boyfriend. What an idiot.

I glance down the path at Holt, Price and Dad talking together next to the food table.

"Berto's special," she says. "Going home will be really hard."

Price looks my way for a second, then back at Dad.

"Uh, huh. I mean, yeah, on all of us."

She traces my stare. "Cute guy talking up your dad," she says, looking back at me. "You know him? Of course you do. Come on, tell. What's up?"

I pull my attention back. "He and his dad helped out when Grandpa had his heart attack." I'm not telling her about the fainting, head-in-his-lap episode. Price never mentioned it. He's friendly at school. Okay, friendly is an overstatement. He smiles and says, "Hi." Why would a junior want to say more than that to a lowly freshman with no observable high school social skills?

Becca taps my hand. "But you're going to do something about him, right?"

"I don't know. Haven't thought about it." That is a lie. Every time I see him, a mini whirlwind kicks up in the center of my stomach.

"He's here, you're here. Looks like a don't-blow-this opportunity to me."

Price turns from Dad again and catches me watching him. The storm spins. I smile and look away. "Don't push."

"Okay." She laughs, then looks serious again. "I want to tell you something."

"What?"

"You changed me."

"I did?"

"You reminded me true friends stick together and call each other on their crap." She puts her hand out. "I really am sorry." Her eyes shimmer. "I missed you."

She's done it. I didn't want to tear up, but it's too late.

"I guess that means we're okay?" she says. "Please say yes."

"Yeah." I wipe my eyes before they leak. "But only if you make a solemn promise."

"What?"

"If you want to ditch me again, tell me first so I can hide your battery."

She laughs and reaches out for a hug. "I promise, now come on, that cute guy and your dad are eating all the cookies."

Dad, Grandma, and I hang up the phone. Mom called and we told her all about the gathering today. She said it sounded wonderful, and was happy so many people came. I'm sure I heard her blow her nose twice while Dad was talking. It never occurred to me that tonight she might be suffering more than us. She's alone. It felt awful when we finally said goodbye.

I push the last of great-great Grandma's napkins into the soak bucket and rinse the sudsy water off my hands. The yard is quiet and in full shade. Price asked if I wanted to get ice cream later—only because Becca kept talking me up, I think. I swear she could make a snail give up its shell. Dad said it's okay, and didn't even set a curfew. Grandma called it my first date. If I call it a date I'll be too scared to go.

I walk through the living room. The house seems empty without Grandpa's grump hovering around his chair. Never imagined I'd miss that part of him. Feels like Roy's hanging around here, too, relieved he and Dad are forgiven.

Grandma hangs her apron on the hook beside the back door and hugs Dad, then me.

"Thank you, children," she says. "It's been a beautiful day. I'm only sorry James wasn't here. We should have thrown a party years ago."

Dad smiles, sadly. "I expect he wasn't ready until now.

CHAPTER TWENTY-TWO

I CHECK MY SHIRT buttons to make sure I didn't miss any, then watch the end of Cooper Street for Price. We resettled in the rental house after Grandpa died. I wish he were picking me up at Grandma's, but she shooed us out after supper, claiming she wanted to be alone. I'm waiting outside so there's less chance Dad will invite Price in to chat. I don't do chat, or "small talk," as Grandma calls it. It feels dumb not talking about real things, but maybe Price likes to keep conversation simple.

The low sun flashes off chrome. I hop off the front steps and get to the gate before Price stops at the curb. A move I regret. Looking over-anxious is bad, looking desperate is worse.

"Hi," he says, as I open the passenger side door. "Sweet tooth getting to you?"

I blush and climb in. "Didn't want to keep you waiting."

"Can we swing out to the dock after we get ice cream?" he says. "I left our player in the boat and if I don't add my music, Dad will have us fishing to classic country all weekend."

"No problem." I look around the cab. Clean for a guy. Dusty, but no junk. "Nice rig."

He laughs and glances at me, like he's not sure if I'm playing with him.

"Truck." I smile back, in chat trouble and we're only to the corner.

"You've only been here since the first of the year." Price says.

Was that a question? "We came to help keep Grandpa out of trouble," I say. "I guess that didn't work out so well." I pick gently at the armrest.

"You worked hard getting him out of trouble that day on the Gulf. You'd really never been shrimpin' before?"

"Nope."

He grins. "Pretty rough start to your career."

A joke. One muscle in my neck lets loose.

"Is there a smooth way to start?" I say. "Thanks, again, for helping us out at the dock. That culling stuff just about killed me. Grandpa was so fast. Not that I think I could ever be, or want to be that fast or a shrimper, Lord knows. I'm done with shrimping, period. Don't get me wrong, I understand wanting to be out on the water. I love nature so that part was cool. But the work, the smell, and I really, really can't get past the by-catch issue. I mean do you like—" I shut up, sure he's going to dump me at the next light.

"Do I like what?" His expression doesn't make fun. He looks more curious about what might come out next.

"Do you like shrimping with your dad?" I say. "Will you work with him after you graduate?"

"Not hardly. I want to study marine biology at Texas A&M."

"Wow." A tune starts up. I look around the cab for the sound, then realize it's the new ringtone I put on my phone yesterday.

"Hi, Bec—"

"Did you see tonight's news?" Her voice is shaking.

"No. What's the matter?"

"They're dragging booms into circles of oil and sargassum grass, then setting them on fire."

"Shouldn't that keep more oil from coming on shore?"

"No!" I jerk the phone away as her voice thunders through the earpiece. "I mean, yes, but they're burning and boiling the turtles and a lot of other animals trapped inside. The rescue boats aren't allowed near enough to collect them before they get torched."

"I'll call Maria and see what's going on." I sound calm but that's because I'm with Price, otherwise I'd be screaming.

"What's up?" Price says when I hang up.

"Hold on a sec."

I tell Maria what Becca said.

"Environmental groups with legal departments are filing injunctions to stop the burning," she says, "and let scientists monitor the wildlife. We just wait and watch."

I grit my teeth and look out the side window so Price won't see my face. Doesn't matter because he can hear me. "This whole thing totally sucks."

"I know," Maria says, "but there aren't clear options for protecting the turtles."

Price turns into the parking lot of the ice cream shop. He shuts off the engine but doesn't move to get out.

"What's going on?" he says.

I explain what Becca told me. "Maria said there's nothing we can do."

"Far as I can tell, the people in charge are short on ideas."

"You're following what's happened?"

"I'd better if I want to be one of those Gulf scientists someday."

"That's so cool." We just blew way past small talk.

Price convinces me a triple scoop will help ease the pain about the turtles. It doesn't, but it tastes good, and him wanting to go into marine science is just too amazing.

We park behind the fish house and head down the dock. I stop in front of the *Linnie Jean* and say a silent hello and good night to Grandpa. I wonder how we'd talk about what's happening with the spill. Likely he'd say the same thing as Maria, only he'd be okay with me being upset.

The sun's gone down behind the horizon but there's still plenty of light to see. The Lungren's boat is at the very end of the dock next to the *Heart's Desire*. I suck the melted remains of mocha fudge out the tip of the cone and walk the line of abandoned buildings while Price rummages around the cabin.

One building looks as big as our school's gymnasium. Painted letters—SAMSON REDFISH HATCHERY— like on Price's hat—flake off the sign next to the front door. I wander over and peek through a dusty window. The large room is filled with eight-foot-round tanks, like the largest ones at the Center. The place looks like workers walked away one day and the last guy out nailed plywood over the door.

"What are you doing?"

I jump. Price stands behind me.

"Becca's not the only one with brilliant ideas. What do you know about this place?"

"My uncle worked here until it closed eight years ago, why?"

"Maria said the breeding-age, female turtles are the most important ones to protect, but the Center is too small to keep them. If this place were fixed up, the turtles could stay here until we're sure the Gulf is safe."

Price walks behind me around the building. I count fifteen tanks and three long cement pools outside under what used to be a lean-to. My gears are smoking. "Needs work, but worth trying, don't you think?" I hear pleading in my voice.

He smiles. "I think you're brilliant."

We talk, mostly I do, about the hatchery idea on the ride home. I barely remember to ask about his life, about growing up here, and his family. I'm jealous he has an older sister and younger brother. He asks about Mom's job, which he thinks is amazing. I tell him it's a mixed bag.

He shuts off the engine in front of the house and turns sideways, his arm sliding across the back of the seat. Every muscle in my body tenses. I've talked a geyser all the way home, now I got nothing left to spout.

"I'm glad we went out," he says.

"Me, too."

"I hope you get somewhere with the hatchery idea."

"Me, too." I rub a palm on my pants leg, worried we're sliding into the dreaded chat zone we've avoided all night.

"You're something else, you know that?" he says.

"I am? Good or bad? I'm sorry I talked your ear off."

"No, I liked it. Besides, I have two of them."

I laugh and hiccup at the same time. Great.

"How about we work on the other ear soon?" he says.

Another hiccup. "Sure." I hold my breath. To stop the hiccups, but mainly because his fingers are stroking the hair on the back of my head. I breathe out and look at him. Pounding heart, no hiccups.

He smiles and gently pulls the lobe of my ear. "Then I'll get to work on yours." He reaches across me and presses the door handle down. "I'll call you tomorrow."

"Oh," I say, sliding off the seat. Wasn't he supposed to try to kiss me? "Night," I say, shutting the door like it's no big deal.

"Later," he says, through the open window. The engine kicks over. I turn and walk to the porch. He waits until I'm inside before pulling away.

Dad looks up from his book. "You're home early. Did you have fun?"

"Yeah, he's really nice."

"I enjoyed talking to him this afternoon."

"That's good," I say. "Well, I'm going to bed."

"You okay, sweetheart?"

"I'm fine. See you tomorrow."

I lie on my bed, staring at the ceiling, my whole body alive. Jittery. I close my eyes and see Price's smile, feel the touch of his fingers against my ear. I flip over and bury my face in the pillow, suck in the pale scent of laundry soap, and toss between wanting the feeling to go on forever and wanting it to go away because it's driving me crazy. I come out for air, roll on my side, and stare at the rectangle of night behind the window.

The boys back home always seemed dumb. Immature. They weren't interested in me anyway. Brad kissed me last year behind the music room after a dance—the only time I've been kissed. I think he was experimenting, prepping for Teresa, maybe. I let him. He didn't make me feel this way. He never tried again.

I replay every scene from tonight. Talking—okay. Outfit—no comment. My whole turtle obsession—way okay. His eyes lit up when he talked about using his shrimping experience to do something more with his life. Something for the Gulf, including the turtles. Then he brought me home. Okay? Five, ten times I run the scene.

Stop it. Who says you have to kiss on the first date?

It would have been nice. Just a kiss.

Then it would be over. Would that feel better?

Yeah. No. I don't know. But what if he doesn't call? Maybe he was just saying he will. He got me out of the truck pretty fast. He can't be that interested.

The movie in my head starts again. I feel his touch.

He's interested; he'll be back.

I squeeze my eyes shut. A ripple, like a giant smile, runs across my chest, up my arms, down and out through my toes.

Monday, May 17

"Maria." She jumps as I fly into her office after school. "Problem solved."

"What problem now?" She leans back in her chair, sounding tired and irritable.

"The female turtles are critical to protect, right, so why can't we keep them in the Samson hatchery until things are safer?"

"That place looked pretty run-down last time I saw it," she says, dropping a file into her briefcase.

"No, really, it's not that bad. Price and I checked it out Saturday night. If we put dividers in the tanks we could keep thirty turtles. That's a lot of potential babies over a lifetime."

Maria squeezes the tops of her shoulders. She's only been back from Louisiana three days. Her in-basket pile is dangerously close to overflowing.

"Bringing a facility like that online would take lots of money and energy we don't have right now," she says, "not with nesting season coming into full swing."

"But you said the government's getting a whole bunch of money to spend on turtles and birds at other wildlife centers. Why not here?"

"First priority goes to facilities dealing directly with oiled wildlife, which aren't near Port Winston. Besides, there is a big gap between an idea and execution."

"Okay." I walk out before she can give me another version of no.

In the atrium, I watch the fish swimming in the display tanks and call Becca. Those fish don't know how lucky they are. It may not be the Gulf, but they've got clean water and guaranteed free meals.

"Hey, E., what's up? How's Price?"

"He's fine, but I could use some good news?"

"Nothing here. I'm reading interviews about what's happening where the oil's hit. A lot more people are getting sick from the dispersant spraying. Something happen with you?"

"I tried to get Maria interested in a great idea to save the Kemp's females, but she turned it down."

"What idea?"

I explain it again, excitement dulling my anger of a minute ago.

"That is a terrific plan," she says.

"High praise, coming from you."

"Go to the top and talk to Barbara."

"I don't like talking to Barbara behind Maria's back."

"Whatever, but we don't give up, remember?"

"I'll think about it," I say.

Maria and I end up going together to see Barbara.

"I like the concept," she says. "But Maria is right. We're not equipped to take on a project of that size. It's doubtful we could get permission from wildlife officials anyway. I'm sorry."

"The answer is still no." I stare at my bedroom ceiling, talking to Becca, but half thinking about Price calling yesterday to ask me out again. The crickets' love songs click in the backyard.

"I've thought about your idea all day," Becca says, "and came up with a contingency plan."

"It better include money, time, and staff."

"Some time and staff, but I'm not sure about the money part."

"Let's hear it.

"Dad was mad enough to melt pavement when he found out about Larry's bribery scheme. And mad at himself for not seeing who Larry was in the first place. Add the oil spill and he and Mom are suddenly super sympathetic to the turtles. I told them sympathy didn't turn me around after the accident. It won't do the turtles any good, either. I laid out your plan and why it got shot down. I pointed out Mom has the legal skills and Dad writes PR proposals so they should volunteer to help put this thing together. They said, yes."

"I can't believe you, that's amazing!"

"You came up with the idea. Besides what are a friend's parents for?" We both laugh. The Calderman crane just lifted a boulder off my chest.

"We have to get busy," she says. "A visit to Samson's better happen tomorrow because we leave for home in a week."

"What? You can't." We just got back together, and for the first time we're working as a real team.

"I've been talking up staying longer. Berto and I have a lot to do."

"Well, work your magic and pick me up after school."

"I'm on it."

Wednesday, May 19

Becca and I sit in Barbara's office with Maria and the Caldermans. We spent half an hour at the hatchery and everyone agrees the place would work great—under the right conditions. "You're making a generous offer," Barbara says, "but putting the money and pieces together could take months, and even then we'll fail if I can't get permission from the owner to use the place and from the feds to collect and keep the turtles. It seems more overwhelming than practical."

"Since when has saving the Kemp's ever been quick or easy?" I say.

"Can't you get permission to keep the turtles you already have," Becca says, "and any new ones that need treatment? Other groups can ship their turtles here once the hatchery gets fixed up."

"Shipping turtles is, at the least, expensive," Maria says.

"Make it part of the financial package," Becca says. "Look, either the government puts the money out or risks losing generations of Kemp's ridleys. A bunch of loggerhead eggs got shipped to Florida for hatching and release away from the spill, even though the scientists don't know if the youngsters will adjust outside their natural habitat. We're offering 100% adult survival, which means generations of egg production. This is such a no-brainer."

"I'm sure it seems that way," Barbara says. She looks at Becca's parents. "You've both got jobs to think about."

"The significance of the oil spill's impacts," Mrs. Calderman says, "convinced my law firm to let me donate hours investigating the legal aspects of the proposal."

"I'll work with you on a presentation plan for the proposal before I head back to New York." Mr. Calderman winks at Becca and me.

Becca hugs her dad's arm. "That means Mom and I can stay longer?"

"We're working out details, but you've bought some time."

"Yay!" Becca and I yell at the same time.

The Caldermans and Barbara stay in her office to talk. Becca leads the way to the atrium.

"Come on," she says, rolling toward the doors to the patio. "We've got some bocce and boy work to catch up on."

CHAPTER
TWENTY-THREE

DAD PICKS ME UP at the Center and we make a quick stop at the super pharmacy for aspirin and sodas. I slide onto the truck seat and drop the bag on the floor. Dad looks at me like I'm an apparition, the cell phone death gripped at his ear.

"Amy, I want you out of there," he says.

"Speakerphone," I whisper.

"The oil broke past the booms guarding the mainland this morning." Mom's voice pops from the phone as he lays it on the dash between us. "It's spread everywhere. You can't get away from the fumes. The breakfast diner by my hotel was full of customers complaining of the same symptoms as the cleanup crews and the people in Venice."

Dad drums the edge of the steering wheel with his fingers.

"Mom? Are you coming home?"

"Hi, Honey. No. This story is breaking wide-open. I can't afford to leave now."

Dad raises his hands toward the ceiling in frustration. "The oil and dispersant fumes are toxic, Amy, you know that."

"What if you get sick?" I stare at the phone, willing her to see reason. My Mom-on-the- battle-line pride is drowning in fear.

"I'll be fine," she says. "Gotta go. I'm late for an interview with a seafood restaurant owner. His business is crashing because he can't get fish."

Dad grabs the phone. "Amy, listen to me, please—"

"I know, Steven, but these people are suffering and their stories have to get out. Try not to worry. Love you guys."

He switches off the phone and starts the truck, eyes flashing. She can be stubborn when she's on a mission. I watch the buildings drop past us as we head for home.

A block from the house, I see a two-toned SUV spilling over the edges of our driveway. Grey on top, black on the bottom, the thing looks like a flat-topped rain cloud.

"Who's that?" I say.

Dad parks at the curb. "I'm not sure," he says, shutting off the truck.

We walk up the drive, but no one gets out. I look through the tinted windows at the pristine, empty inside. The gate into the backyard is partway open.

"Stay put." Dad brushes past me into the yard. "What the devil are you doing here?" he says from beyond the fence.

I peek around the gate. Larry Wilkes, out of jail "on ~~his own recognizance,~~" turns from surveying the dull green lawn. I cross behind Dad and take cover behind the Adirondack chair.

Wilkes sits down ten feet from me on the end of the picnic table, resting one deep blue, snakeskin cowboy boot on the bench. I hold onto the top of the chair to stop my hands from shaking. So much for thinking he couldn't scare me.

"I'm here to pay my respects over losing Papa James." He glances back at me. "Given the circumstances, I didn't want to upset Mama Linnie by showing up at the gathering."

It grinds at me, hearing him talk about Grandpa and Grandma like they're his own parents.

"Not after all they did for me as a kid," he says to Dad. "Our families once looked out for each other."

"What's that got to do with now?" Dad says.

"More than you've thought through, I imagine, since Elizabeth got me arrested over a misunderstanding."

"Pardon?" I say, my fingers tightening on the chair.

"Avery and the others approached me for campaign funds in exchange for guaranteed approval on Tortuga Sands."

"That is *so* not what's on the video."

"There's a much bigger picture here than your movie." He shifts his weight on the table and adds the other boot to the bench. "You weren't here to see the tough times, Steven. Folks losing shrimping as a way of life, desperate for jobs." Wilkes's face shifts from cloudy to alive. "Tortuga Sands is a huge shot of daylight for this county. People can get back to work, pay the bills, even get ahead and give their children a future. Elizabeth takes the stand, talking about stuff she doesn't understand, everybody loses."

Dad sits down on the other end of the picnic table. "You're driving this truck of yours where exactly?"

Wilkes sweeps a hand around the yard and at the house. "Managing landscaping crews twelve hours a day is getting you nowhere. That's sad. I'd like to see you comfortable, living in a real house. Send that smart girl of yours to a good college someday. Even give your wife a chance to quit working."

"You know nothing about Amy," Dad says.

"Between the Internet and a high school girl's gossip, I've learned enough." He looks at me. "Your Mom's in Louisiana reporting on the oil spill, right?"

"What she's doing is none of your business," I say, wondering why Dad doesn't tell him to get lost.

"No need to get hostile. All I'm saying is she could be on the safe side of things. Work locally instead." He switches back to Dad. "I know the owners of all the big newspapers in this state. Lots of people owe me favors one way or another."

"Get down to it, Larry. What are you offering?"

"Dad!"

He stands, holding up a hand to shush me.

"Dad, come on." His expression locks me out.

"My lawyers will deal with the unfortunate video," Wilkes says. "If Elizabeth agrees not to testify, you'll run a brand new project I'm putting together for the north side of Deer Creek."

I storm around the chair, wishing Grandpa were in it. He'd give Larry a big hunk of what-for. I move close to Dad, searching for signs he hasn't gone completely stupid.

Wilkes stands, a gentle shake dropping the pant leg over his boot. "We were like brothers once."

Dad looks at the ground.

Larry steps toward him, hand out. "Roy'd want us to share the dream he missed. You don't have to live small."

Dad looks up and drops an arm around my waist. "I already don't. Now get out."

Wilkes lowers his hand. "I knew you were a coward the day you slunk out of town. Don't add un-wise."

"He's not the coward," I say.

"Let's see, after I spell it out," Wilkes says. "Tortuga Sands was always big business, but the bad economy was an unexpected bonus—made people around here extra needy. It took years, but I earned my name, pooled together influential people, and built up little ones. Now that the time is right, they'll cash in their chips to make this thing go." He runs his hand along the edge of the table, watching Dad. "This project dies, when people hear the Barker name they'll think lost jobs and lost opportunities. What's your kid's testimony going to mean when you can't find work?"

"Are you threatening me?" Dad says.

"Quite the opposite. I'm holding out the chance for you to finally stare reality in the face and be somebody. The end of the day, my lawyers negotiate a slap on the wrist. The fine will be ugly, but I'll be back in business before anyone blinks. Where will you be?"

Wilkes takes a few steps toward the gate and stops. "There's something else you should consider."

"I believe I told you to leave." Dad says.

"Not yet. You may have poisoned my parents against me, but they're my dependents. You think shrimp paid for their new house and Dad's nice boat, the one that helped rescue Papa James? They'd be living like you if it weren't for what I've done with this town. You willing to risk killing them with a trial?"

"I'm not worried about your folks—we're square," Dad says. "As far as finding work, I've built my reputation with a different crowd."

"Then, if not yourself, realize the trouble Elizabeth's going to face."

"Threatening me now?" I say, feeling Dad's hand tighten on me as I start to move.

"Julia says you've had trouble fitting in at school. Testifying won't make it easier. Not with so many kids' parents tied to the future of this project. Then, I'm not surprised your father raised an outcast."

I squirm loose from Dad's grip. "At least he didn't raise a daughter who lets her boyfriend knock her around."

Wilkes takes a quick step back, eyes dark. "You're a vicious liar."

I step toward him. "Want pictures?" A bluff I'm guessing he won't call. I give him my best Grandpa stare. "Or is Pete swimmin' in that special pool you were braggin' about?"

Wilkes doesn't look back or bother slamming the gate behind him.

"Good riddance!" I yell as the engine roars and gravel skids under the tires.

Dad wraps me in a hug.

"I was scared for a minute you were gonna throw me over," I say.

"Not a chance."

"We've got to call the DA."

"Really?"

"I'm pretty sure we just witnessed 'witness tampering.'"

Dad laughs out loud.

Monday, May 21

Ten classrooms pile out of seventh period onto the quad. Shawna and I head toward the library for the photography club meeting. I'd rather go home or to Grandma's. Mom called this morning before Dad and I left the house. She's really sick. Huge headache, throat and eyes burning, and weird skin sores after being out on an oiled beach a few days ago. She barely has enough strength to get out of bed, but the diner waitress is putting her on a plane home tonight. All I've done today is worry.

My phone hums with a text message. It's from Maria. *Sunny's hatch is starting.*

"Yipe!"

"What?" Shawna stops when I lean against the corner of the building to call Maria back.

"Sunny's eggs—" The phone rings in my hand. "It's Becca."

"See you inside," Shawna says and retreats into the library.

"Did Maria call you?" Becca says.

"She just texted me."

"Aren't you excited to see the babies?"

"Yeah, but not about putting them in the Gulf."

"Don't think about that."

"I'll try. I've got a meeting. Call you later?"

"Wait, Can you and Price come over for dinner tonight? The parents are going out and I want to see you two in action. Leftover lasagna and salad. You don't care what we eat, do you?"

"Your mom's food? You kidding? I'll have to ask Price, though." I'm nervous about Becca getting to know him better. There won't be a bunch of people around, like at the gathering. Maybe she won't like him because he isn't out there or funny like Berto. What if he doesn't like her 'cause she tends to take over?

"Seven o'clock," she says.

"Okay, I'll let you know."

I hang up and reach for the library door. Julia's image shimmers in the glass, not ten feet behind me. I duck inside. The news is full of her dad and the Commission corruption. Now she's the trash-talk target at school.

"Hang on to that guy," Becca whispers when I hug her goodbye at the condo door.

I grin. "I'm glad you like him. We had a great time."

Price pushes the elevator's down button. "Where should we go now?" We watch our reflections in the mirrored walls as we ride twelve floors to the parking garage.

I check my phone. "It's nine-thirty. Dad's picking Mom up at the airport at ten-thirty, and you need to get me home by ten forty-five. Plenty of time."

"For what?"

"To check on Sunny's hatch. It'll take fifteen minutes, tops."

"Lead the way."

We head down Forster toward the Center. I hook my finger through the loop on the clutch purse Becca gave me. Feels odd not having my camera, but this thing's only big enough for my phone and the tube of barely-pink lip gloss.

"Now that you've got a guy," Becca said, as we stood in front of her bathroom mirror trying out colors, "spiff it up a little." I took the lip gloss not knowing whether to be insulted or grateful.

"How many nests from the Landing so far?" Price says.

"Seven, including Sunny's."

We pull into the Center's back lot and park.

"Good, Tom's here," I say, noticing his truck and the light on in the back room. We try the door into the rehab area to let him know we're checking out the hatch. It's locked.

"Well," I say, "volunteers check her nest every hour, so we'll probably see him before we leave."

"It's kind of dark to see much."

The quarter moon cuts a sliver of white into the clear night sky. "We'll be fine." I don't need much light to feel close to Sunny's babies one last time. Before they belong to everyone on release day.

We cross the dimly-lit front patio and walk the darkened boardwalk to the beach. The night is warm and quiet except for the rhythmic slapping of waves on the damp sand.

Price's arm bumps me. I move aside. My breath catches as his fingers slide between mine, closing our palms together. That jittery feeling slid in, too. I move my fingers a little. He doesn't let go. Our steps match, wrists and arms riding against each other.

"Great lasagna, wasn't it?" he says.

I don't answer and his grip tightens. I stop, making him turn to face me.

"What?" he says.

I close the gap between us, my heart pinging against my chest. "I want to find out something."

"And that would be?" he says, eyes gentle, mouth turning up in a smile.

I pull myself into him, eyes closed, and miss, catching his top lip between mine.

Let me die where I stand.

His grin against my mouth fixes the kiss. Soft, then firm. My insides slurry. Arms around me, the breath from his nose quickens against my cheek. I draw back, only for a second. Then eyes open and tight in his arms, I meet his lips again. On target this time.

"You smell terrific," he whispers, kissing my ear. "Not at all like turtles."

I push him away.

"Just kidding." He smiles and rests my face in his hands, running his thumbs lightly over my cheekbones. "You know I love turtles." We kiss again and longer. When I come up to breathe, he pivots out of my arms and stands next to me. I try to hug him, but he stops me.

"What's the matter?" I search his face for hints. I'm a rotten kisser.

The waves beyond us roll against the dark shore. He faces me, hands on my shoulders, keeping us an arm's length apart.

"I've never met anyone like you," he says, eyes diving deep into mine, like he's looking for home base. "This may sound stupid or way too early, but I want us to take our time." I shiver and he pulls me close again. "I want us to have lots and lots of time together."

My head swims. "Okay." I pull back to look at his wonderful face. "One more?"

He kisses me hard and short, then pushes us apart, his sigh more a soft groan.

"Before my resolve gives out," he says, "we better get back to . . . what was it?"

"Sunny's nest," I manage to croak. Right now turtles are a million light-years from my mind.

"Come on, so we don't blow your schedule."

I settle in the wrap of his arm, searching the dark for the corral ahead. A boxy form emerges fifty yards down the beach and stops. Truck headlights flick on, lighting up the corral.

"Must be the volunteer," Price says.

"No." My heart is double-thudding and not the good, rushing feeling of a minute ago. I recognize the walk, the rounded shoulders, and blond hair as he passes into the light. "It's Pete."

"What's he up to?" Price says.

Pete leans a pole against the fence. His hands reach for the gate lock. I squint. Not hands, bolt cutters. The gate slams back. Pete slings the tool aside, and steps inside the corral.

I pull Price into a run. "Get out of there!"

Pete turns, hesitates, then walks to the back of the enclosure. A bag drops beside him. The high beams glint off the rising, then falling blade of a shovel. It stabs the sand and lifts.

"The nests!" I yank my hand from Price and sprint ahead. Sand and eggs drop toward the bag.

"Elizabeth, stop!" Price yells close behind me.

I fly through the open gate. Pete whips the shovel through the air, coming at me. I stop six feet from the tip. Price grabs me from behind, arm locked across my chest, and pulls me back toward the gate.

"Yeah, stop, Elizabeth." Eyes wild, Pete waves the shovel toward an open gunnysack on the ground. "Or your head'll be in there, too." My stomach twists. The severed heads of three adult Kemp's ridleys lay inside under a dusting of sand and broken eggs.

"Why?" I screech.

"You blew up everything."

"What?"

"My future, idiot! The one I ain't got, thanks to you and your damn turtles. But they're fish food now."

I wrench myself free of Price.

Pete raises the shovel and steps toward me. "Back off."

Price swings in front, hands out. "Put the shovel down."

"Stay out of this, shrimper boy."

"I said, put it down." Price moves, tracking the augering motion of the shovel. Pete swivels, his back to the nests, his attention glued on Price. I scan the row. Sunny's nest is untouched in the corner. Ten feet from it, where Pete stood a minute ago, whole and broken eggs lay jumbled around a ragged hole in the sand.

"Get out." Pete hisses, still twisting the shovel back and forth at Price.

"Put it down," Price says, "before you do something even more stupid."

"Who's stupid?" Pete lunges forward, sweeping the shovel low. Price jumps. Pete's knees buckle. He jams the shovel point down, stopping his fall, then whirls up from a half crouch, slamming the shovel handle across Price's stomach, doubling him over onto the sand. The shovel lays trapped underneath. Pete drops onto Price's back, swinging blows into his head and shoulders.

I plow my body into him. "Stop it!" I scream, tearing at his face with my fingers. His elbow jab to my ribs throws me backwards. I grapple to my feet, desperate for a weapon. The sack. I grab the ends together. Praying to the ocean mother, I bring it smashing down on Pete's head. He falls forward, then rears back, fist raised, eyes blazing. I swing the sack over my head and slam it broadside into his face. Something cracks. Head shaking wildly, he shoves himself off Price and rips the sack from my hands. A solid ridge of knuckles connects with my left temple. Pain shoots behind my eyes. The light from the truck disappears.

CHAPTER
TWENTY-FOUR

VOICES. SOMETHING BULKY PRESSES around my neck. The top of my head's splitting, like my brain wants out. Now.

"Elizabeth, can you hear me?"

Who's that? Lights. Red, blue, red, blue, red—

"Elizabeth, if you hear me, open your eyes."

No. Dark is better. Light blinds. Never see again.

"Honey." The next voice is weak and raspy.

Mom? I mouth.

"Yes, Baby. And Daddy, too. Come join us."

I force my lids open a slit and look around. I see Mom's mouth, Dad's worried forehead, and pairs of legs in white pants.

"Hey, champ," Dad says, low and soothing.

I smile, but it hurts. "Sunny's eggs . . . " I whisper.

"Don't talk," Dad says. "Tom's here and Maria's on her way. The first hatchlings peeked their heads out a few minutes ago. Must be all the excitement."

"Want to see." I say, reaching out. My head throbs like a car speaker, throwing high notes full volume.

"Folks." The white pants set a stretcher on the sand beside me. "One of you can ride along, but Elizabeth needs to get to the hospital." Arms in white sleeves cradle my shoulders and legs, slide me onto the stretcher, and lift me into the air. Dad walks on one side, Mom on the other. The flashy light thing is an ambulance.

"Price?" Images flood in. The shovel slamming into his stomach. Pete beating him.

"He's gone to the hospital." Dad says. "Nasty cut on the back of his head and badly bruised, but he seems okay."

The thing on my neck won't let me move my head. I strain my eyes sideways to look at Mom. Her face is pale. Red blotches cover parts of her cheeks and forehead.

"Look rotten," I croak, my throat dry. *So thirsty.*

She smiles, weakly. "We're a pair."

The EMTs lift me through the ambulance door.

"Wait," I say. "Pete?"

"Price decked him going out the gate," Dad says, "then called 911. Lucky I'm on speed dial in your phone. He caught us leaving the airport."

I'm slipping. "Daddy?"

"Yes, sweetheart."

"I'm so sleepy."

"Elizabeth," a voice says close to my ear. "You can't sleep."

"I'll go with her." Maria's words drift in from nearby.

"Only family," someone says.

Mom climbs in beside me. Straps tighten.

"Talk turtles," Maria says from the door.

As we roll down the sand, then up onto pavement, Mom asks questions about how long it will take for all the turtles to hatch and where they'll go from here. I manage bits and pieces. Every time my eyelids start to close, she calls my name.

And the siren screams.

Mom lies in the hospital bed across from me. The emergency room doctor took one look and admitted her for tests and observation. They haven't got a room ready for her yet.

I have a concussion. Doctor's orders: I can go home, school's okay in a week, but no P.E. or rapid movement for at least a month. I can go to the hatchling release, but only because I wouldn't let him tell me no.

He said it's safe for me to close my eyes now, so I do. It feels great. A tiny snore slides up the back of my throat. I hear a voice.

"Hi again," the voice says.

Go away. I open my eyes enough to see a uniform at the foot of the bed.

"Remember me?"

I squint against the glare of the florescent lights. Officer Kirkland. The one I lied to about the photos.

"Yeah," I say, trying not to groan.

"I need to know what happened, if you're up to talking?"

Dad helps me scoot up on the pillows. I grit my teeth against the pain thundering through my head. "I owe you some pictures."

Wednesday, May 26

The parking lot at the Landing is filling with cars when Price and I roll in behind the Calderman's van. It's five fifty-six a.m. The sun is rising, dissolving the deepest dune shadows. A crowd of fifty waits in a semi-circle behind yellow caution tape on stakes set twenty-feet back from the breakers. A patch of clouds hangs mid-sky and a light breeze flutters colored ribbons on poles held by volunteers. A few hungry gulls dart above the flags.

Edging out of the truck, my head pays me back for not staying home. I'm sad Mom and Dad aren't here, but no way. She's home in bed and he's taking care of her. The doctors don't have a sure diagnosis—probably chemical poisoning from the oil and dispersants, but not all the tests results are back. In my backpack is her good camera and wide-angle lens. She's already planning her next article. On the turtles, and kids, and conservation.

Becca lowers her chair lift to the pavement. Berto obviously is not the early riser she'd hoped, since he's nowhere in sight. Her mom closes the door to the passenger seat and walks toward Price and me.

"Oh, dear." She raises her hand toward my bruised face and swollen eyelid, then looks beside me. "You must be Price."

My arm's linked through his. "He got the worst of it. Show them your head and the bruises." Price shoots me an embarrassed look. "Okay, just your stitches."

He lifts off his ball cap and turns around so they can see the back of his shaved head. Wearing a hat's uncomfortable, but he thinks walking around bare-headed with a sewed-up bald spot is worse. I think it's a mark of an eco-soldier and way cool.

"You two made quite a catch," Mr. Calderman says, shaking Price's hand.

Price winks at me. "Elizabeth gets the credit, I just did cleanup."

Becca eases up beside me. Mr. Calderman shakes his head. "It's amazing what these women get us to do."

Price smiles. "I really don't mind."

The Caldermans lead him away toward the surf, peppering him with questions about the fight. He glances back and shrugs. I wave so he knows leaving me behind is okay.

"I don't have makeup for that," Becca says, softly. She tilts her head toward the crowd. "Ready for this?"

"Guess so. I just wish there was another choice." I wrap my arms together to warm away the goose bumps that aren't from feeling cold.

Light off the red-orange sky washes across Becca's cheeks. "Me, too." She points to the back of the chair for me to grab on. "Come on, Auntie E." This time I do.

Two coolers sit beside Tom inside the release area. Eighty of Sunny's eggs hatched. I trudge slowly across the deep sand, remembering the day almost two months ago when Maria, Tom, and I took the eggs away from here.

Tom waves Becca and me to the center. Commissioner O'Connor clears a space in the crowd and lifts the yellow tape so we can get through. She stops me, her hand on my arm.

"As soon as the Commission has three new members," she says, smiling, "I'm putting forward a resolution to recognize your fight to protect the Landing and the Kemp's ridleys."

I look at Becca, waiting for me a few yards away. Price stands in the surf at the end of the tape.

"A couple of other people deserve credit, too. If it's all right."

"I'm sure," she says. "We'll talk soon."

I've thought some about Larry Wilkes the last few days. About what Grandma said he was like as a kid. I might get why he went wrong, but it's still no excuse. I'll never feel sorry for him. Julia dumped Pete, so I guess she'll have another chance, if she takes it.

Maria walks the line. A dusty grey hatchling lays quietly on her palm. The crowd jockeys for position, moving kids up to the tape or setting the little ones on shoulders so they can see. People snap pictures. "Flashes off, please." Tom follows with the container of hatchlings. Sunny's kids are wide-awake, squiggling and climbing over each other.

Maria stops in front of a little boy. It's Joey from Kroger's the day Noel and I collected signatures. His chin nestles the head of a small, stuffed turtle.

His mom smiles, her eyes sleepy. "He's been up since three-fifteen."

"What do you think?" Maria says, lowering the hatchling so he can see. He nudges his turtle toward it, then hugs the toy back to the safety of his chest.

We walk back to Becca, sitting beside the other cooler.

"Price Lungren, please join us," Maria says.

Price walks out of the water and stands beside me. Our shoulders touch. I breathe and press against him.

"This morning," Maria says, "we have two young people to especially thank. Two months ago, Elizabeth Barker put herself in great danger defending the mother of these hatchlings against three hoods. The other night, she and Price stopped one of them from destroying the nests in our protection. Without Elizabeth and Price's intervention there wouldn't be a release today."

The crowd claps. I turn toward the Gulf and breathe deeply, trying to keep it together.

"We are excited," Maria says, "to help the next generation of Kemp's ridleys start their life's journey. They carry their mother's genes, her tenacity to keep going despite wounds, fatigue, and hunger. Her offspring that survive will pass on those genes. Their strength and determination will keep this beautiful species moving away from extinction."

Becca is the first to cheer. She pats her *Rock and Roll* armrests. I use one and Price for balance as I kneel beside Maria, the coolers between us.

"Go," Maria says. We tip the containers and the two-inch long, slate-colored turtles slide onto the beach. After all the commotion in the coolers, at first only a few move.

"Hurry, put them in the water," a little kid yells.

"They have to imprint the Landing in their memory," Becca says to the crowd, "so they'll know to come back. And the Landing will be here, just like it was meant to be." She smiles. I know she couldn't stop herself from adding the last part.

People clap and cheer. A shrill whistle bursts above the noise. I grin. Whistle-lady.

Six hatchlings take their first steps. Front flippers alternate with back ones, their bodies scuttling forward like little turtle robots. After a few feet, they stop, rest, then one-by-one they scurry faster toward the Gulf. Price sweeps his ribbon-topped pole through the air, scaring off a bold and hungry gull.

The first turtle touches the water. The edge of a wave rolls it over and pulls it in. Its marble-like head breaks the surface. A second wave tumbles the hatchling back to shore, before sweeping it out again. More turtles take their first dips. Each wash moves them farther from shore. They flap and rest, flap and float.

"Make your momma proud," someone calls.

When the shore is finally empty of hatchlings, the crowd quiets. The trail of hundreds of tiny flipper prints dissolves under the incoming waves. Dozens of tiny black heads bob along the water's surface, moving toward the horizon's light. I follow them with Price until we're waist deep in the Gulf. My toes squirm into the sand and I lean my head against his. We watch until we're sure they're gone.

Price hugs me close as tears run down my cheeks. I wanted to be happy for Sunny's babies. I have to settle for hope.

CHAPTER
TWENTY-FIVE

Saturday, May 29

TODAY IS MY BIRTHDAY and we're having a big celebration at the Blue Moon. Later tonight a bunch of us are going to the Latin dance at the temporary stage the city built on Highland Beach. I caress the silver turtle hanging around my neck, my birthday present from Price. He got a huge kiss for it—in front of Mom and Dad and everybody.

I sit under the HAPPY BIRTHDAY sign draped above the banquet room door and greet people as they come in. Scents of ginger, sesame, and hot peanut oil drift out of the kitchen every time a waiter swings the doors open to deliver food to other tables. I'm past ready for our sit down and eat part of the evening.

Becca motors over, her grin as wide as one of Grandma's flowers.

"Happy birthday, you."

"Yay, for me." I turn my smile into a pout. "But no samba lessons tonight really sucks."

"And slow dancing all night with Price is terrible, why?" She winks. "We've got time for samba after your brain heals."

Dad points me to the chair at the head of the table. Grandma sits on my left, Mom on my right. She's pale and moving slowly. Her head tilts and rests her check briefly on Dad's arm when he touches her shoulder. "We have an idea to run past you," he says.

I look back and forth between them, suddenly nervous. "What? It's my birthday, so this better be good."

"We think so," she says. "When I'm better, the magazine that hired me for the Gulf assignment wants me to produce more pieces for them." She catches the instant panic that crosses my face. "I'm not going back," she says. "I've got plenty of notes and photos to work up the oil spill stories from here."

"Okay, that's a relief. So . . . ?"

"So, Dad and I talked it over with Grandma, and we wondered how you'd feel about us moving in with her?"

"Are you kidding? I am so already packed."

"I penciled it out," Dad says. "With saving money on rent, and the connections I've made since we got here, I can restart my landscaping business. I'm going home to get my equipment out of storage in a couple of weeks."

"I knew you were up to something."

"It's hard to hide anything from you," he says. "Shall we get this party started?"

Price eyes me from the other side of the table, but keeps talking to Berto. That ripply feeling goes through my chest.

I touch my necklace. "It already has."

Dad taps his chopsticks on the edge of his beer glass and the room quiets. "Thanks for coming to help celebrate Elizabeth's birthday. Several people have asked to speak, but I'm first.

"Our family hit more than a few rocks since moving down here in January." He looks down at me. Didn't we?"

I roll my eyes. "Uh, yeah, but it's practically smooth sailing now." Except for the trial, testifying, the spill . . . hey, now's not the time.

"Well, not smooth, exactly," he says. "but I never imagined a night like tonight was possible four months ago." He lays a hand on my shoulder. "Your Grandma talked me into coming back here, but you and Grandpa helped me come home. Thank you." He holds out his hand for me to shake.

"You're welcome," I say. "Don't make us do it again."

He laughs. "Not a chance."

"My turn," Mom says, reaching for a hand to hold. "On your ninth birthday, we gave you a camera so you could safely wander around Picketts Pond after flowers and frogs." She shakes her head and smiles. "Can't imagine what got into you. Now, we're thrilled you made it to fifteen."

I lean over and wrap my arms around her. "Me too." I hold her extra long, hearing her crusty breathing, feeling the rise of her chest against my arm, her effort to be here. My Momma warrior.

"Elizabeth," Barbara says, standing and passing an envelope down the line to me. "You and Becca certainly live up to that *Rock and Roll* credo." Becca pats her chair arms and sends a thumbs up salute across the table. Barbara points to the envelope. "In there is a $125 check for your photo sales."

Becca raises her glass of iced green tea. "Here, here. A camera around the neck *is* more than a fashion statement." The table erupts in laughter. Berto claps her a high-five.

"And," Barbara says, "we're ready for more. However, if you've a mind to also kick up more trouble, I'm assigning Tom as body guard."

I lock my eyes onto Price's warm gaze. "Thanks, but I'm covered." I slip the check from the envelope. "This is my down payment on a new camera."

Grandma shifts in her chair, resting a hand on the edge of the table as she stands. I watch her strong back, the straight line of her shoulders. She's the root of everything. All of this. Without her, well, what would our family be now?

"Happy birthday, Darlin'" she says. "Your daddy's right. I got him to bring you all home, but you brought me back my James. Forced him to remember what really matters, and he was more grateful for that than you'll ever know." She scrunches the handkerchief in her hand, then motions toward the envelope. "Put that check to some other wish."

Dad sets a box in front of me. The wrapping is pale yellow paper she's painted on top with Grandpa's favorite hydrangeas.

"James knew he wouldn't likely be here to celebrate your birthday," she says, "so he asked your mother to pick this out. It's his gift to you, with all his love. And mine, too."

I carefully pull off the paper, not wanting to ruin it, and lift out what's in the box. A brand new camera, the latest, compact model, with tons of functions. On top are two more boxes. A wide angle for landscapes and a macro for my smallest bugs and flowers.

I stare at it all, pushing down the lump in my throat, on the edge of embarrassing tears. "Wow." Deep breath and I turn with a wink at Mom. "I can get into real trouble with these."

"How about you don't," Dad says.

"Speech!" Berto calls out.

"Yeah," Shawna echoes, her camera flash lighting the room.

I blush and blink everyone back in focus. Maria's at the other end of the table. A chopstick twirls slowly between her fingers. She looks up and smiles.

"You guys, I'm terrible at speeches."

"Yeah, right," Becca says. "That dodge is over."

"Okay, unrehearsed, here goes. Thank you, Grandpa, for giving me the first kick in the butt. Thank you, Sunny, for hooking my heart. Becca, when you told me New Yorkers don't whine, I was stuck. With the turtles and you guys. You kept me going. Will keep me going, whatever comes." I look at Dad and Grandma. "I'm happy to be home, too. That's it, let's eat so we can get to the cake!"

"Hold up," Maria says. The clapping drifts off. Eyes follow her as she walks around the table and stops at my side. "You're not too swelled up from all this nice talk and reaching the mighty age of fifteen, are you?"

"Me?"

"Good. I get the last word." She looks out at the crowd. "When Tom and I met Elizabeth, she was a scared young woman in trouble. During our journey together, a few folks may have called her a bit wayward. None of us foresaw her unstoppable spirit." She turns to me. "Not even you."

I look down at the table.

"Birthdays," she says, "are about gifts—those you give and those you get. I don't want to tie up too big a ribbon here. Turtles are still in trouble, and Elizabeth has accepted no small burden, testifying in the upcoming trial. That is her gift to us and to the Kemp's ridleys; we're with you every step." She pulls me to her side. "I took a poll and all here agree. In gratitude—and in perpetuity—Sunny's beach will be called Elizabeth's Landing."

END

Acknowledgments

My small claim to Texas heritage rests with my mother, Virginia, an East Texas farmer's daughter. I am grateful to my Texas family for keeping her memory and our connection alive.

Three environmental clashes frame Elizabeth's story: 1) fishing practices and species decline, 2) development and habitat loss, and 3) ocean oil production and pollution. The complex, decades-long battle in the U.S. between shrimpers, private fishing groups, agencies, and environmental advocates is far from over. Coastal development and climate shifts are key players in habitat loss—for wildlife and people. Still under scientific and economic study, the full environmental, social, and economic impacts of the 2010 Gulf of Mexico oil spill are unknown. Within each conflict sea turtles, countless ocean species, and coastal residents remain caught among the crossfire and uncertainty.

The vigilance and hard work to save sea turtles, worldwide, are the heart and breath of Elizabeth's Landing. The following experts generously expanded my understanding: Dr. Donna Shaver, Chief of the Division of Sea Turtle Science and Recovery at Padre Island National Seashore; Jeff George, Executive Director, and Shane Wilson, President, Seaturtle, Inc.; Barbara Gregg and Mike Ray, Texas Parks and Wildlife Department; Dr.

Charles Manire, DVM, Mote Marine Laboratory; and Carole Allen, Gulf Director of the Sea Turtle Restoration Project. Thanks to my dear friend Sherry Cook for introductory guidance on the Coast Guard rescue.

Diane Wilson, fourth-generation Texas shrimper, international social activist, and author was invaluable in helping me portray shrimp fishing. Her spirit and persistence live in Elizabeth — in one person's power to shift the tides.

Credit for Elizabeth's mother reporting on the impacts of immigration on families goes to Stephanie Elizondo-Griest and her eye-opening, engaging memoir, *Mexican Enough: My Life Between the Borderlines.*

Since the late 19th century, members of my family have worked and advocated for people with disabilities. Becca's character honors this heritage and progress in our understanding since those early days. Life Coach and Ms. Wheelchair Florida 2005, Becky Blitch, read early drafts. Her openness and insights helped clarify specific aspects of living with physical disabilities. I also appreciate the Abell family's example, encouragement, and introduction to beach bocce.

Elizabeth's Landing grew from my own ten-year environmental fight over local gravel mining. I am forever grateful to Sally Oliver, who taught me to stand up and care. And to Dr. A.G. McLellan, who helped me understand the social justice consequences and social responsibilities of extracting and using natural resources. These generous mentors opened doors to my future. The Yolo County Resource Conservation District board deserves credit for hiring a 42 year-old fresh out of college. Former Director John Anderson, DVM taught me to capture the big picture by looking through smaller frames.

The story idea for Elizabeth's Landing came quickly; the book took six years. I had to learn how to write—to become a writer—in spirit and practice. Many fostered this humbling—and continuing—experience. My thanks to Charlotte Gullick, who encouraged my first noodlings. To author Ginny Rorby, for believing in my ability—once I understood, "more tension." My earliest writers groups gave their keen eyes, friendship, and laughter: Ginny Rorby, Jeanette Stickel, Karen Lewis, Nona Smith, Fran Schwartz, and Marie Judson. To my daughter, Erin, for reading from a young person's vantage, and for her loving good cheer. The manuscript and my writing evolved tremendously from professional critiques by Ellen Sussman, David Corbett, Helen Pyne, Molly Dwyer, Nancy McLelland, and editor Annette Jarvie. Thanks also to zoologist Adrienne McCracken for her careful, final reading.

Talented graphic designer, Laurie MacMillan, put her heart—and great patience—into the challenging task of capturing my vision of the story's dramatic essence in the cover art.

The joy of completing Elizabeth's Landing is shared with my husband, Robert. His commitment to nurturing Elizabeth as she grew up, his perceptions, pragmatism, and loving partnership enriched my journey, as always.

Former Executive Director of the Yolo County, CA Resource Conservation District, Katy Pye lives and writes on California's North Coast. Elizabeth's Landing is her first novel. She volunteers for the Mendocino Coast Writers Conference, at the Point Cabrillo Light Station, and with the Threshold Choir. Camera in hand, her daily walks along the ocean or redwood forest trails provide inspiration and entertainment. Known to talk to local tree frogs, hummingbirds, turkeys, and sometimes coyotes, she is delighted, yet not surprised, when they talk back.

Katy's website and blog have more about sea turtles and young people making a difference in all sorts of ways. You can reach her through the site's CONTACT ME page.

http://katypye.com
Facebook page: Katy Pye-Author
Twitter: Katy Pye@Katy4Pye
YouTube Channel: Katy Pye-Author

A PORTION OF BOOK SALE PROFITS SUPPORTS WORLDWIDE SEA TURTLE CONSERVATION AND EDUCATION PROGRAMS.

CPSIA information can be obtained at www.ICGtesting.com
Printed in the USA
LVOW04s1400210415

435476LV00001B/191/P